Underground

Underground

by

Gayle O'Brien

Hookline Books

Bookline & Thinker Ltd

Published by Hookline Books 2011
Bookline & Thinker Ltd
#231, 405 King's Road
London SW10 0BB
Tel: 0845 116 1476
www.hooklinebooks.com

The right of Gayle O'Brien to be identified as the author of this work has
been asserted in accordance with the Copyright, Designs and Patents Act
1988.

A CIP catalogue for this book is available from the British Library.

This book is a work of fiction. Names, characters, places and incidents
are either a product of the author's imagination or are used fictitiously.
ISBN: 9780956847645

Cover design by Gee Mac
Printed and bound by Lightning Source UK

For Ziggy and Sam

Chapter 1

Annie lay down on her bed and scrutinized her work. The ceiling didn't look bad, considering. She would have preferred dark blue for the sky and gold for the stars, but black and yellow had been the only two colors on the darkened Wal-Mart loading dock. It was no use being picky.

If Annie was still in Virginia, she would have called Jenna and Marcy and told them to come over and see how she'd transformed her bedroom ceiling into a starry night sky. They would, she knew, tell her it was amazing, be jealous that she thought of it first and go home begging their parents to let them do the same.

The truth was she wouldn't have been allowed to do this in Virginia. A year ago, she'd asked her mother if she could.

"Absolutely not," she'd said.

"Why not?"

"Because it's a complete waste of time and money and, when you get sick of it, we'll only have to paint over it."

"I won't get sick of it," Annie argued. "It'll be an educational exercise. I'll make sure all the constellations are right."

"You're not painting your bedroom ceiling. This conversation is over."

I'll ask Dad when he gets home, she remembered thinking. *He'll let me.*

But that was the night everything changed. She never got to ask him.

Annie got off her bed and looked out the window. Clumps of snow lay scattered over the brown grass in the front yard and small, icy puddles filled divots in the muddy driveway. The gray mountains were swallowing the setting sun. Across the street, a frozen river glistened.

"So, this is Vermont," she said, pressing her fingers on the glass and feeling the icy air force its way in. She shivered and reached for the fraying J.Crew sweater she'd found at Goodwill.

Never could she remember being this close to freezing. In Virginia, it rarely got this cold and, when it did, she'd crank up the central heating to 85 °F and pretend she was in Florida. Compared to all the places they'd lived over the past year, Battenkill, Vermont was the coldest and the most remote.

What made it worse was realizing that in Virginia it was spring. It was the middle of March, which meant daffodils would line the highways and bluebells would lurk in the woods next to the football field. Cheerleading would start again, and Jenna would be pressuring everyone to "burn off that winter weight." It made Annie think of the high school cafeteria, where Jenna would spend the entire lunchtime dissecting the calorie content of everything at the table, then take a vote on who had the "fattiest food."

Annie made sure it was never her, but it didn't go unnoticed that her meal was a close second or third. What could she say? She loved food. Her father loved to make it, and she loved to eat it: enchiladas, fish tacos, chicken with dumplings and beef brisket in the winter; BBQ pork ribs, marinated steak, pasta salad and grilled corn on the cob in the summer.

"Healthy," her dad would say when Annie asked him to describe her shape.

"Ooh, I got more than an inch!" Jenna would shriek, pinching Annie's sides as they changed for cheerleading practice.

If only Jenna could see her now.

A rumbling noise came from Annie's stomach and she tried to recall when she'd last eaten. *Yesterday,* she remembered, at the 7-Eleven in Troy where she'd half-filled the tank of the Dodge Dart and had a hot dog smothered in ketchup.

Since then she had driven the hour to Vermont in the dark, stolen several cans of paint, and helped her mother into their new house. Add painting her bedroom ceiling into the equation and she had more than earned her one meal of the day.

Annie's stomach rumbled even louder. She grabbed her backpack and a pair of mittens and went downstairs.

Her dad always said, "If something sounds too good to be true, it probably is." Annie had never understood what he meant until they'd arrived at this house. The newspaper ad had read: *House for rent. Cash only. No lease.* Now she could see why.

It was an old farmhouse. There were houses like this in older parts of Virginia, but Annie had never seen one this close to falling down. At least

2

it wasn't as bad as the barn out the back, where Annie reluctantly put the Dart after the drive from Troy. She feared the wind would blow the wrong way, the barn would collapse and she'd be stuck having to steal yet another car. For now though, the Dart needed to stay hidden. Just in case.

Everything in the house was filthy. Whoever lived here last either had no interest in dusting or the place had been empty for a long time. Standing at the bottom of the stairs, looking at the dirt-encrusted skirting boards and murky windows, she knew she should have spent the day cleaning instead of painting.

She went into the kitchen. Dead flies littered the counter. She opened the oven and the smell was rancid. The house was dirty enough it could make her and her mother ill. Doctors and hospitals weren't an option. Even though there was only so much effort she wanted to put into a house that she might have to leave at any time, Annie resolved to find a store and buy some bleach.

And food. She needed to do something about food.

She peered into the living room and saw her mother still curled up on the couch, asleep. Her hair hung limp and defeated over her face. Over the past year it had grown, her original brown color pushing out her old blonde highlights until only the ends were yellow, as if she'd dipped her hair in paint. She thought of the ceiling upstairs and wondered if her mother remembered forbidding it on the night everything changed. Had Annie painted the ceiling in their old house, there would have been screaming and yelling and threats and privileges taken away. Now Annie was lucky if her mother even opened her eyes.

She slid her feet into her red cowboy boots, basking in the familiarity of their soft leather. As she unbolted the front door she caught her reflection in a large foggy mirror on the wall. She looked older. The gray circles under her eyes and the paleness of her normally rosy skin made her appear older than her 17 years.

How much longer could they live like this?

She braced herself against the cold and threw open the door.

With the Dart sentenced to the barn, Annie set to walking. She thought she remembered seeing a store on the way back from stealing the paint and headed in that direction.

The narrow, windy road was flanked by clumps of trees and the occasional herd of cows. She passed a total of four houses and a brown historic marker. She reached a crossroads and there, overlooking the intersection, was a two-story building covered in gray clapboard. A large painted sign hung from the columned porch: *Store at Five Corners.*

Annie walked across the small parking lot and pushed the door open. A bell clanged overhead. The store was quiet and dark. Tall mahogany shelves held assorted bottles, boxes and cans. A refrigerated cabinet glowed from the back wall. Pine floorboards croaked under Annie's weight as she sought out bleach and cleaning cloths.

At the freezer section, she logged the price of each pizza, burrito and pot pie, standing there for so long she was soon cold again. The cheapest item was a vegetarian burrito – buy one, get one free. She put a dozen of them into her basket. For her mother, she got M&Ms and Diet Coke.

At the counter, a bell sat next to the cash register, asking to be rung for attendance. Next to it was a laptop, its screen glowing with the familiar white and blue of a Facebook news feed. Annie had to stop herself from reaching out to the keyboard. She last checked her Facebook page a week ago. Her status was as she'd left it on the night everything changed: *...is watching a re-run of Gossip Girl. Not as good the second time around.*

Then she thought of her other Facebook page. Private, with only one friend. She felt for the memory stick in her pocket. Still there.

Soon, she thought. *I'll take care of it soon.*

A teenage boy shot up from behind the counter. "Sorry," he smiled. "Re-lacing my shoes."

Annie's hand leapt to her heart.

"Sorry," he said again, "didn't mean to scare you." He began punching her grocery prices into the cash register. "I'd say you're just passing through, but we don't get many tourists buying bleach."

Annie cleared her throat. "Excuse me?"

"I was wondering if you'd just moved here."

"Oh. Um. Yes. We live just down the road."

"Ah, so you're the ones who've moved into the old Jennings Farm."

"I don't know whose house it used to be."

"Gray farmhouse? Stained-glass 1850 above the front door?"

Was there an 1850 above the door? She hadn't noticed.

"No one's lived there for a while," he added.

That explains all the dust, she thought.

"Do you need a bag?"

She put her backpack on the counter and pushed everything in. "No, I'll just use this."

"An environmentalist," he said. "I like you already."

Annie blushed. The bleach fell off the counter and onto her foot.

4

"Ow!"

The boy came out from behind the counter.

"Here, let me help," he said, leaning over to pick up the bottle. "Hey, cool boots! Where'd you get 'em?"

The day her father gave her the boots flashed behind her eyes.

"Happy Birthday, sweetheart," he had said. "They're authentic. Look, they've even got a knife loop on the inside of the right boot."

She remembered she had laughed. "What the heck do I need a knife loop for?"

Her dad had laughed, too. "Hey, you never know when something like that might come in handy."

Annie took the bleach and hurried to the door. The boy followed her.

"So," he said, "will I be seeing you at school?"

"I don't go to school."

"You don't? How old are you?"

"I'm 17."

She didn't hold the door for him. He followed anyway, bursting out into the cold without a jacket. *Why is he following me?* she thought.

"Did you graduate early or something? Don't tell me you're some kind of child prodigy."

"No, I just don't go to school," she said, fumbling with her mittens.

If he heard the impatience in her voice he didn't respond to it. "Wow. I'd heard there were kids that didn't have to go to school, but I've never actually met any of them. Are you part of some religious cult or something?"

"No. Just a decision I made."

The boy laughed. "Oh, man. I can just see my old man's face if I decided I wasn't going to school anymore. You've gotta tell me how you convinced your parents."

"Actually, it's just me and my mom, and she's fine with it." Annie's whole body shook against the cold as the boy followed her across the parking lot.

"Call me old-fashioned," he called out, "but I think you forgot to pay."

"Oh, I'm so sorry!" She pulled $20 from her pocket.

"Just give me a sec and I'll get your change."

Annie needed the change. But what she needed more was to end this conversation. "Keep the rest."

"Oh, come on, let me at least give you what you're owed."

"No, really," she said, backing towards the street.

5

"I'm Theo," said the boy, holding out his hand.

"I'm sorry," said Annie, reaching the road and setting her pace. "I have to go."

Chapter 2

Samantha Weston couldn't breathe.

"Don't pull so hard!"

"Miss Sammy, you knows I's gots to pull hard. What's the point of wearing this thing if you ain't gonna wear it right?"

Nessie put her foot on Samantha's behind and yanked hard on the corset strings.

"Be careful!" Samantha snapped. "You'll make me fall over!"

"Arms up, Miss Sammy."

Samantha lifted her arms. Nessie threw the hoop skirt over her head. The wire circle hit the floor. The skirt blossomed out from Samantha's waist.

"I feel like the Liberty Bell," she moaned.

Nessie mumbled something under her breath as she tied the skirt's belt around Samantha's waist.

"What did you say?" Samantha snapped.

"I said, 'Buck up, Miss Sammy. This here is the price of becoming a young lady.' "

"You can go now, Annessa." The cold voice of Samantha's mother froze the room.

Nessie curtseyed and made a hunched exit. At the Weston plantation, it was common knowledge that if a house slave got too tall, she was sent directly to the cotton field. Even Samantha knew Nessie would be as tall as Samantha's mother if she stood up straight.

"It hurts," Samantha whispered.

"Good," said her mother, inspecting the corset. "Then it's tight enough."

"How am I supposed to sit down?"

"You won't have time for sitting. You'll be lucky if you have time to breathe."

"But Mother…"

Her mother raised her hand. "I don't want to hear another word. You're 17 years old. I started wearing a corset when I was 13."

7

Samantha rolled her eyes. Her mother raised her hand to strike her, and Samantha winced. Since the planning for Samantha's debutante ball began her mother's fuse had burned down to its crackling base. It wasn't that Samantha did not want her debutante ball – indeed, she wanted it very much. She wanted the music, the dancing, the swishing of ball gowns and the smell of men's cologne. She wanted to be the center of attention, the envy of her female peers and the desire of every man in the room. Never mind that she already knew who she wanted to marry – in fact, had known since she was five-years old – but a debutante ball was a rite of Southern passage and she intended to enjoy every second of it.

If only her mother would remember that this was Samantha's debutante ball, not hers. Or Georgia's.

Her mother snapped her two fingers. Oma and Chimi, two house slaves, entered carrying Samantha's debutante gown like it was rice paper. Samantha's mother had brought it back from Paris. The pale silk bodice was fortified with whalebone, making it practically stand on its own. The skirt was made of a dozen layers of organza and chiffon, embroidered with hundreds of tiny, dark pink roses. It was, quite simply, the most beautiful dress Samantha had ever seen. She reached out to touch it, and her mother slapped her hand.

Oma and Chimi lifted the dress over Samantha's head and guided it over the hoop skirt. She watched their dark hands manipulate the pale, delicate fabric. Oma stood behind with a button hook and began fastening the 120 satin buttons up the back of the bodice. Samantha tried to ignore the corset digging into her ribs.

Halfway up the bodice, Oma stopped. "I can't do no more, ma'am," she said.

"What?" said Samantha's mother. "What do you mean?"

Oma gently turned Samantha so her mother could see the back of the dress.

A terrible pause filled the room.

"Why doesn't it fit?"

No one dared answer.

"Measure her."

Oma pulled the cloth measure from her apron and wrapped it around Samantha's waist.

"21 inches, ma'am," she whispered.

"Give me that." Samantha's mother snatched the measure and pulled it tight around Samantha's middle. No one breathed.

Samantha braced herself. If her mother slapped her for anything, it would be this. Instead she shouted: "Get the dress off her. Now!"

Oma quickly undid the buttons. The dress was lifted over Samantha's head.

"Leave us," she said. The two slaves exited quickly and quietly.

Samantha stood while rage seeped through her mother's low voice like smoke out of a cigar. "Do you want to explain to me how your waist got to be 21 inches?"

Samantha opened her mouth, but nothing came out. How could she explain the inexplicable? The truth was that most days her body behaved independently of her intentions. It was changing, almost daily, and with those changes came an ever-evolving list of desires. Her body wanted food, in all its scrumptious shapes and forms: corn bread, caramelized peaches, creamed collard greens, maple-cured pork, biscuits and gravy. It wanted water, milk, lemonade and tea so steeped and sweetened it resembled Virginia soil after a thunderstorm. Her mother had always made clear the correlation between food and a woman's figure, but even on the days and weeks when Samantha resisted her cravings, her body still seemed determined to mature. The mirror did not always catch these modifications, but Samantha could feel them: the widening of her hips, the slight narrowing of her waist, and the ballooning of her chest. She knew the latter was the real reason her bodice was now too small, but how could she justify this to her mother, who was repulsed by the human body's needs and functions?

"Mother, I..." she stammered.

Her mother's expression shifted from rage to disappointment.

"How could you, Samantha? How could you do this to me?"

"I...I didn't mean to, Mother. I just..."

"You come out in one week. Don't you realize how important this is? Do you know how much money your father spent on the gown alone?"

"I know, Mother. I wish I could..."

Her mother sighed. "There is only one thing to do. Nessie!"

The slave appeared so quickly it was as if she'd never left the room.

"Until the cotillion on Friday, my daughter is only allowed water, apples and plain bread. Understood?"

Nessie curtseyed. "Yes, ma'am."

Samantha's mother left the room. Samantha fought back tears while Nessie quietly untied the ribbons of the hoop skirt and let it fall to the floor.

"Come on, Miss Sammy. Step on out."

Nessie held Samantha's elbow as she stepped outside the frame.

"Get me out of this corset, Nessie."

Nessie stepped back. "But Miss Sammy, you know your mama wants it on all…"

"I said, get me out!" Even Samantha was surprised by the volume of her voice.

Nessie undid the knot and loosened the strings. Samantha took in several deep breaths, as if she'd been under water too long.

Nessie put her hand on Samantha's shoulder. "You want to talk, Miss Sammy?"

Samantha sneered. "Leave me alone, Nessie. You definitely wouldn't understand."

Nessie left the room and closed the door. Samantha pushed the corset off her body and kicked it across the room.

Samantha's palomino was waiting for her in front, just as she'd instructed. Free of the corset and hoop skirt, she wore her canvas riding dress, durable for riding, but cool compared to the silks, wools and taffeta her mother wore regardless of the weather.

Milo, the horse slave, held onto the palomino's bridle. When Samantha burst through the front door with her saddle bag, he took one look at her dress and shook his head.

"Oh, no, Miss Sammy."

"Take the saddle off, Milo."

He slowly undid the straps. "You know your mama wants you riding side saddle. And in your real riding outfit." He set the saddle onto the ground and made a stirrup with his hands. Samantha pushed her bare foot into his pale palms. "Miss Sammy, you trying to get me whipped?"

"Give me my saddle bag," she said.

Milo tisked. "Saddle bag, but no saddle. Honestly, Miss Sammy. What's your mama gon' say?"

"She won't say anything because no one is going to tell her." Samantha kicked her feet into the horse's sides. As she galloped away from the main house, towards the cotton fields, she turned her face toward the sun.

Spring had arrived early in Virginia. The grass was dotted with daffodils, and the woods were blanketed in bluebells. In a little over a month, cotton planting would begin. For now the field contained row after row of dry branches and brush. Every field hand she'd ever known had scars on their hands from those sharp cotton bristles, miniature versions of the whipping scars that streaked across bare, black backs like the trail of a dozen shooting stars. "The marks of insolence," her grandfather used to call them.

Once past the cotton fields the landscape gave way to lush woodland. Mont Verity, Samantha's family's plantation, was 500 acres in all, 100 of which were filled with ancient trees that her grandfather claimed had been inhabited by Indians before the family bought the land. Samantha guided her horse towards the stream that marked the property border with Dominion Royale, the Fabre family plantation, and dismounted.

While the horse drank from the stream, Samantha stepped over stumpy rocks to reach a large, flat boulder in the center. Had it been summer, she could have waded in and let her feet dangle in the rushing water. But even on this mild spring day, she knew the water would be too cold. It didn't matter – Samantha was just happy to be out of the house and out of that stupid corset. This part of the stream was where she came every day, and where no one from her family ever bothered her.

"Hold it right there."

Samantha looked up and saw Eli Fabre standing on the other side of the stream. His pistol was pointed straight at her, concealing his blue eyes and his blond curls. "You're trespassing on Fabre family property."

Samantha stood up. "I think you'll find that since the stream marks the division, the stream officially belongs to no one."

"I think if you check the deed the dotted line runs right down the center of the stream, thereby making one half mine and one half yours. You, Miss Weston, are on my half."

Samantha laughed. "So what are you going to do, Mr. Fabre? Shoot me?"

Eli cocked his pistol. "You know, I just might."

Samantha put her bare feet in cold water and began to cross the stream. "Well, I can foresee a number of problems with that."

"Stay where you are, Miss Weston. Or I'll shoot you."

Samantha ignored him and kept walking. "One, my daddy will kill you. Two, when my daddy kills you, your daddy will try and kill my daddy. Three, if I'm dead, then there's no one to inherit my plantation. And four," Samantha swiftly pulled her pistol from her cleavage, "you can't kill me if I kill you first."

Eli let down his pistol and bowed.

"Touché, Miss Weston. Touché."

They stood awkwardly, knowing what they were meant to do, but unsure who should initiate it. After several excruciating seconds,

Samantha leaned in to kiss him. She missed his mouth, and kissed his nose instead.

"You're late," she said, blushing.

They sat on a fallen tree at the edge of the river.

"I'm sorry. But you'll never guess what happened? Father took me to the auction!"

"A slave auction?"

"Obviously. What other kind of auction happens around here? Your father was there, too."

This came as a surprise, but she did not say so. As far as she knew, her father wanted to replace slave labor with the industrialized methods used up north. Why was he buying more slaves?

Eli continued. "One of the ones Father bought has the biggest hands I've ever seen on any man, which will be good for some of the hard labor Father needs doing. But a man that big might have a big attitude, so we'll just have to keep an eye on him. And then we got a young thing who'll probably have a baby in a month or so."

"Two for the price of one," she said, absentmindedly. It's what her grandfather always used to say when a slave was pregnant.

"Nah, we'll probably sell the baby on. Father's had enough with black babies running around the place. He says at his age he only wants the ones that can be put to work. Then there's two your father bought. A husband and wife, but he isn't going to have them right away."

"Why not?"

Eli sat up straighter, pleased – it seemed – that he had something to teach her. "I think the wife is sick or something. Actually, I don't know why your father bothered with her. He could have just had the husband and left it at that. If you ask me, he's just asking for trouble."

"What do you mean?"

"Well, the slave will know that your father is soft and that is the worst thing in the world a slave could think about its master, especially this one. I could see he had an independent streak. Father tried to talk him out of it, but he wouldn't listen. It'll cost him one way or another."

"You talk like you're an expert on this stuff."

"I've got to be if I'm going to run my plantation."

"Our plantation."

Eli gave her a gentle nudge. "You know a woman can't own property."

"And you know you wouldn't have the prospect of a plantation if you don't have mine."

Eli cleared his throat and shifted on the log. "So, what's been happening in the world of Samantha Weston today?"

"My dress fitting," she said. "It didn't go so well."

"No?"

Samantha told him about her mother and the small amount of food she was now allowed.

"Well, I'm just going to have to start bringing you some cornbread. I can't have you looking like you're ripe for the picking."

"It's not funny, Eli. You've got to talk to Father soon."

"Don't you worry, I've got it all planned."

Samantha perked up. "You do?"

"I've just got to get him at the right time," said Eli.

So he doesn't have a plan, Samantha thought.

"I was hoping I could talk to him at the cotillion actually," said Eli. "He'll be looking at all those suitors who've come from Lord knows where, and that's when I'll present myself. It's an offer he can't refuse – keeping his daughter and his plantation."

Samantha wasn't so sure, but didn't say. She didn't know what to do, either.

"Oh, I almost forgot!" She opened her saddlebag and pulled out a slim, rectangular box made of smooth wood.

"Here," she said, handing it to Eli. "Happy Birthday."

Eli smiled. "You remembered."

"Of course."

Eli pushed the lid off the box. Inside, resting on folds of deep red satin, was a Bowie knife. Samantha watched him wrap his hand around the wooden handle and pull the hold off the blade.

"Well, my, Samantha," he said. "It's a beauty." The steel blade was almost a foot long. He tapped the tip of the clip point.

"Ow!" he said, as blood oozed from his fingertip.

"It's sharp," she said.

"I can see that."

"You like it?"

Eli put his bleeding finger in his mouth "I sure do."

"Look," she said, "the handle is inscribed."

Eli took his finger out of his mouth and held the knife flat over his palms. An oval copper plate shone against the wood.

He read: "To Elijah Fabre, With Love from Samantha Weston, 1861."

Chapter 3

Annie ran barefoot across the highway, darting in and out of cars. Lights blazed and horns blared. Beyond the highway, her father stood in front of their house in Virginia.

"Dad!" she yelled.

He held out his arms to embrace her. As she took a step towards him, an explosion ripped through the air. She waved her hands to clear the smoke and there it was: the Virginia State Police car, set against her house as it burned to the ground.

"No!" yelled Annie, jolting upright as she woke from her dream. Sweat dripped down her back as the stained wallpaper surrounding her came into focus. Outside, icy rain tapped angrily at the window as if wanting to be let in. Footsteps came slowly up the stairs.

He's here, she thought. *We're dead.*

She thought about screaming, but if he'd found them, there was no point fighting it. She was tired of running.

Her door creaked open, and Annie held her breath. Her mother appeared at the bedroom door, an apparition in the gray light on the upstairs landing.

"I heard a noise," she said, her voice almost imperceptible against the sound of the rain.

Annie released her shoulders from where they'd crept up to her ears. "Sorry. I stubbed my toe."

Her mother turned and slowly made her way back down the stairs, not noticing that Annie was in bed and therefore couldn't have stubbed her toe. If they'd been in Virginia, Annie might have told her mother she'd had a bad dream, because then her mother would do what mothers do – take Annie into her arms, rock her back and forth, and tell her everything was going to be okay.

Instead, Annie fell back onto the bed and yanked the quilt over her head.

Her empty stomach woke her several hours later. She glanced at her father's watch – it was 2pm, a full hour before she usually allowed herself to eat.

Annie had been scrutinizing what she ate since the night everything changed. It wasn't that she was deliberately starving herself or trying to make herself ill – it was pure necessity. She and her mother had a fixed amount of money and when it ran out they would have nothing. Eating one meal a day was her way of making the money last longer.

Still, she couldn't deny she liked the effect this regime was having on her shape. Her jeans were looser, she could count her ribs and her cheekbones dominated her face. When she stood with her feet together, there was a few inches of space between her inner thighs. She could just imagine Jenna and Marcy's reaction when they saw her again. "Oh my god, you're so skinny!" they'd shriek. They would notice and they would be jealous.

As she lay in bed, she imagined herself returning home, the center of attention, the past year nothing but a good story that everyone wanted to hear. Both guys and girls would admire Annie for surviving it all, even Jenna and Marcy, and they would envy that Annie got to see the country while the rest of them were stuck in high school.

Who am I kidding, she thought. Even if she could go back to Virginia tomorrow, all her friends would be on the verge of graduating, something she could not do after missing a year of school. She'd have a lonely senior year while all her friends went to community college or Virginia State. No matter what happened now, her life was ruined forever.

Her friends had forgotten her already anyway. It was obvious. No one had posted anything on her old Facebook page for months. On the night everything changed, almost everyone she knew posted something.

Where R U????
I just saw your house – WTF?!?
Please call me. We're all worried sickkkkk.
I just want to know that you're okay. Please know that NO ONE believes your dad could have done such a thing. Get home safe.

Within a month, the posts stopped. These days, when she had access to a computer, she devoted her time to her other Facebook account.

She reached into her jeans and pulled out the memory stick, holding it in the palm of her hand. This flimsy piece of plastic was the only thing that had kept Annie going over the past year. But it was useless without a computer. Maybe Theo, the boy at the Store at Five Corners, would know where to find internet access in this town.

Theo.

Annie spent hours replaying their meeting in her head. Could she have acted more rudely? More foolishly? He'd been so nice and full of smiles, and she'd reacted the only way she knew how: by running.

Her only comfort was that had she been a normal girl, with a normal life, she might have been able to carry on a normal conversation with a perfectly normal boy.

At least, this is what she kept telling herself.

Annie forced her feet to the cold floor and got up, taking the quilt with her like a shroud. She knelt over her small pile of clothes and searched for anything that did not smell. Except for one clean pair of underwear and a pair of mismatched socks, everything else was dirty.

"Guess I need to do some laundry," she said to no one.

As Annie scooped the clothes into her arms, she could hear Jenna's reaction to the thrift-store clothes she now wore – "Since when are you going for the homeless look," or "I think you need to return those to the trash can where you found them."

Annie carried the clothes downstairs, past her mother sleeping on the couch, and to the basement for the first time. Each step down felt like it might give under her weight. There was no railing, so she ran her hand along the wall.

The basement was one large space, exactly the same size as the first floor above. A pile of defeated boxes littered one corner; in another stood a set of rusted metal shelves. A washing machine and dryer sat against the wall at the bottom of the stairs.

Annie blew at the dust on the washing machine and lifted its lid. The drum inside was old, but intact. She pulled the dial to *Normal*. Nothing happened. She pulled out the mini flashlight she kept in her pocket. Cobwebs clung to her arm as she reached behind the washing machine to retrieve its plug and put it into the one socket she could find. The machine rumbled to life. No sooner had Annie turned around to retrieve her clothes than a loud pop sent the basement into blackness and silence.

"Great," Annie groaned. She scanned the room with the flashlight and located the fuse box. As soon as she flicked the errant switch the fluorescent lights came back on, but the washing machine did not. Annie pushed and pulled at the dial until it came off in her hand.

She stared at the piece of plastic in her fist. Why were things that should be so simple so difficult? All she wanted to do was get out of the house and do what she needed to do, in clean clothes. And now she couldn't, because nothing was working. She thought about her father. This – fixing a washing machine – was his job, not hers. He should be here, doing what dads were supposed to do, but he wasn't. He'd done what he'd done and no amount of wishing was going to change that.

Then she thought of her mother upstairs: why wasn't she down here doing the laundry? Why was Annie, by default, the responsible one?

I didn't ask for this, she thought. *I didn't ask for any of this.*

Annie took one step back and kicked the washing machine with the flat of her foot. It rocked slightly, then settled back in its place. She kicked it again, harder this time. Before it had the chance to settle, she kicked it again and again and again.

"Stupid, stupid, stupid," she chanted with each blow. It rocked and rocked, until it finally fell sideways onto the floor, hitting the edge of the bottom step as it fell.

The door to the basement creaked.

"Is something wrong?" Her mother's feeble voice.

Annie cleared her throat. "No, Mom. I'm doing laundry."

"I heard a crash."

"Just the drum vibrating."

The door closed. Annie sat down on the stairs and put her face in her hands.

That was when she noticed the gap between the bottom two steps and the rest of the staircase.

Annie turned on the flashlight, got up and crouched down to look through the gap. The sight of something white made her throat tighten. She angled the flashlight down to the floor, but couldn't see anything else. She reached her hand through and pulled, falling backwards when the bottom two steps came away from the rest of the staircase.

Underneath was a space about six feet deep. A small ladder led to the ground. She put one foot onto the first step and bore down to assure herself of its solidity, then she slid through the hole and climbed all the way in.

Annie crouched in the middle of the small space. The white she'd seen through the gap was a rectangular piece of canvas. A mixture of hay and green dust trickled out from underneath. A gray blanket was folded at the foot. A sunken pillow, yellowed with age, lay at the head.

"A bed," she whispered.

Next to the bed was a wooden crate. On top of it was a lantern, its glass black with residue, and a small Bible no bigger than the iPhone Annie used to carry everywhere. She got on her knees and picked it up carefully like a rare piece of china. Flashlight in one hand, she opened it, the pages as delicate as dry leaves on autumn ground. Her eyes marveled at the minuscule print and the familiar names it formed: *Genesis, Exodus, Deuteronomy.*

Then something caught her eye on the inside of the front cover.

AK - 12/4/56
JS - 12/4/56
MB - 4/17/57
CT - 7/4/57, GB
ZT - 7/4/57, FD
AA - 1/8/58
DF - 3/12/58, M
HY - 9/23/58
GK - 7/4/59, DS
BR - 2/13/60
HN - 6/29/60, FD
GR - 7/13/60
HJ - 9/17/60, M
EF - 3/27/61
SW - 3/27/61

Annie blinked, as if blinking would transform the handwriting into an idea she could understand. *Bible passages?* she thought. *A code?* She flicked to the back cover to look for more. As she did, a small, unsealed envelope fluttered to the ground. A faded but perfectly curved script read:

Mr Sanford Weston
Mont Verity
Nr. Beckwith Station
Virginia

Annie was almost afraid to touch it. It seemed otherworldly, like a ghost or a phantom. She scooped it up gently, as if it were a baby bird.

"Virginia," she whispered.

Inside the envelope was a folded piece of paper. Annie struggled to steady her hand as she slid her fingers in to pull it out and unfold it.

March 27, 1861

Dearest Papa,

There is so much I want to tell you that I don't know where to begin.

Firstly, I want you to know that I am safe. For now. It has been a long journey here and I have seen places and people I'm not sure I could have even dreamed of. This is a beautiful country, Papa – do you know this? The beauty runs in the rivers and over purple mountains; it is in the soil on which animals graze and food is grown. And the people who inhabit this country, Papa – they, too, are a spectrum of colors. Our world is more than black and white. I know this now.

I cannot tell you where I am. I do not want to endanger those around me. No doubt this letter, when it reaches you, will have a postscript. I will be long gone by then, so please do not try and find me here.

I have changed, Papa. I am certain you would not like what you would see if you were here. I have had my eyes opened to the real workings of the world, in all its cruelty and wonder.

We will probably never see each other again. After all that has occurred, there are many reasons why a return to my old life in Virginia is impossible.

But what I really want you to know is that I am in love. Never did I think the love of my life would come in the shape and form that it has. I do not know what will become of this love, but just to know that there exists in this world someone so kind, so strong, so extraordinary – that is enough for me. Loving him, being able to love him – it has made me happier than I can describe. Know, Papa, that whatever happens to me now, whatever you may think of what I have done, the last few weeks have been the happiest of my life.

I love you, Papa. None of this is your fault; nothing you or Mother could have done would have changed the outcome. Please ask her to forgive me. And if it's appropriate, please tell the Fabres I am sorrier than I can say, and that I await God's judgment on my actions.

All my love,

Samantha

"Samantha," said Annie, running her finger over the name.

She sat on the bed and read the letter again, willing it to tell her the rest of the story. Then she looked around the small space, the hidden space, wanting the room to have more to say.

So many questions flew off the page in her hands. They whirled around Annie's head, so loud and demanding it was as if they could be reached for and held.

It felt like some kind of trick. How could this have been here, all this time, and no one ever noticed? She half-expected a television personality to jump out and tell her she was on candid camera. "Ha, ha!" he'd say. "You fell for it! You thought you'd found a letter written by a Virginia girl, just like you. And you thought it funny that the some of the contents of the letter could have been written by yourself? Fooled you!"

There was no television personality. *Of course there isn't,* she thought. The longer she sat in the room, the more real it became.

She carefully put the letter back in its envelope and inserted it in between the pages of the Bible. As she crawled out of the room and put the two stairs back into place she felt guilty, like she was closing the door on a newly discovered friend. She let her hands rest on the edge of the stairs and pressed her fingertips into the worn wood.

There were many things that Annie did not know. How long would they be in Vermont? Where would they end up next? When would she see Virginia again? Would it ever be possible to go back to her old life?

But this is what she did know: a Virginia girl named Samantha had written a letter over 150 years ago and never sent it.

Annie had to find out why.

Chapter 4

Samantha stood up and lost her balance. This now happened several times a day. She knew it was down to the lack of food. Her mother told everyone it was Samantha's intolerance of the heat and increasingly weak disposition.

The cotillion was tomorrow and it couldn't come soon enough. Samantha had floated through the week on a hunger-induced haze. Every day the routine was the same. Chimi and Oma pulled her out of bed and splashed cold water on her face. She was given one apple for breakfast accompanied by a cup of weak tea. Her teeth were brushed, her nightgown pulled over head, and her hair taken out of cotton wraps and tied back. After this, her face was powdered, even though it all melted off by 10am, and she was doused with perfume that went stale in an hour.

Next, she was dressed. The dreaded corset. Fifteen minutes of pulling and tightening until her ribs overlapped across her heart. The hoop skirt, and then a dress made from fabric that did not breathe, which Samantha thought gave her and her dress something in common.

She was then brought downstairs for her lessons with Miss LeMonde, who gave Samantha endless instruction on how not to laugh loudly, how not to share her true thoughts on people and places, how not to reveal her talents in shooting and riding – in short, how to stifle her every inclination. She was primed to ask questions about an individual's accomplishments and property, even when she had no interest in the answer. She was taught to stand unnaturally straight, forcing her shoulders back even though it made her feel exposed, like her chest could be opened and her heart lifted out. In previous lessons, she was made to practice taking small bites of food, fighting her natural desire to eat as much as she could, as quickly as she could. That lesson had been banned since the disastrous dress fitting.

"You're not eating until the cotillion is over, so there is no need," her mother had said.

Samantha felt she bore the marks of a tree that had been axed, one delicate branch at a time.

Lessons ended at noon, when the smell of freshly baked bread wafted in from the kitchen. At the beginning of the week, such smells made Samantha's mouth water. Now, after a week of not eating, they just made her feel ill. Oma brought her back up to her bedroom where she was given her second apple and a thin slice of bread, while those downstairs had beef stew and fried okra, with strawberries and cream for dessert. After lunch her dress and hoop skirt were taken off so she could rest for an hour on the chaise while Oma waved palm leaves to circulate the air. Today she did not resist. The room swayed. Closing her eyes only made it worse.

There were many elements of the cotillion that should have made her nervous. Would she trip in those ridiculous shoes? Would the heat in the room be too much to bear? The truth was none of these things concerned her. Her main worry was that Eli would not be brave enough to talk to her father and make his proposal. In the meantime, she was expected to make every bachelor in the room believe she might be theirs for the taking.

Her mother's fast step broke through such thoughts. "We need to go through the list," she said as she sat on the end of Samantha's chaise.

"Do we have to?" Samantha moaned.

Her mother read from the piece of paper she held. "Jeremiah Stanton."

"Too fat."

"Enjoys shooting and riding horses. Tobacco plantation."

"You just described every bachelor in Virginia."

"Davidson LaRoue."

"Pompous."

"Heads the Plantation Owners' Society at the church."

"He just likes hearing himself talk."

"Clemens Casey Cantor-Carlson."

"Sounds like a tongue-twister."

"Acceptable dinner conversation topics include the weather and the church. You are not to mention books or politics, and for God's sake don't mention secession. If the conversation turns to shooting you are to say you know nothing about it."

"I'm a better shot than most men in Virginia."

"That's your father's doing. Men despise being shown up by a woman."

Samantha yawned. Her mother yanked her arm and pulled her upright.

"I do not accept this behavior. You come out tomorrow. You must smile, you must laugh, and you must charm. You must do everything that is expected of a girl in your position or there won't be a single man in Virginia who will have you."

"I already know who I want to marry, Mother," she blurted.

Her mother glared. "Who?"

Samantha straightened, even though it made her dizzy. "Eli."

Her mother laughed. "You can't be serious."

"Think about it, Mother, it's perfect! There's no one else to inherit Mont Verity…"

"There was," her mother whispered.

"…and Royal Fabre will inherit Dominion Royale. So that means Eli is free to take over our planta…"

"Elijah Fabre is just a silly little boy," said her mother. "I have tolerated the time you spent with him as a playmate, but now I see I let it go too far. It is a foolish idea, Samantha, and you must get it out of your head."

Samantha sank. "But Mother, I've decided…"

"You think you get to decide? Women never get to decide. The sooner you accept that, the better." She handed her the list. "Memorize this. When I come back, you will recite it to me word for word. If you do that, I might even let you have some say in who we choose. Cooperate and you might get someone you could actually learn to love."

"Like you love Father?"

Her mother pursed her lips. "I'll be back in an hour," she said, and closed the door behind her.

Samantha crumpled the list and threw it at the door.

"Best do as she says, ma'am," said Oma.

"What do you know?"

She crossed her arms, furious that her mother had dismissed her idea so quickly. Marrying Eli was best for everyone. Surely her mother and father had realized by now that they couldn't marry her off to someone with his own plantation. Then Samantha would have to go live with her new husband, wherever he was, and then what would happen to Mont Verity? This was her home and she was determined it always would be. Surely her father understood that.

"Oma, where's Father?"

"Don't know, ma'am. Though I heard he was heading out to the shooting range."

Her father never went to the shooting range without taking her with him. Why was he there on his own? "What's he doing out there?"

"Don't know, ma'am."

Samantha stood up. A wave of dizziness brought her straight back down. She slowly moved her feet.

"What are you doing, Miss Sammy?"

"I have to talk to Father."

Oma held Samantha's arm. "Miss Sammy, you knows your mama wants you in here resting."

"Don't touch me," she pushed Oma's arm away. "Now untie this corset."

"Miss Sammy…"

"Just do it!"

Oma meekly did as instructed. The strings loosened and Samantha felt her ribs and lungs shift back to their rightful place. She took several deep breaths then eyed her open window.

"Oma, go and get me some tea."

Oma's eyes darted to the teapot on Samantha's dressing table. "Miss Sammy, you gots tea already."

"Well, I want more."

Oma's eyes pleaded. Samantha knew that disobeying her mother's orders was not in Oma's nature. "Please, Oma, it's the only thing I'm allowed at this time of day. Now go."

"Miss Sammy, your mama will have me whipped…"

Samantha grabbed Oma's arm. "I'll whip you myself if you don't do as I say."

As soon as the words were out, she regretted it. She'd scared Oma – the look on her face made that clear. She eased her grip. "Please, Oma."

The slave gave a meek curtsey and left. With the door closed Samantha wriggled out of the corset and let it fall to the floor. She reached under the bed for her riding dress and put it on. From her window she could see her palomino in the paddock. A few slaves worked in the driveway trimming the shrubbery, their backs largely turned. Samantha climbed out of her window and onto the roof of the terrace. Over the years she'd mastered swinging herself onto the pillar at the end of the terrace, stealthily and quietly. Leg muscles made strong by horse riding served her well as she shimmied down to the ground. A house slave was clearing the remnants of lunch from the terrace and Samantha's landing startled him.

"Miss Sammy, what you doing?" he asked.

Samantha put her finger to her lips before running towards the paddock.

Her father had presented her with the palomino on her 11th birthday. It had been too big for her at the time, but that didn't stop Samantha from mounting it and digging her heels into its cream-colored sides. Six years later and the palomino was a dear, old friend. She climbed the fence, mounted him bareback and pointed him towards the shooting range. As they rode, she told him about her mother's reaction to marrying Eli. The palomino was well versed in Samantha and Eli's plans. She'd confided in him the day Eli told her they were destined to be together, and since then nothing nor nobody had come along to make her change her mind. Sure, Eli had his faults, but who didn't? "We're the same, you and me," he'd said at the time. "We're both living in someone else's shadow. Mine is Royal; yours is Georgia."

Royal was Eli's older brother – an accomplished horseman, marksman, and businessman. Anything Royal tried, he mastered. He was socially adept and showed, some said, strong business acumen. According to many, he was the most eligible bachelor in western Virginia. To Samantha, he was the most boring man she'd ever met. And he was mean to Eli. According to Royal, Eli always said the wrong thing, would never shoot a rifle with precision, and would never possess the skills necessary to ensure longevity of the Fabre family name and reputation.

Samantha had to contend with a much larger shadow. Her older sister, Georgia, was a natural beauty, an effortless conversationalist, and – as her mother put it – a Southern belle to her very core. Georgia was also dead. Scarlet fever had killed her four years ago, a month before her cotillion. After she died, Samantha's mother locked herself in her dressing room for six months and refused to come out. When she finally emerged, she wore black for three years and passed the days sitting by the window looking out toward Georgia's grave. She had very little to do with Samantha during those years, which suited Samantha just fine. Her mother made it no secret that Samantha should have been the one to go, that Georgia had so much more to offer the Weston family name and that she'd never be half the lady her sister once was.

In the years that followed, Samantha did everything to stay away from her mother. On rainy days, she passed the time in her father's study, reading the books on his shelves while he conducted the business of the plantation. Men coming in were always surprised to see a teenage girl sitting on the chair by the window, but her father always maintained there was nothing concerning the running of Mont Verity that could not be said in front of his daughter. This was how Samantha learned about her father's plans for industrializing Mont Verity, pretending to read while listening to everything that was said.

25

The only time Samantha was asked to leave her father's study was when her father's slave overseer, Clement Durant, came in. For reasons she never understood, her father didn't want her witness to anything concerning the business of owning slaves.

On sunny days, she would mount her horse in the morning and only come back when she was hungry or when it was getting dark. Most of the time she'd meet Eli in the woods, where they'd build forts, climb trees and swim in the creek. They'd catch fish with their bare hands and fry them over a small fire. They'd play hide and seek, they'd wrestle, and they'd have horse races. (Samantha and the palomino usually won.) Even as they got older and Eli's voice dropped and Samantha's girlish figure became soft and curved, they still spent their days much as they'd done when they were children. As far as Samantha and Eli were concerned, it made perfect sense that they get married. They were companions. Their land shared a border. They would spend the rest of their lives doing the same things they'd done when they were children. Eli would never expect Samantha to be a lady, and Samantha would never ask Eli to stop being himself.

Then Samantha turned 16. Her mother shed the black taffeta and threw herself into planning Samantha's cotillion. Samantha went along with the formalities. After all, what girl didn't want one of the grandest parties of the season thrown in her honor? But it quickly became apparent that her mother meant this to be a proper coming out, where suitors would arrive and assess her and her plantation, and her parents would check credentials against their own desires for the family's future.

All of this meant she hadn't been in her father's study for months. She'd neglected him, replacing their time together with dress fittings and etiquette lessons. As she raced to the shooting range, trying not to feel hurt that he was there without her, she realized that even though it was Eli's role to ask her father for her hand, her mother's reaction to the idea of Samantha marrying Eli made one thing clear: Samantha needed to talk to her father, and soon.

Gunshots rang through the air. The palomino bucked.

"Whoa, steady boy." Samantha calmed him. She arrived outside the perimeter of the shooting range, which sat in a clearing in the woods. Four horses were tied to the range's hitching post. One was Eli's.

"What's he doing here?" Samantha wondered out loud. She dismounted, tied her horse to the post, then trod quietly over the pine needles and stood behind a wide maple so she could observe without being spotted.

A scarecrow stood crucified in the middle of the clearing. Her father, Eli, Royal and Major Fabre stood at the gun table packing pistols. Samantha watched Eli sneak glances at Royal, looking for clues as to how to pack his pistol better. She knew he'd been asking his father for months to take him shooting, yet he always refused to let Samantha show him. Her own father had brought her to the shooting range as soon as she was strong enough to hold a pistol. She could pack one with her eyes closed.

"What happened to those slaves you bought last week?" she heard Major Fabre ask. "Have you got 'em yet?"

"Not yet," said her father. "They told me tomorrow, but I can't spare any resources tomorrow to fetch them. Not with this godforsaken cotillion nonsense. I'll just have to wait a few more days."

"That sure is a shame, Master Weston," said Eli.

"One of those things," said her father. "I think they'll be the last slaves I buy though."

"Thought so," Samantha muttered.

"Why's that, Sanford?" asked Major Fabre.

"I don't think slavery is going to be around much longer. If Lincoln is elected, I imagine that would be his first action."

"Lincoln?" said Major Fabre. "That old coot wouldn't dare free the slaves. He'd have every Southern man worth his salt marching to Washington and personally putting a gun to his head."

"Besides," said Eli, forcing his voice into a lower register, "who says Lincoln gets to be the boss of us? We'll secede before we let some northerner tell us how to live our lives."

"Elijah," warned his father.

"You're just repeating what everyone says at the Owners' Society," Royal snorted, not taking his eyes off his task. "We'll all suffer if we don't come up with an alternative to slave labor."

"Do you think so, Royal?" asked her father.

Eli wedged himself between her father and Royal. "Father, don't you think we could spare Cudgen? He could fetch the slaves on the night of the cotillion. You know, as a favor."

All three men looked at Eli. He cleared his throat and continued. "Our overseer could bring them as far as ours, then I'll personally escort them to your place, Master Weston. That way you get them sooner."

"You'll miss part of the ball if you do that," said Royal. Even from a distance Samantha could see Royal was laughing at Eli.

Eli stood straighter. "I'd rather do a favor for Master Weston and be late for the cotillion. Please, Father, let me do this."

Master Fabre's brow was furrowed. Then his face relaxed, and he put a hand on Eli's shoulder. "Well, that's mighty noble of you, son."

What's he doing? Samantha wondered. *If he misses the ball then he won't have the chance to talk to Papa.*

Royal elbowed Eli. "Your turn," he said, handing Eli the pistol.

Eli held the gun with both hands. It looked two sizes too big for his thin arms and feeble wrists.

"You're supposed to shoot with it, not cradle it," snorted Royal.

Eli approached the scarecrow, then put his back against it. Samantha could no longer see him – the scarecrow was taller and wider than he was. She heard him cock his pistol. Her father counted. With each count Eli took a step.

"One, two, three, four, five, six, seven, eight, nine, ten!" Eli turned and shot.

A tree next to Samantha lost its bark. Samantha screamed.

"Hold fire!" her father shouted. "Who's there?"

Samantha meekly stepped out from behind the tree.

"Samantha!" Eli and her father exclaimed at the same time. Samantha walked to the packing table. Despite overhearing the entire exchange between the four men, none of it explained what the Fabres were doing there. In all the decades of their living nearby, not once had they been shooting together. It was a pastime reserved for actual friends, not for neighbors who could barely tolerate each other. The only explanation for the Fabres' presence was that her father had invited them, yet nothing in their conversation gave Samantha any clue as to why.

She arrived at the table. Her father put his arm around her.

"Darling," he said, "what are you doing here?"

"What are y'all doing?" she said cheerfully, even though she knew the answer.

"Dueling!" Eli said.

"Except Eli's as bad a shot as a girl," Royal sneered, and Major Fabre shared in the cruel laughter. Eli's red face turned downward.

Samantha wasn't sure what offended her more – the slight against Eli or his insult to women in general. *Typical Royal,* she thought, and threw her shoulders back.

"Are you saying a girl can't shoot?"

Royal smirked and crossed his arms. "Haven't yet met one who can. Besides, everyone knows women and guns don't mix."

"And why's that?" she said. "I have eyes to see the target, a hand to hold the pistol and a finger to pull the trigger."

"Samantha..." said her father sternly.

"Let her try," said Royal, offering his pistol. "I want to see what I'm dealing with here."

Had Samantha not been hit by another wave of dizziness she would have demanded to know what Royal meant. Instead she had to wait for the swaying to subside before taking Royal's pistol and walking towards the scarecrow. She caught Eli's eye as she went, but couldn't read what he was trying to convey.

The sun blazed overhead and Samantha felt surrounded by its heat. She put her back to the scarecrow and leaned on it for support, ignoring the grinding noises emanating from her stomach. She cocked her pistol and took a deep breath.

"Count me," she yelled. Her father hesitated, then began. Samantha walked in time.

"One, two, three, four, five, six, seven, eight, nine, ten!"

Samantha turned and, just like her father taught her, waited that crucial extra millisecond for the target to come into focus. Her finger was on the trigger. She knew, if she shot now, her bullet would go straight through the scarecrow and shatter the pole. Then she remembered what her mother had said that morning and realized what Eli's face had been trying to convey: "Men despise being shown up by a woman."

"Might as well do as I'm told for a change," she thought, and fired. The bullet went exactly where she'd intended – into the sky, free and fast.

Behind her, Royal laughed. "Told you so!" he said. Samantha turned to face them and concede her defeat.

Then everything went black.

Chapter 5

Annie sat facing the door of the Laundromat and its condensation-lined windows. Behind her, half a dozen washing machines whirred. The smell of flowery fabric softener rode on the heat from the dryers. She had done her best to wear clothes that smelt the least and feared that if it wasn't for the pervading smell of laundry detergent it would be obvious how much she hadn't succeeded. Her plan was to finish her laundry, change her clothes, then head to the Store at Five Corners. Hopefully Theo would be home from school and she could ask him where she could have access to a computer.

She'd half-hoped it wouldn't be necessary, that she'd turn up on Main Street and find an internet café. While her clothes were washed in the Laundromat she'd find out everything there was to know about Samantha Weston, the place where she lived, how she'd ended up in the middle of Vermont and what had happened to her afterward. Annie would even have time to log onto Facebook and do what she needed to do.

There was no internet café. Aside from the Laundromat, all Main Street had to offer was a bakery, a post office and a hardware store. It was a wide road built for horses and wagons with small, Colonial houses dotted several feet back from the edge of the road.

All so different from where she lived in Virginia.

Clinton, Virginia did not have a Main Street. It had townhouse developments and mini malls, one after the other, stretching along the highway that ran from the Potomac River in DC all the way to the Blue Ridge Mountains. There was a point, Annie knew, somewhere after Manassas, where the townhouses ended, but Annie had never been past Manassas. There was never any need to go that far. Everything she'd ever needed was right in Clinton County – her friends, her high school and a mall with all her favorite stores. After all the moving around they'd done when she was little, Annie had been happy to stay in one place.

She pulled out Samantha's letter and looked at the address. *Beckwith Station, Virginia.* She wondered where it was, if it was anywhere near Clinton. For all she knew it could be in the next county. Annie had never been good at paying attention to geography or maps. *Boring,* she would have said to anyone who tried to convince her differently.

She opened the letter and re-read it again and again, until she soon knew it by heart.

...I cannot tell you where I am...

...I have changed, Papa. I am certain you would not like what you would see if you were here. I have had my eyes opened to the real workings of the world, in all its cruelty and wonder...

...We will probably never see each other again. After all that has occurred, there are many reasons why a return to my old life in Virginia is impossible...

Memorizing the words did nothing to help her read between them. She decided there were no answers to be gleaned from it, only more questions, and she put the letter away in frustration.

She studied the letters and numbers on the inside cover of the Bible. Perhaps the numbers were dates, but she couldn't work them out.

Another thing I need the internet for, she thought.

"So this is where you hide."

Annie jumped and then looked up into the green eyes of the boy from the Store at Five Corners.

"It's me, Theo. We met last week?"

Annie blinked as if to make him disappear. This was not how she had planned their next meeting. It would be at the store, she would be in clean clothes, and at least have run a comb through her bobbed hair.

"Why aren't you at school?" she croaked.

"It's Saturday."

Annie had completely lost track of the days.

"Whatcha doing?" he said.

She cleared her throat. "Laundry."

"Really? I thought maybe you were here for some sort of religious experience."

"What?"

"You're the first person I've ever met who brings the Bible to the Laundromat."

Annie looked at the book cradled in her hands.

He sat next to her and let out a mock gasp. "I was right! You are part of a religious cult."

Annie let out a little laugh. "It's not mine."

"Oh my God, you stole it! Thief! We've got a thief!" The other two people in the Laundromat took no notice. Annie resisted the urge to grab his arm. She didn't know how to tell him not to draw attention to her.

"So, what have you been up to?" he said.

"Um…nothing."

He leaned in. "Do you want to know what I've been doing?"

Annie shrugged.

"Going to high school. You should try it sometime."

She opened her mouth. Nothing came out.

"Relax, I'm joking," he said. "But you know what you could tell me?"

"What?"

"Your name."

Annie couldn't remember the last time anyone had asked that question or the last time she'd given a truthful answer. "It's Annie."

Theo held out his hand. "Nice to meet you." His handshake was gentle.

"Can I ask you something?" she said.

Theo smiled. "Of course you can."

"The first time we met, you mentioned the people who used to live in my house. Can you tell me anything about them?"

He shrugged and shook his head. "I can't tell you much. It's known as the Jennings Farm, but I can't ever remember anyone named Jennings living there. It's always been families or couples who don't stay for very long. I don't even know who owns it. We could find out though."

"What?"

"Who used to live there – the Town Hall has census data going back to the early 1800s. Let's go have a look." He stood up.

"What, you mean, now?"

"Sure."

"But my laundry…" said Annie.

Theo laughed. "No one will steal your stuff. This isn't that kind of town." He motioned towards the door and grinned. "Shall we?"

As soon as they left the Laundromat it began to snow and Annie became painfully aware of how inadequately she was dressed. She'd taken off some of her layers to wash them and wore just a button-down under her sweater. The black Chinese shoes she wore felt as thin as tin foil and her feet slid over the ice hiding underneath the new white flakes.

It took them ten minutes to get to the Town Hall, and Annie was frozen by the time they entered.

The Town Hall was a brick building perched on a small hill at the end of Main Street. Four pillars propped up the overhanging roof. Three rocking chairs sat frozen to the porch.

Inside, Theo and Annie's footsteps echoed on the marble floor. The foyer was two stories high. A stained-glass window above the wide staircase threw primary colors onto the walls. Underneath the staircase was a large wooden desk. Theo approached the gray-haired woman sitting behind it. "Hey Shirley," he said.

"Well, hey there, Theodore. How's your Dad doing?"

"He's okay."

"And you boys?" said Shirley.

"We're okay. Noah and Matt are both back at college, so it's just me and Dad now."

"Do you need anything? I can drop off another casserole tomorrow if you do."

"No, thanks."

There was something in Theo's tone that Annie couldn't quite place – a sadness, disappointment.

"Now, what can I do for you today?" said Shirley.

Theo put his hand on the small of Annie's back. Without thinking, she moved away.

"This is my friend, Annie. She just moved into the Jennings' place."

"Oh, that's nice," said Shirley. "That place could use a little TLC."

"She wants to find out more about the history of the place. Do you mind if we have a look at the town census records?"

"Of course you can, Theo. As long as you remember…"

"…put everything back when I'm done. I remember."

"Nice meeting, you dear," said Shirley.

"Thanks," said Annie.

She followed Theo up the stairs and down a long hallway. Sunshine streaming through the windows caught the dust dancing in the air. Theo entered a room at the end of the hall. A card table sat in the middle, surrounded by four metal foldout chairs. Wooden filing cabinets lined every available inch of wall space.

"Let's see," said Theo, running his fingers over the number plates on the front of each drawer. "It's an 1850 above the door, right?"

"Um…right," she said, even though she wasn't sure.

Theo opened one of the cabinets and started flicking through the files. Annie stood in the doorway, unsure of where she belonged.

"Found it!" he exclaimed, laying a manila folder onto the table and carefully angling a piece of paper so Annie could see it. The paper was thin and brown, the writing thick and faded. He pointed to an entry halfway down the page.

Jennings Farm, River Road.
Jennings, Z., head of household. 51.
Jennings, R. 49. Matron.

"I wonder if they knew my great-grandfather," said Theo.

"Is that possible?"

"Sure. My great-great grandfather built the store. The first Mason is in the 1785 census." He rolled his eyes. "And we've been here ever since."

"Wow," said Annie.

"What?"

"It's just....I was wondering what it feels like to be so rooted to one place."

"Hey, where are you from anyway?"

"Oh, all over, really. No place in particular."

"So you're a nomad?"

Annie pretended not to hear the question.

"So is this all there is to know?" she said. "That there was a couple living there in 1850?"

"No, I'm sure we can find out more. It just might take a little while."

"I really should go back for my laundry. But thanks for your help."

Theo put his hand on her arm. "I've got an idea. You go finish your laundry. It'll take, what, another hour? There's a little café in the bakery, about three doors down from the Laundromat. I'll see you there."

She knew she shouldn't. She should find out where to find a computer and then tell him she probably wouldn't see him again. She should finish her laundry, then go home and hide until it was absolutely necessary to come out again.

Instead she said, "Okay, see you there."

Annie watched from the café window, her clean laundry in a garbage bag by her feet. In the time she'd been to the Town Hall and back the snow had come down hard, then stopped, leaving everything covered in soft white. The sun reflected the snow, making the surroundings brighter.

It was, she surmised, a beautiful winter's day in New England.

Annie was one of four customers in the café. Two were a couple in their 50s, sharing a newspaper, wearing matching waterproof boots. The other was a girl, about Annie's age, intently making her way through a stack of college brochures.

Annie thought about the brochures that had come unsolicited through their old mailbox, all places her mother wanted her to look at, but that Annie only glanced at. Jenna and Marcy had showed her their lists, all large universities that had, as Jenna put it, "the best sororities ever." Annie's mother's list was all small, private colleges in the middle of nowhere.

Kind of like here, Annie thought.

The smell of food in the café was overwhelming. Standing at the counter ten minutes earlier to order a mug of tea – the cheapest item on the menu – had been agony. Freshly baked bread sat on high shelves, as if daring Annie to take them. In the display case were blondies, bagels, muffins, tortes, cheesecakes and strudels.

Just wait until you get home, she repeated to herself. *Your one burrito is waiting.*

Theo entered the café as if on a breeze, his face flushed and glowing. Annie clasped her hands around her hot tea.

"Hey Steph," he said as he passed the girl with the college brochures.

She looked up. "Hey, Theo," she said brightly. Annie watched as the girl opened her mouth to say more, but by then Theo was already at Annie's table.

"Good, you're still here," he said, sitting down next to her. Their thighs brushed. Annie shifted away. Theo didn't seem to notice or care.

"Can I get you something?" she offered.

"Maybe in a minute, first things first." He took a folded piece of paper out of the pocket of his fleece and laid it flat on the table. "Here's what I've got. The Jennings moved to Battenkill in 1835 and they started building the house you're now in. It wasn't finished until 1850, which explains the stained glass above the door. Mr. Jennings disappeared from the census list in 1865, which probably means he died that year. But at least one or two members of the family stayed in the house until the 1940s. Then a family trust was set up, and the house has been owned and managed by it ever since. However," he turned the page over, "the house's inhabitants have been sporadic. It's been empty for the past five years. I asked Shirley about it. She said the people who manage the trust are in some kind of legal battle over whether to sell it or keep it."

35

She looked at the list of names and her shoulders sank. No Samantha Weston.

"What's the matter?" said Theo. "You seem, I don't know, disappointed or something."

"Sorry. I really appreciate your help. Thank you. I was hoping you'd find a particular name, but it's not there."

"Which name?"

Anne shook her head. "It doesn't matter."

"Oh, come on. Consider it payment for my effort. You can't just dangle something like that in front of my face and then take it away."

Annie feared she'd angered him, but then saw that his eyes were laughing.

She reached into her backpack and pulled out the Bible.

Theo held up his hands. "Oh, no," he teased. "Don't think you can distract me by preaching a sermon."

Anne pulled out the envelope from where she'd wedged it into the book's binding. She removed the letter, unfolded it and gently placed it on the table.

"Whoa," said Theo, leaning over and squinting at the faded ink. Annie watched his eyes move over the handwriting, then back up to the top of the page.

"1861!" he exclaimed, and a few people in the café turned to look. "Where did you find this?"

Annie hesitated, unsure of how much should she tell him. It was better, she knew, to be overcautious than not cautious enough. Still, she reasoned, the house was its own entity; its history had nothing to do with her or her mother or how they'd ended up in Battenkill. And she wanted to find out more about Samantha Weston. What could be the harm in sharing the mystery?

"I found a hidden room in my basement. It's underneath the stairs. There's a bed and a lantern and a wooden crate. On it was this Bible, and in it was this letter."

Theo's fingers hovered over the letter, as if fearing it might disappear. Annie waited for him to laugh, to say it was obviously a fake, or at least that it was nothing to get excited about. Instead he said, "This is amazing!"

"Really?"

"I mean, look at this! A real letter from a real person, written – what – over 150 years ago? I've never seen anything like this. We've got to find out more."

"What do you mean?"

"Like who she was, where she went afterwards, and why this letter was never sent, don't you think?"

"How?"

"There's lots of ways. Internet, for one."

If only, Annie thought.

Theo stood up. "Come on."

"Where are we going?"

"I don't know. I can't decide what I want to do more – see this room of yours or go home and start searching the Web."

"You can't come to my house," she said quickly.

"Why not?"

"My…my mother. She doesn't like to have visitors."

"How come?"

Annie's head flooded with the truth. *Because she's frightened of every strange sound and shadow. Because she's been scared to death so many times that in some ways she's actually dead. Because she's been so scarred she can't actually feel anything anymore.* And yet, for the first time, Annie had found something to make her rise above the fear of the past year: Samantha Weston.

"My mother's not very well. It's better if I can go home first and see how she's doing."

"Well, how about this, then. You go home and make sure she's alright. Then come to my house."

Annie gulped. "Your house?"

"I'm going to find out everything I can about Samantha Weston and Mont Verity." He paused. "Don't you want to know too?"

Annie stood up to meet his eyes. "Yes. Of course I do."

"Good," he said, and turned to go. At the door, he paused. "Oh, and Annie?"

"Yes?"

"You are going to show me this room. Don't think you're getting out of it."

Annie felt a smile fill her cheeks. "I won't."

Chapter 6

Samantha was dreaming. Even though she knew it, she couldn't make it stop. Everything was blurry, like looking out of the window during a thunderstorm. Voices surrounded her, but they could not be deciphered. A horrible sensation burned across her senses until she felt she might explode.

Consciousness slowly won over unconsciousness and the pieces of her dream found their real-life counterparts. She blinked until the blurriness gave way to clear vision. Oma waved smelling salts under her nose.

"Come on, Miss Sammy, wake up."

Samantha was in bed. The clock on her mantelpiece read half past five. *I don't remember coming in here to lie down,* she thought. She searched her memory, then the images hit her: the gun, the scarecrow and Royal's vapid presence.

Outside her bedroom door, voices raged.

"You have the audacity to starve our daughter without even consulting me?"

"Oh, don't be so dramatic."

"How could you do such a thing? She's still a growing girl."

"Growing in the wrong direction, if you ask me..."

"All this fuss, Madeline. The cotillion, the dress, the list of men I wouldn't let near my daughter under any other circumstances, and for what? We've already decided who she's marrying."

Samantha shot up.

"Lie down, Miss Sammy," said Oma.

"Shut up, Oma," Samantha whispered. "I need to hear this." She strained towards the door.

"You know perfectly well why we're doing this. A cotillion isn't just for potential suitors. A debutante's coming out sets a precedent for how she'll be received in society for the rest of her life."

"Look around you, Madeline. There's a war coming. Everyone knows it."

"Don't be ridiculous. Even the Fabres aren't worried. Major Fabre says it will be over before it's even started."

Samantha heard her father sigh, as he often did when talking to her mother. "I'm going to talk to our daughter. I want her to have a real meal in her room by the time I'm finished or so help me Madeline I will stand at our front gate tomorrow and turn away every single guest, and I will tell them it's because you're flatulent."

Her mother gasped. "You wouldn't..."

Samantha stifled a giggle.

"Yes, I would. Now if you'll excuse me, I have to talk to my daughter."

Samantha lay down. "I've been asleep this whole time," she whispered to Oma, closing her eyes before the girl could respond.

Her father's heavy footsteps entered the room, and Samantha felt the comfort of his familiar scent. He always smelled of the outdoors, like freshly scythed grass slowly drying in the sun.

"Leave us, Oma," he said, and the slave quietly obliged.

Samantha felt her father's weight on the end of her bed and it reminded her of being a little girl. Her father would sit with her almost every night and tell her stories about when he was a little boy, running barefoot through the fields and woods. There was no main house then – just a small wooden cabin where they lived while the main house was being built. He would tell her how the grand white house in which they now lived literally grew out of the land, its foundations laid when he was no more than knee high, the whole house completed by the time he entered manhood. He would tell her how he stood behind his father in the cotton fields, watching him plan rows and spacing between plants, determining which fields were fertile and which ones needed to rest. He would tell her that he was never happier than when he was at Mont Verity, in his fields, smelling the freshly-budded cotton blossoms and inhaling the moist air. Samantha and her father had this in common. She, like him, never had any desire to leave this land and this house.

Her father placed his gentle hand on her shoulder. "Samantha," he said. "I need you to wake up."

She opened her eyes. Her father looked exhausted. Dark blue pockets sat under his dull eyes. His posture was bowed, as if his broad frame and shoulders had lost their ability to stand in strong, straight lines.

"What is it, Papa?"

"First of all, I'm sorry about this... the food thing your mother dreamt up. If I'd known..."

39

His voice faltered. "It ends now. Oma will bring you something shortly."

"Thank you, Papa."

He folded his hands over his crossed knee. "And I'm sorry about this whole cotillion nonsense. But thank you for going along with it so far." He paused. "It means a lot to your mother."

"I know," said Samantha.

"I need to tell you something, Samantha. Something I should have told you the minute the decision was made. Your mother didn't want you to know until after the cotillion. But I think you have a right to know."

Samantha held her breath.

"You're going to marry a Fabre."

Samantha threw her arms around her father. "Oh, Papa, thank you so much. Eli and I..."

Her father pulled her arms away and held them tightly in front of her. "Samantha," he said. "It's Royal."

Samantha waited. Her father had just made a mistake. Any second now he would correct it.

He didn't. She thought of Royal at the shooting range, mocking Eli and undermining her. Now she regretted not shooting the scarecrow into smithereens. Royal was everything she despised: pompous, self-important and too focused on being good at everything to know how to laugh.

"But...but, Papa. I hate Royal."

"You don't hate him, Samantha."

"Papa, he's awful. He's mean, he's boring, and...Papa, how could you do this to me?"

"I promise I have good reason. Your sister is gone. You know Mont Verity will go to you. I need you to stay close, to make sure that everything our family has worked for over the past fifty years wasn't for nothing."

"But, Papa, that's exactly why I should marry Eli! Royal will inherit Dominion Royale. How can he manage two plantations at once?"

"Royal and I are still working out the details. It looks like the best course will be for you to reside at Dominion Royale after the wedding. When I'm gone he will hire someone to inhabit and oversee Mont Verity until such time that an heir is ready."

"An heir! You mean you'll wait until I have a son and he's old enough? Papa, I am a suitable heir. Eli is a suitable heir."

Her father shook his head.

"Samantha, there's something about that boy I've never liked or trusted. I really do think this is the right decision." He stood up. "Now, you rest. Oma should be here soon with your supper, a proper supper." He turned to leave.

Samantha's eyes burned. "Papa, please don't make me marry Royal. Let me stay here."

Her father paused at the door, and Samantha exploded in desperation.

"I won't even marry Eli! I'll stay a spinster and I'll run Mont Verity better than any man. You know I can, Papa. You know what I can do."

She watched her father sigh and lower his head. "You know that can't happen, Samantha. It's the law."

"Then change it!"

"Samantha," he said sternly. "There are far greater concerns now than altering long-standing traditions so that you can get what you want."

"Like what?"

"Samantha, it is possible that our country is on the verge of a great change. I don't know for sure, but I have a feeling things are going to get worse before they get better. This is just how it has to be."

"I hate Royal!" she shouted. Her father left, leaving Samantha to fall onto her bed in a heap of tears.

When supper arrived an hour later, Samantha planned to reject it. Did her father really think that such a gesture mitigated his larger offense? She imagined leaving the tray outside her door, untouched. Or even better, dropping it from the upstairs landing and letting it crash onto the marble floor below. The whole house would hear it, maybe even some of the slaves working outside, too.

But Samantha weakened. Faced with fried chicken, browned potatoes, creamed corn, two biscuits still warm from the oven and pecan pie drowning in cream, she forgot everything Madam LeMonde had taught her about table manners and etiquette. Never had food tasted so good. Samantha did not stop until all plates were clear. Outside her window the sky flooded with the best God had to offer: purple and blue streaks against the vibrant orange of the setting sun. Sated for the first time in days, she lay down on the chaise, put her hands on her full belly and fell asleep.

When Samantha awoke from her food-induced slumber, it was dark. She lay on the chaise, wondering if she should muster the strength to move. Downstairs, the grandfather clock chimed ten times.

"Eli," she whispered. "I have to get to Eli."

She jumped up and threw open her bedroom door. Oma and Chimi rose from two chairs that straddled the entrance to Samantha's bedroom. Behind them, the house was eerily silent.

"I'm going out," she said.

Oma and Chimi stood together, blocking Samantha's exit.

"Sorry, Miss Sammy,' said Oma, "but you gots to go back in."

"What?"

"We's got our orders, Miss Sammy," said Chimi. "And we can't let you out. You staying put until the cotillion tomorrow."

Samantha looked past them. The hallway was quiet. A faint light emanated from the stairwell, yet no sound or movement accompanied it.

"Where is everyone?"

"They all been tol' to get an early night, since we all gonna be up befo' dawn and prob'bly not back in bed until the next dawn."

Samantha rolled her eyes. "I meant Mother and Father."

"They at the Fabres, Miss Sammy," said Oma. "Said they had matters to discuss."

Samantha spoke through gritted teeth. "Well you send Mother a message that she can't keep me locked up in here like some... some...slave."

Oma ignored the slight. "It ain't your mama's orders, Miss Sammy. It's your daddy's."

"Papa?" The idea made Samantha's knees shake. Not only had her father ordered her confinement, but he was at the Fabres right now planning...she didn't even want to contemplate what he was planning.

Samantha lunged forward. Oma and Chimi grabbed her.

"Let me go!" she screamed. The two slaves pinned her to the wall, surprising her with their strength.

"Now you listen, Miss Sammy," Chimi hissed. "We gots our orders. Your daddy says we can tie you up if that's what we gots to do to keep you here. Now, I don't want to have to do that. So for once, Miss Sammy, do as you are told and sit tight. It'll make it easier on everyone."

Samantha's eyes darted between the two women. She looked for a weakness, for a hint of wavering resolve. But there was none. She turned around and closed the door behind her, disbelieving what had just happened.

She waited until she heard Oma and Chimi sit back down in their chairs, then tiptoed across the room to the window. She opened it, bracing herself for a creak that would give her away. There was none. She lay down on the windowsill to push herself through. Her back brushed the

42

frame and the window shifted slightly in its place. Her bedroom door flew open. Oma's voice halted her.

"Don't even think about it, Miss Sammy." The slave strode into the room, grabbed Samantha's arm and pulled her back in.

"There ain't no point tryin' that again. Your daddy's got Milo and Zeke down there and they got the same orders as we do."

Samantha looked out of the window and down to the ground. Milo and Zeke sat in the front garden, facing Samantha's bedroom window.

Oma left the room. Samantha slumped to the floor and put her face in her hands.

Samantha stayed there all night, failing to figure out what to do. She had to convince her father that marrying Royal wasn't what was best for Mont Verity. Or, for that matter, Samantha. Running away was not an option and her father knew it. She loved Mont Verity too much to ever leave it voluntarily. She briefly contemplated refusing to attend the cotillion unless her father changed his mind, then conceded that such a move would be disastrous. Whether she liked it or not, her mother was right: a debutante's cotillion set the tone for how she would be perceived for the rest of her life. There had to be another way.

Samantha heard a click at her window. She got up and peered out, just as a small pebble hit the glass. Outside the night sky was letting in the blue of dawn. Down below, Milo and Zeke were asleep in their chairs. In front of them was Eli.

"Eli!" she exclaimed. He put his finger to his lips. He motioned for her to open her window. She did it slowly and quietly. Eli held up his slingshot. Samantha smiled. It was the one sport in which Eli was a good shot.

She saw him pull something from his pocket. From where she stood, she couldn't tell if it was a piece of paper or a scrap of cloth. She watched him wrap it around a small object, then shoot it towards her window. Samantha held out her hands to catch it, but misjudged its weight. It sailed between her open palms and hit her hard in the chest. Only the knowledge that Oma and Chimi were outside her door kept her from cursing.

She lit the candle by her bedside table and saw what Eli had delivered – a note wrapped around a rock the size of an apple. She unwrinkled the damp paper, held it up to the dim light and squinted at the inky scrawl.

I overheard it all – I know they want you to marry Royal. I want you to know that I WILL NOT LET THIS HAPPEN. I know how to change your father's mind. But I need your help.

Meet me tomorrow at midnight, by the stream. I'll explain everything.

Samantha ran back to the window. Eli was gone. The hand holding the note fell to her side. How could he ask her to meet him tomorrow night, of all nights? It was her cotillion, for goodness sake. How would she escape? She hadn't been able to escape past four incompetent slaves this past night; how was she supposed to steal away when every person – guest and slave – would be watching her? And how on earth would she get to the stream in that blasted hoop skirt?

"Men," she sighed in frustration. "They never think of these things."

She read the note again.

I know how to change your father's mind.

"I hope you do," she whispered.

She held the note over the candle, letting it burn in her hand.

"I will meet you," she said, forcing her resolve to harden. "I'll figure out a way."

She threw what was left of the note into the fireplace and watched it wither into ash. The clock on the mantelpiece chimed six.

Her mother then entered the room, fully dressed and painted. She danced across the room to close the window, her hoop skirt swaying.

"Oh good," she said, cheerfully. "You're up. Oma will be here with your breakfast shortly, then we'll put your hair into wraps. Then there's the interview with the *Beckwith Station Gazette*, putting you into your corset, painting your face – oh, we've got so much to do." She put her hands on Samantha's shoulders and made Samantha meet her eyes.

"Remember this day," she said. "Because after today, your life will never be the same again."

Chapter 7

Annie emptied the bag of clean laundry onto her bed and rifled through the pile. If she was really going to Theo's house she wanted to make herself presentable. She threw off the two-day-old button-down shirt and picked up a long-sleeved V-neck. Once it was on, she checked herself in the mirror. It was tighter than she remembered, clinging to her waist and chest.

Defying the cold draft coming in from the thin window, she took off all her clothes. Goosebumps rippled over her skin as she inspected her full shape. There was undeniably much less to her than there used to be, but somehow there still seemed to be too much.

She shivered and pulled the V-neck back on. It was too revealing on its own. She didn't want Theo to think she was the kind of girl who flaunted herself. She pulled on a clean button-down shirt, a bulky blue sweater and her jeans, now satisfied she was well hidden underneath the layers.

She tried to remember the last time she'd dressed up to meet a boy. The answer, she realized, was never. *Girls dress to impress other girls,* she thought. In Virginia, Annie dressed in what she knew would meet with Jenna's approval. It had never occurred to her to change or challenge it. She realized for the first time that she was now free from those restrictions, at least until this nightmare was over.

Her stomach roared. It was nearly three in the afternoon, the time she usually allowed herself one meal. But she needed to get to Theo's house. She would just have to eat later.

Annie went to get her mittens off the radiator in the kitchen. From the living room came the low rumble of the television she'd found in a closet and reluctantly set up, knowing it would never be turned off and give her mother even less of a reason to get off the couch. She wondered if her mother remembered not allowing that in their old home, how if Annie had the television on for too long her mother would come in and turn it off, telling her to go rot her brain somewhere else. It was typical of grown-ups. The rules they threw around like boomerangs never came back on them.

She poked her head into the living room. To her surprise, her mother was sitting up, her legs crossed and the blanket on her lap.

"Mom?"

She looked over at Annie and smiled faintly. "Oh, hi sweetie."

"You okay?"

Her mother looked confused. "I think I'm hungry."

"Really? That's great! Do you want something?"

"I don't know. Anything. Please."

Annie went into the kitchen, turned on the oven and took her last burrito out of the freezer. *Great,* she thought, *now I'll have to buy more food when I'm at Theo's store.* She had been hoping to use it as an excuse to go back there tomorrow. Why did it suddenly feel like she was back in Virginia and her mother was getting in the way of what Annie wanted to do?

She went back into the living room. "There's a burrito on the counter. The oven should be warmed up in about ten minutes."

"Where are you going?"

"Just to the store. We're almost out of food." She gritted her teeth. "Is there anything you want me to get?"

"How much money is there?"

"A thousand, at least."

"It's going to run out soon," she said.

Annie crossed her arms. "What do you want from the store?"

Her mother looked out of the window. "Where are we again?"

"Vermont. Battenkill, Vermont."

"How much longer?"

"I don't know."

"Do you think we're safe here?"

"As safe as we can be. No one knows we're here. Our names aren't on anything. If he finds us, it'll be pure luck."

"Good." She pulled the blanket up to her shoulders.

For a brief moment Annie considered telling her mother where she was going and why. She and her mother had never had much in common, but she thought Samantha Weston and the room under the stairs might be something that would spark her mother's interest. After a few brief seconds of contemplation, she decided against it. The less her mother knew about what Annie did, the better.

"So, you're okay waiting until the oven warms up?"

46

"What? Oh, yeah. Then what do I do?"

Annie felt a familiar rage seep into her bones. "The burrito needs twenty-five minutes. The timer's broken, so you just need to keep an eye on it."

"I think I'll wait until you're back," she said sleepily.

You can't bring yourself to put a burrito in the oven? Annie thought. "I might be a while. It's a long walk," she lied.

"No rush. I'm not going anywhere."

Annie stomped into the kitchen and turned the oven off. She didn't want to rush her time with Theo because her mother refused to make her own food. Even here, even now, somehow her mother managed to ruin everything.

"I'm glad I didn't tell her what I was doing," she muttered to herself as she opened the front door. "I'm taking as much time at Theo's as I need to. She can wait for me for a change."

Annie entered the Store at Five Corners and saw Theo behind the glass deli case, absorbed in the process of making a sandwich. She suddenly felt giddy and nervous, like every move she made or word she spoke could make him change his mind about wanting her there.

"Hi," she said, approaching the counter. Theo looked up.

"Hey! I was just thinking about you."

"You were?"

"I was trying to figure out what a girl like you would want for a snack." He motioned to the contents behind the deli counter. "You can have anything you want. We've got ham, turkey, roast beef, hummus, tuna, cheddar, American, provolone, Monterey Jack, lettuce, tomatoes, sprouts and onions. And for bread we've got white, wheat, multigrain, oatmeal, rye or pumpernickel."

Annie's mouth watered. It all looked too good to be true, all that food. But accepting it felt wrong, even though she knew the freezer at home was bare. The food regime she'd established a year ago was so ingrained she almost feared veering from it. It was better to stay in control.

"I just ate. What are you making?"

"Theo's Triple," he grinned. "Three of everything: ham, turkey and roast beef in between one slice of rye, one slice of pumpernickel, one slice of oatmeal, and all the trimmings."

He put the sandwich on a paper plate and arranged the other sandwiches in the deli case.

"You do that like you've had practice," she said.

"Yeah, I guess you could say my brothers and I learned to crawl back here."

"How many brothers do you have?"

"Two. They're both older. One is a junior at Wesleyan and the other is in law school at Northeastern. What about you? Any brothers or sisters lurking in the bowels of higher education?"

"No," she said.

He motioned with his head for her to follow. "This way."

"Where are we going?"

"The computer is in my bedroom."

Annie gulped. *His bedroom?*

Annie followed Theo through the back of the store and up two sets of wooden stairs. His bedroom was the attic room on the third floor of the house, its walls sloping with the roof line. A bed without a frame sat in the middle of the floor, covered in a blue and green flannel quilt and various wool blankets. His desk was a thick piece of oak clamped to two weathered trestles. A poster of Ziggy Stardust hung over his bed, the edges weathered and worn.

She went to the dormer window and looked out. Theo's top-floor vantage point provided a long view of the property behind the store. There were at least two acres of lawn. In the middle was a tired red barn. Its loft hatch lay open and Annie could see small hay bales through the gap.

"What's that over there?" said Annie, pointing to bumps in the landscape.

Theo looked over her shoulder. "That's the old town cemetery. Some of the graves go back to the 1700s. The more recent ones are from the 1940s. After that they opened the new cemetery in the middle of town. But most of my family are in there."

"Which Theodore Mason are you again?"

"I'm the fifth. Or the sixth." He laughed. "I can't remember."

"Guess you'll just have to count the graves."

"I suppose. Although lately I don't like looking at them."

"Why?"

"It's kind of weird to see so many gravestones that have my name on them."

As she turned something caught her eye. On his chest of drawers was a small black and white photo in a silver frame. A woman smiled through the shades of gray, clearly Theo's mother. The eyes, the high cheekbones and the perfectly round dimples – all of this he inherited from her. She was

48

young in the picture – mid-twenties, perhaps. Her smile stretched from one thick curtain of hair to the other.

Annie felt the heat of Theo's body behind her and wished he wouldn't stand so close.

"My mother," he said, reaching around her to pick up the photograph.

"She's beautiful."

"Thanks."

There was a sadness in his voice that rang familiar, but she struggled to place it. Then she saw his notes from the Town Hall on his bed and remembered: she'd heard it when Shirley mentioned his family. She wanted to know more, but didn't dare ask. It might make him think he could ask questions of his own.

Theo put the picture down and went to his computer. *His computer,* Annie thought. She felt in her pocket for the memory stick; it was there, like always. Maybe she'd be here long enough that he'd go to the bathroom or something. She only needed a five-minute window to do what she had to do.

She thought about the different ways she could trick him into leaving, then stopped. Theo was her only friend. Friends didn't do such things. No matter how badly she needed his computer, she didn't want to take advantage of him. *I'll just have to come up with something else,* she thought as she sat on his bed.

"So, have you found anything on Samantha Weston?"

Theo jiggled his mouse and brought the computer to life. The excitement in his voice was palpable.

"Okay, so I started by looking for Beckwith Station, Virginia." He motioned for Annie to look at the screen. It was a modern day map of Virginia. Her eyes zeroed in on Clinton, sitting just below the Beltway.

"That's my home!" she wanted to scream. *"That's where I want to be, not here in the Ice Age. I want my friends, I want my house. I want everything back the way it was."*

"The thing is," said Theo, "Beckwith Station doesn't exist."

"What? How is that possible?"

"Well, here's the thing I found out about the South. In the old days, before the Civil War, they didn't really have towns. They had cities, like Charleston and Atlanta, but outside of cities they really only had plantations and farms. It's only after the war ended that a lot of the plantation land started to be built up as towns. But before that, addresses were linked to railroad stations, which is why Samantha's mailing address said 'near Beckwith Station'."

Annie felt stupid for not knowing this. She'd lived in Virginia – how could she not know all this? "So Beckwith Station is not a town?"

"No."

"What is it now?"

He looked at the computer screen. "It was in an area that's now known as Clinton County."

The room swayed.

"You okay?" said Theo.

"Sure."

"Now, Beckwith Station – the actual train station – was destroyed in a slave rebellion right around the start of the Civil War. The area around Beckwith Station was renamed during Reconstruction."

Annie tried to figure out why she felt she was in a bad dream.

"What about Mont Verity? Did you find anything on that?"

Theo grinned and picked up a notebook covered in blue-inked handwriting. "Mont Verity was built by an Abraham Weston, and when he died it went to his son, Sanford. He married Madeline Jacobs in 1829 and they had two daughters. The eldest, Georgia, died in 1856, but the youngest was a lovely little girl called…"

"Samantha!"

"Yes."

Annie couldn't stop herself. "Is the house still there? Did you find out why she left? How did she end up here? Where did she go after? When did she die?"

Theo laughed. "Easy there, cowgirl. I've only been at this for an hour. There's still a lot more I can do though. But in the meantime, I think you should see this."

He opened a document and hit *print*.

"Right before you got here I found this website. It's all about old Southern society, so it has minutes of Plantation Owners' Society meetings and reports from slave auctions. But then there's this one section that is old who's-who announcements about cotillions and weddings."

He took the paper off the printer and held it up proudly. "On March 6, 1861, Samantha Weston had a debutante ball."

Chapter 8

Beckwith Station Gazette
Society News and Views
March 7, 1861

Cotillion season had its grandest coming out so far this year when, yesterday, Samantha Ashton Weston, only daughter of Sanford and Madeline (née Jacobs) Weston, was introduced to society.

The young debutante wore a Charles Worth original gown of champagne silk and tulle, embellished with embroidered pink rosettes. Hot-house roses and baby's breath were woven into her coiffure, which this society reporter deemed a magnificent defiance of gravity.

The first guests to arrive were Major Louis Fabre of Dominion Royale, his wife Narcissus (née Main) and their eldest son, Royal. Other guests and eligible bachelors travelled from near and far, with Colonel Jeremiah Stanton making the furthest journey from the Carolinas.

Miss Weston graciously met and greeted every single guest, engaging each of them with a few minutes' pleasantries. She remained at the door for over two hours without ever breaking her stance or smile.

Dinner was served promptly at 8 o'clock. Master and Missus Weston put on a sumptuous feast of roast pig, honeyed swede, collard greens, tomatoes and beans, and baked rhubarb and cream. Every one of Sanford Weston's slaves rushed to ensure the comfort of each guest. Never has this society reporter been offered so many mint juleps!

The dinner conversation in this reporter's corner, led by Miss Weston, was surprisingly tame given that our beloved state of Virginia has only just held its first secessionist convention. It shows just how well-bred we Virginians are that we are able to maintain civility and courtesy in these trying times.

One of the highlights of the evening was the gathering of the entire party onto the back terrace so that the occasion might be immortalized in tintype. The photographer charged with capturing this wonderful event has assured me that the resulting photographic image will be supplied to both Sanford Weston and myself.

The dancing began at 10pm, with Miss Weston and Mr. Royal Fabre sharing the first waltz. Despite the increased heat in the ballroom, Miss Weston then proceeded to dance with every eligible bachelor present (this society reporter counted 26 in all). It is no surprise then that shortly before midnight Miss Weston swooned while sharing a dance with her father. That she had to then excuse herself and be escorted to her bedroom suite was an unfortunate finale to an otherwise perfect evening. Master and Mrs. Weston, ever the most gracious of hosts, insisted their guests stay until the mint juleps ran out. This reporter also has it on good authority that Master Weston was generous with the cigars and bourbon on the back terrace.

All in all, a spectacular event, which will no doubt be followed by an engagement announcement from the Weston family. Who will be the lucky bachelor to secure Samantha Weston? You can be sure to hear it from this reporter first.

STOP PRESS: Just before we went to press, this reporter heard that on the night of the cotillion two of Master Weston's slaves – newly purchased – managed to escape while in transit to his plantation. It is also rumored that Major Fabre's slave overseer, Miles Cudgen, was killed in the escape. Typical of the Negro to take advantage of his white savior at what was supposed to be a time of celebration. We wish Master Weston luck in tracking down the heathen fugitives.

Samantha kept her eyes closed as her father carried her upstairs and into her bedroom. Oma and Chimi followed.

"I'll leave her in your hands," he said, easing her onto the chaise. She felt his breath on her face. "You were wonderful, darling," he whispered, then left the room. Samantha opened one eye.

"Dress...corset..." she murmured. She turned over to let Oma unbutton the dress while Chimi pulled the flowers from her hair. The hoop skirt was removed and the corset loosened.

"Light..." she whispered. "Too bright."

Oma lowered the lantern and Chimi appeared with her nightgown.

"No," said Samantha. "Too hot." Samantha was not lying. Before she pretended to swoon, there had been several moments when she feared she might pass out for real. It was an unusually mild evening for March. Every guest glistened, even the women who did nothing but stay in the corner to be fanned by the slaves. By the time her father carried her upstairs, most of the guests were seeking relief on the back terrace. She'd checked the front terrace briefly before the dance with her father: it was empty, save for the slaves guarding the front steps and the dozens of carriages collected outside.

"Please," she said. "Let me sleep." Even Oma and Chimi didn't think to doubt her exhaustion. They quietly extinguished the lantern and left the room. Samantha listened to them close her door and settle into the chairs outside her room.

"I think even her mama will let her be now," she heard Oma say. "That girl done everything she s'posed to do."

All night she had waited for Eli to turn up at the ball. He didn't. At 11pm, Samantha approached Royal.

"You want another dance already?" he joked.

Samantha did not smile. "Do you know when Eli is expected to arrive?"

Royal stood too close. "If all goes well, never."

"Why must you be like this?"

"And why must you bring up my stupid little brother at what is effectively the only engagement party we're going to have?"

Samantha sighed and turned away. Royal grabbed her arm.

"Well, if you're going to be like that I suppose I can tell you this: he's set-up some cockamamie scheme whereby he's going to bring your father's slaves here, since everyone is too darned busy to do it themselves."

Samantha started to remember. Dueling practice, yesterday. Eli offered his father's overseer to bring the slaves as far as Dominion Royale, then Eli would bring them the rest of the way himself.

"So he's not coming," she said, unable to hide the disappointment in her voice.

"Guess you'll just have to settle for me," said Royal, his voice a mixture of hope and sadness. He reached to put his arm around Samantha's waist, but she'd already walked away in the direction of her father, ready to share the dance in which she would pretend to swoon.

Downstairs, the grandfather clock chimed for 45 minutes past the hour. Samantha reached under her bed and pulled out her riding dress. Once dressed, her pistol secured in her bosom, she crouched by her bedroom window to check if it was clear. A carriage went down the drive. When it was gone, she slipped through the window, shimmied down the fat pillar and landed like a cat upon the dewy grass. Horses and their carriages were lined up six-deep along the side of the house. She maneuvered her way through the rows of carriages until she reached the border where the scythed grass ended and the wildflowers and reeds began.

It was only once she was sure she was out of sight that her pulse quickened.

Did Eli want her to run away with him? No, surely he would have mentioned that in his note. What if he meant for them to elope? And then, consummate?

No, she thought, repulsed by the idea. *Eli knows we'll never have Mont Verity that way.*

No matter which way she approached it, she simply couldn't reconcile why she was running through the woods instead of charming that insipid bunch of bachelors at the cotillion. Maybe this was Eli's way of helping her get away from it, even if for only a few hours in the night.

She arrived at the stream and looked for Eli's horse. It wasn't there.

It must be midnight by now, she thought. *Where on earth could he be?*

She looked up at the sky. The moon glowed through the trees. A light breeze swayed the high branches and Samantha caught sight of the North Star.

Twigs cracked under footsteps and Samantha turned. Eli emerged from behind a tree. Samantha ran to him and gasped. Blood covered his shirt. He smelled of kerosene. He did not look at Samantha, but instead looked through the woods behind her.

"Eli! What happened?"

"It's nothing." His voice was flat and unfamiliar.

"But your shirt!"

"It's not my blood."

"Then…whose is it?"

"I'll explain in a minute." He turned around. "You can come out now."

Two figures emerged from the darkness. Slaves, one male and one female.

They couldn't have been much older than Samantha, maybe even younger. The male was tall and thin, with sharp cheekbones sitting high on his slender face. Even by moonlight she could see the bones protruding under the skin of his wrists and the muscles in his sinewy legs. His large, bright eyes made contact with Samantha's and she quickly looked away. The girl was small and slight, her worn, cotton dress made for someone twice her size. Her hair was hidden under a handkerchief and her eyes were as dark and watery as the stream over which she stood.

"Samantha," said Eli, "this is Odus and Amira."

"Eli," she whispered, "what are they doing here?"

"I need you to hide them."

"What?"

"These are the slaves your father bought last week, the ones that Cudgen was supposed to bring to my plantation so I could bring them here."

"I don't understand."

"Cudgen was intercepted before he made it to our place. I need you to hide them somewhere. And I need you to make sure that no one knows where they are."

"But...but why?"

"I don't have time to explain right now. Just do this for me, Samantha. Meet me back here with them one week from today, at midnight."

"What? Where are you going?"

"I'm going to give your parents every reason to change their minds about me. Do as I say and I promise we will be married before Easter."

"But, Eli, where on earth am I going to hide them?"

"Somewhere in the house. Think about it, Samantha, the last place anyone would think to look for escaped slaves is in the main house of the plantation they were running away from. Your attic, or even your dressing room." He looked at Odus and scowled. "Someplace where you can keep an eye on them."

"How am I going to get them into the house?"

"Now is the perfect time. Everyone is at the ball. The upstairs should be clear."

"But how do I know they're not going to run away from me?"

Eli looked at Odus. "Because we have an understanding, don't we, nigger?"

Odus nodded so slightly Samantha wasn't sure he actually moved. Eli slid something into her hand. She looked down – it was the knife she'd given him for his birthday. The blade caught the moonlight.

"Why are you giving me this?"

"In case you need it."

"Eli, you know I always have my gun."

"And now you have this, too. You can never be too careful with these niggers. You never know what they might get up to."

Samantha shook her head. "I don't want it. I gave it to you. It's yours, not mine." She thrust it into his hand, tears welling in her eyes. "Eli, I don't see how I can..."

"Dammit, Samantha!" he shouted, and even the two slaves jumped. "I can't do this all by myself. If you can't figure a way to do this one thing for me then maybe you and Royal deserve each other."

"I'm sorry. I'll find a way, Eli. I will. And I'll be back here with them in a week. I promise."

"Good." He kissed her forehead. "Now, get going." He turned to Odus. "Don't let me down, nigger."

"Yes'suh."

They watched Eli run into the woods. Samantha stared into the space he'd just left. She couldn't even begin to imagine how she could keep the two slaves hidden, never mind how doing so would convince her parents that she should marry Eli.

She turned to the slaves. "You both do exactly as I say or we'll all be whipped within an inch of our lives. Do you understand?"

They nodded.

She motioned towards the house. "Okay, follow me."

Chapter 9

Annie hadn't planned on doing it.

In the time she'd been sitting in Theo's bedroom, watching him print off all he'd found on Samantha Weston with the excitement of a child on Christmas morning, she'd tried to hold onto the decision that she wouldn't use his computer.

But then his father called from downstairs. "I need to take a delivery," came the voice from below. "Can you just watch the counter for fifteen minutes while I unload?"

"Darn, I was just getting going," Theo said. "I'll be right back. Feel free to have a look yourself – you might find something I missed." He picked up his empty plate. "Are you sure you don't want something to eat?"

Annie knew she needed to extend his time downstairs. "Actually, could I have a sandwich? I guess I am kinda hungry."

"Sure. What do you want?"

What's the most complicated sandwich I can ask for? she thought.

"Um…can you do something grilled? I guess I'm craving something warm."

"I'm not surprised. I'd be cold too if I went outside wearing as little as you. Don't you have a winter coat or something?"

"Um, no, I haven't got one yet."

"Why not?"

She failed to come up with a good lie. "I guess I didn't know it would be this cold."

"Well, you can't keep going out without a coat around here. You'll freeze, especially being as thin as you are."

Annie felt a bitter twinge of satisfaction. *He thinks I'm thin.*

"Anyway, one grilled sandwich coming right up."

"Don't hurry, I can take care of myself."

He grinned. "I'd believe that if you weren't the girl who just admitted to not having a winter coat in Vermont."

She listened to his footsteps disappear down the stairs and tried not to look at the computer screen. But this was her chance.

"I can't do it," she decided. "It's not fair to Theo."

She pulled the memory stick from her pocket. It contained over 100 photographs, all taken within the space of a minute. Half of them she'd already posted on Facebook – one a week, in chronological order, starting from the beginning.

The process of posting was always the same. Log into the account she'd created at the bed and breakfast in Charleston. Read the new messages – there were always new messages. Post the photo. Double check the privacy settings (the page, the photos – everything was for his eyes only). Send a message of her own. Log off and clear the history of whatever computer she was on.

If she had time, she sometimes checked the pages of her old friends. From what she could tell, not much had changed. Life went on. People dated, they broke up. Girls fought, they made up. Games were won and lost. As she sat on Theo's bed she realized there were ways in which her old life seemed like a daytime soap opera you could miss for years and still know what was going on once you started watching again.

She knew there wouldn't be time for checking anything else now. The only action she could take would be to log on to her other account, post a photo, and log off.

She stood up, went to the door and listened. There was no sign that Theo was on his way upstairs. She went to the window and looked down. A tractor-trailer sat in the loading dock and she could see crates and boxes being carried off. She closed her fist around the memory stick and went to Theo's computer.

She opened a new browser window and logged on to Facebook. She had three new messages.

I'll get to those later, she promised herself.

The memory stick slotted into the USB port and Annie tapped Theo's desk while she waited for the computer to read it.

Finally, a pop-up box appeared, listing the photos. Annie checked the Facebook page to be sure of the last photo she loaded. Her eyes caught a glimpse of what was already there, the grainy green of night-time exposure reminding her of seasickness. She went to *Photos*, and clicked on *Upload*.

"Dad, I'm just going upstairs to give Annie her sandwich," she heard Theo yell from downstairs.

Annie selected the next photo in the sequence and double clicked.

"Come on, come on," she whispered through gritted teeth.

The photo finished loading just as Theo's footsteps hit the stairs.

Annie quickly typed a caption. *In case you think I forgot....*

She yanked the memory stick out of the port and closed the browser window.

"Any luck?"

"What?" Annie snapped. She only then realized she'd been holding her breath.

"Are you okay?" he said, handing her a plate. It smelled divine.

"Yes. Fine. Thanks." She held up the plate. "What is it?"

"Grilled mozzarella, tomato and pesto. I was going to put chicken in it, but I wasn't sure if you were a vegetarian."

Annie smiled. "I'm not." Without thinking she sank her teeth into the toasted bread and melting cheese, their flavours assuaging an ailment she didn't know she had. Warmth surged, and she became painfully aware of how much her body ached for this kind of relief.

Theo sat on the edge of his bed.

"So, did you find anything?"

"What?"

"Samantha Weston. Did you find anything while I was downstairs?"

Annie checked the computer screen and was relieved to see it showed only Theo's desktop.

"No, not really. I think we've done all we can for now."

"Okay. Well, when you finish your sandwich, we can go."

"Go where?"

"To your house. I want to see this room."

"Theo, I don't know…"

"I'll be quiet. Your mother will never know I'm there." He stood and opened the door of his closet. "Here," he said, handing her a black pea-coat. "It doesn't fit me anymore."

Annie picked it up, and the wool scratched her skin. She slid her hands through the satin-lined arms and wrapped herself in its folds. It smelled of Theo – a mix of sawdust and freshly baked bread.

"Come on," he pleaded. "You owe me."

Annie gazed at his desk and his blank screen. She looked at the still-warm sandwich and felt the weight of Theo's coat.

"Okay, we'll go."

Annie pulled as hard as she could.

"Are you sure I can't help you with that?" Theo watched Annie try to shift the bottom two steps of the basement stairs. On the day she'd found

Samantha's letter she'd put the steps back in place, but now they were stuck. The wood cut into her hand.

"It's jammed, somehow," she said, her breath laboring from the effort.

"Here, let me," said Theo, crouching next to her. She watched him cup his hands around the corner of the steps and gently wriggle them. He pulled a small flashlight out of his pocket and Annie couldn't help but smile. *So he has one, too,* she thought.

"Ah, this is the problem," he said, and Annie craned her neck to see. "There's a divot here and the corner is stuck in it. I'll take this side and you take the other."

Annie did as she was told.

"On three – one, two…"

The steps moved on their hinge to the side, as if they had been waiting for Theo all along.

"I think you need to be careful how you put the stairs back, especially if you're in there when you do it. I'm not sure you could get it out of that divot from the inside."

Annie smiled to herself. He sounded just like her dad.

Theo shone the light through the gap. He looked at Annie. "Shall we?"

She watched him crawl backwards, on his stomach. By the time she followed he was already sitting on Samantha's bed, shining the light around the small space.

"This is amazing," he said.

"What do you mean?"

"Gosh, where do I start? The fact that this is here. That it was so well hidden. That some girl was writing a letter while sitting in this very spot over 150 years ago and that it's been here ever since, waiting for you to find. I mean, don't you think it's incredible?"

Annie didn't have time to answer. Theo was on his knees, unwrapping the canvas sheet from its hay bed.

"What are you doing?" she asked.

"Exploring. Do you mind? I mean, you found the letter in the Bible – who knows what else she might have hidden in here?"

Annie hadn't thought of that. She watched Theo pat his hand over the hay. The smell of mold permeated the space.

"It's incredible that this is so intact." He wrinkled his nose. "A little on the smelly side, though. So, where's your Mom?"

60

Her mother was in Annie's bedroom. Annie was only able to convince her to let Theo in under the guise of him fixing the washing machine. Her mother conceded, but only if she could hide upstairs.

"We probably shouldn't stay down here for too long," she said.

"Well, there's nothing under here," he said, folding the sheet back over the hay.

He shone the flashlight onto the lantern, still as Annie had found it sitting on the wooden crate.

"Wow, this is a relic." He picked it up. Annie watched its shadow dance on the wall. "I'm sure I've never seen one this old. We've got some old ones in our barn, but I'd be amazed if any of them could compete with this." He lifted it to his nose. "You can still smell the kerosene."

He set it down on the floor and handed Annie the flashlight. "Can you hold this for me?"

He put his hands on either side of the crate and gently pressed.

"What are you doing?" she asked.

"I want to pick it up, but I want to make sure it won't fall apart if I do." He lifted it up and Annie shone the light on its empty imprint on the floor.

"Darn," he said. "I was hoping she'd have put something under here. Oh well. Too much to hope for."

As he set it down, the flashlight's beam caught a reflection.

"Theo, wait," said Annie. She handed him the flashlight and turned the crate over. As she reached in, she felt a wooden handle. She pulled, but it didn't give. She jiggled it a few times until it broke free and she could bring it out into the light.

"Whoa," said Theo.

It was a knife, the silver blade about ten inches long with no hint of rust. A few small dark stains marred the cutting edge. Annie put her finger to its tip.

"Ow," she said. Blood oozed out of the small puncture the knife made in her skin.

"Careful," said Theo.

She laid the knife flat on her palms. On the wooden handle was an oval copper plate, tarnished green with age.

"There's an inscription on it," said Theo, leaning over and shining the light.

Annie read. "To Elijah Fabre, With Love from Samantha Weston, 1861."

"Fabre," said Theo. "That name rings a bell."

He crawled back into the main part of the basement. Annie followed and found him rifling through his backpack. He pulled out a piece of paper. "Yes, here it is."

Annie stood next to him. As he showed her the paper, his arm brushed against her shoulder. For the first time, she didn't mind.

"When I looked up plantations in Beckwith Station this one actually came up first – a place called Dominion Royale that was owned by the Fabre family. During the war the family were evicted and the house was used as a hospital by the Union Army. When they no longer needed it, they burned it."

"Elijah Fabre," Annie muttered. Something about his name struck a chord, but she couldn't immediately place it. There were two townhouse complexes near Clinton – one was called Dominion Heights and the other was called Royale Acres. Somehow they weren't what felt familiar.

"I wonder..." She pulled the Bible out of her bag and opened it to the page with the letters and numbers. Theo stood behind her and read over her shoulder.

"Here," she said, "at the bottom. SW and EF. They're initials. I can't believe I didn't see it before."

Theo took the Bible and Annie watched his eyes scan the page.

"Why didn't you show me this earlier?" The anger in his voice startled her.

"I...I don't know. I guess I didn't know what to make of it and thought I'd wait until I did."

Theo looked at the page like it was a ghost.

"Theo, what is it?"

He studied the page one last time. "I've seen this before," he said. "There's something exactly like it in my barn."

Flakes of icy snow fell from the gray sky as Theo drove back to the Store at Five Corners. James Taylor played through the speakers. Annie looked out the window at the mountains covered in white and felt, for the first time since the night everything changed, like the past year had been merely a dream. Here she was, riding in a truck with a boy, wearing his coat. It was almost like she was normal.

"I mean, it's just always been there," said Theo. "I used to wonder what it was. I even asked my dad once, but he didn't know. He guessed they were measurements or a log of some kind."

Theo pulled in behind the store. Annie followed him up a small hill in the backyard. The ground was a mix of ice, mud and snow. The old graveyard she'd seen from Theo's bedroom window was nothing but bumps in the snow. Despite Theo's coat, Annie felt her hands going numb under her mittens.

He pulled open the doors to the barn and three kittens scattered.

"My grandfather kept horses in here until the 1950s. I used to play in the hayloft a lot when I was a kid, but, well, I'm not a kid anymore."

Annie followed him to a set of disused horse stalls. Theo swept away the hay and dirt with his foot, revealing the outline of a square trapdoor. He grabbed a crowbar hanging from the wall and pried the door open. It popped out of its frame, and Theo leaned it against the wall of the barn.

"See?"

Annie sat down, her feet dangling into the hole Theo had just revealed. On the underside of the trapdoor lay a list of letters and numbers in exactly the same format as the ones Annie had. She opened the Bible to the inside cover and held it up. Theo ran his finger down the list.

AK - 12/4/56
JS - 12/4/56
MB - 4/17/57
CT - 7/4/57, GB
ZT - 7/4/57, FD
AA - 1/8/58
DF - 3/12/58, M
HY - 9/23/58
GK - 7/4/59, DS
BR - 2/13/60
HN - 6/29/60, FD
GR - 7/13/60
HJ - 9/17/60, M
EF - 3/27/61
SW - 3/27/61

Then he compared it to the ones on the door.

AK - 12/4/56
JS - 12/4/56
M - 4/17/57
CT - 7/4/57, GB
ZT - 7/4/57, FD
AA - 1/8/58
DF - 3/12/58, M
HY - 9/23/58
GK - 7/4/59, DS
BR - 2/13/60
HN - 6/29/60, FD
GR -7/13/60

AF - 3/27/61
BV - 4/12/61
TG - 6/26/61, ESF
MO - 9/1/61
VX - 11/16/61, ESF
OY - 12/31/61
KJ - 2/13/62
GR - 6/25/62, ESF
VC - 1/6/63, ESF
KA - 1/6/63, ESF
HA - 1/6/63, ESF
PT - 4/11/63, ESF

"They're not exactly the same, but they're pretty close."

"Until here," said Annie, pointing to the list in the Bible. "Mine ends at SW."

"And mine keeps going. Although the date that yours ends matches the date here on mine – with initials AF." His eyes darted between the two and he sighed. "I don't get it."

Annie closed her eyes and thought about the contents of Samantha's letter. "She was in love. In her letter she talks about this great love, about how she is content to live in a world knowing such love exists. Maybe she was talking about Elijah Fabre. Maybe her parents didn't want them to get married so they ran away."

Theo considered this. "If Dominion Royale was the Weston's closest neighboring plantation then her father must have known Elijah Fabre. Why doesn't she just tell him who it is?"

"Maybe because she knew he wouldn't approve."

They sat in silence, both unsure of what to do.

Theo slapped his hands onto his thighs. "Come on. There's still so much more to know." He took her hand and they helped each other up.

"Hey, where did you leave the knife? We should find a safe place for that."

"I already have," she said and looked down. The handle was just visible above the knife loop in her cowboy boot.

Her father had been right. You never knew when something like that would come in handy.

Chapter 10

"Stay close," Samantha whispered. "And for Heaven's sake, don't make a sound."

Samantha, Odus and Amira peeked through the edge of the woods, looking over the tall grass to the scythed lawn and towards the main house. Yellow light emanated from the downstairs windows. Dozens of darkened figures lingered on the back terrace. Samantha looked at the rows of carriages lined six-deep along the side of the house, above which sat Samantha's bedroom window. All they had to do was get to the carriages unseen, then climb up the pillar and into safety.

She was about to lead them back the way she came, through the tall grass, when she saw that it was still matted down from where she'd run over it earlier. She couldn't risk taking the slaves back that way – what if someone noticed in the morning that the grass had been trampled? She looked across the lawn and decided the safest way back was also the most dangerous: they would have to crawl across the lawn.

"We need to get to those carriages," she whispered. "Do as I do."

Samantha got onto her stomach and began crawling on her elbows. The dampness from the grass permeated the cloth of her dress. All she could hope was the light from the house made it hard for those on the terrace to see what was happening on the lawn.

The more she crawled, the more infuriated with Eli she became. What was he thinking? This was complete madness, anyone could see that. They were sure to be caught. She doubted he'd even stopped to think of the repercussions if that happened. How this could possibly make any difference to her parents' decision that she marry Royal completely eluded her.

After what felt like a lifetime, they reached the nearest carriage, unseen. Samantha crouched under it and waited. Odus and Amira were a few feet behind, and she could hear Odus gently urging Amira on.

"We almost there. Just a bit more."

Samantha was about to shush him when Amira's face came into view. The girl was clearly tired and in pain.

"Okay," Samantha whispered, "we're going to crawl under the carriages until we get to the side of the house. Stay as close as you can to the back wheels and for God's sake don't spook the horses. See the corner window at the edge of the front terrace? That's my bedroom. We need to climb up the side pillar to get there. Can you do that?"

Odus looked at Amira, who looked as if she might cry. "We can do it, ma'am. I'll help Amira." He put his hand on her arm. "It's gon' be okay."

Samantha rolled her eyes. "Come on."

They crawled under the carriages. Samantha's dress got stuck under her knees, making her stumble. She stifled the urge to curse. As they got closer to the side of the house, the two slaves who had been guarding the house's entrance now sat on the side railing of the frontterrace. Their backs were turned; their legs dangled. One sat leaning against the exact pillar Samantha, Odus and Amira needed to climb.

"Dammit," she whispered.

She turned to Odus and Amira. "Don't move until I say so. But when I do, you have to move fast."

They both nodded.

She crawled under the carriage closest to her window and positioned herself between its two front wheels. It was in the first row, so the horse – she hoped – would have a clear and long run. She reached up the left-hand side of the wheel shaft and felt for the brake lever. Visions of the many ways in which her arm might get torn off flashed through her head.

I'm going to kill Eli, she thought.

The brake would not budge. Samantha knew she needed to reach higher, to get more leverage, but she couldn't risk the slaves on the terrace seeing her. She reached up and pulled again, her muscles shaking with exertion. She could not get it to move.

A hand slid onto her shoulder and she nearly screamed. Odus had crawled next to her and motioned for her to take his place with Amira underneath the other carriage.

"Be careful," she whispered. "You could lose your arm if you aren't quick."

"Better mine than yours, ma'am."

Samantha crawled back. She watched Odus' sinewy arm reach up, his lean muscles bulging as he pulled back the brake lever in one clean motion.

The horses bucked immediately, then darted from their position, racing down the drive and past the gatehouse.

"Holy Moses!" yelled one of the slaves, jumping from his perch and running after the carriage. "That be Master Fabre's." The other slave ran inside. Samantha rolled out from under the other carriage and pulled Amira with her.

Odus was nowhere to be seen. Samantha panicked, fearful his arm was stuck in the wheel shaft or his shirt caught in the mechanism and he was being pulled along down the drive.

Or, it hit her, he had taken the chance to run away.

"Psst," she heard, and looked up. Odus was on the terrace's roof, extending his hand.

Samantha hoisted Amira up on the railing. Amira hugged the pillar and attempted to pull herself up, but it was clear she did not have the strength to pull her own body weight.

"What do you mean the horses just ran off? What on earth did you do?"

The voice of Royal Fabre approached the front door. Samantha jumped onto the railing and cupped her hands around Amira's left foot. She heaved, and almost immediately the weight of the girl was lifted. Samantha looked up to see Odus pulling Amira up without making a sound. He then held out his hand to Samantha.

"Well, this isn't what I expected to see out here."

Samantha froze. Royal Fabre stood in front of her, his face level with her waist. A slave stood behind him. She quickly glanced up to the roof. Odus had disappeared.

"Mas'suh Fabre, what you want me to do about your carriage?"

Royal spoke to him without taking his eyes off Samantha. "You go and get it. I'll wait here."

The slave obeyed and ran off the terrace.

Samantha felt ridiculous, stuck in the position in which he found her – toes balanced on the railing, arms extended, her hands holding onto the edge of the flat roof of the terrace above. Royal's eyes ran over her outstretched body and the damp riding dress that clung to her skin. If she covered herself, she might fall off the railing. If she climbed up onto the roof to escape, he might tell her parents.

Royal stepped forward and put his hands around her waist. Her own hands clamped onto his and she dug her fingernails into his skin.

Royal laughed. "Easy there. I'm just helping you off." He lifted her as though she weighed no more than a sunflower and gently set her down.

"You want to tell me what you're doing out here?"

"Fresh air," she said.

"I see. Would you like me to fetch your mother?"

"No."

He motioned to the bench swing on the terrace. "Sit down."

Samantha did not move.

"Please," he said.

She sat. Royal pulled a piece of paper out of his inner jacket pocket before joining her on the bench.

"Here."

Samantha held the paper up to the light.

Master and Mrs. Sanford Weston of Mont Verity are delighted to announce the engagement of their daughter, Samantha Ashton, to Evans Royal Fabre, son of Major and Mrs. Louis Fabre of Dominion Royale.

The wedding will take place Friday, March 15 at the bride's residence. The couple will take a brief honeymoon to New Orleans before settling at the Fabre plantation.

The hand that held the piece of paper collapsed into her lap.

"It's being sent to the *Beckwith Station Gazette* and the *Richmond Courier*," said Royal.

"March 15 is a week from Friday."

"Yes."

"Royal, I hardly know you. And I don't love you."

"I know."

"I want to marry Eli."

"Why?" he said. It seemed a genuine question.

"Because… I love him. And he loves me."

Royal sighed. "With all due respect, Samantha, Elijah doesn't love anyone but himself."

"He's going to prove you wrong, and my father, just you wait."

She was trying to bait him, to get him angry. But he remained steady and looked at her calmly.

"I don't want to live at Dominion Royale," she blurted. "I want to stay here. Mont Verity is my home."

Royal reached for her hand. She pulled it away. "I have nothing but Mont Verity's interests at heart. It is my intention to run both plantations, perhaps even merge the two. I'm thinking of felling the woods that join our land to make more pasture. The stream running through it is perfect for irrigation. With two sets of slaves, there's no end to what we could do."

Samantha remembered what she'd overheard him say during dueling practice. "I thought you said slavery wasn't a viable long-term option. That it would only hold the South back over time."

Royal blushed. "How do you know I said that?"

"I listen more than people think I do."

Royal cast his gaze to the ground. "I said it to impress your father."

Samantha wanted to ask him why, but then she remembered Odus and Amira.

She stood up. "I'm going."

Royal held her arm. "Kiss me," he said.

"What?"

"Whether you like it or not, a week from Friday you will be my wife. So, kiss me."

Samantha resisted the urge to slap him. "No."

"Okay," he said, getting up. "I'll just go tell your parents that you snuck out of your room when you were supposedly too faint to attend your own debutante ball."

She thought about the gun in her cleavage. How she would have loved to brandish it and prove what a good shot she was. But she thought about the two slaves on the terrace above and how, whether she understood it or not, they were vital to Eli's plan of convincing her father that they should wed. As with everything else today, Samantha went along with what was asked of her.

She lifted her face, waiting for Royal's lips. Instead, he grabbed her and pulled her to him with such force that her breasts hurt as they were pressed into his hard chest. The kiss was horrible, his tongue swishing around the inside of her mouth. She pushed him away, fearing she might be ill.

"Good night," he said.

Samantha watched him go inside. Before lifting herself up onto the terrace roof, she wiped her face and spat Royal's kiss onto the ground.

The slaves weren't on the roof of the terrace. Had they gone to the other side and jumped? Part of her hoped they had. This was all too much. She just wanted things to be simple, to be easy. But it seemed her life would never be simple again.

She crawled through her window and found the two slaves huddled in the dark corner by her bed. As Samantha got closer she saw that Amira was shivering. *For goodness sake, it's not even cold,* Samantha thought.

"If you make a sound, we'll all be hung. Now follow me."

She took the lantern from her bedside table and walked towards the doors to her walk-in wardrobe. She struck a match and lit the lantern, leading Odus and Amira past rows of dresses worn once and shelves of shoes too impractical to walk in. At the end of the wardrobe, she crouched down and pushed several hat boxes to the side, revealing a hatch to the eaves that was smaller than she remembered. It popped when she pushed it out of its hinges, and Samantha and the two slaves held their position while waiting for signs that they were about to be discovered. After several seconds, satisfied that no one had heard, she crawled into the eaves.

The space under the eaves was a long corridor about four feet wide, running the length of the house. Its ceiling sloped in line with the roof above, making it hard to stand. There were no windows or ventilation, rendering this the hottest or coldest part of the house, depending on the season and time of day. The lantern's light threw eerie shadows over her rocking horse and the old doll house she'd inherited once Georgia lost interest in make-believe. The cradle her grandfather had made held a small blanket and a pillow. Samantha picked them up, blew the dust off and handed them to Odus, his long figure hunched against the lean of the ceiling.

"This is the best I can do. I'll come back as soon as it's safe in the morning."

She crawled to the hatch opening.

"Ma'am?" said Odus.

"What?" she snapped.

Odus' eyes darted between Amira and the rest of the small space. "I'm sorry to ask you to do more than you've already done, but we gon' need water in here. And a place to..." He cleared his throat. "You know."

Samantha wanted to scream. Was it not enough that she was risking everything just having them here? "Typical Negro," she could hear her mother say. "Never knows when to just shut up and be thankful for all we do for them."

"Wait here," she said.

She emerged from the walk-in wardrobe and a wave of fatigue washed over her. All she wanted to do now was sleep and hope to wake up to have this nightmare over. Instead she had to procure water and a chamber pot. It was all too much. *I'll just lie down for a minute,* she thought, *and figure out what to do. An extra chamber pot? Who ever asks for such a thing?*

As she lay on her bed, listening to the rumble of conversation drift up the stairs, she decided to tell Oma and Chimi that she felt sick and might throw up. That would justify an extra chamber pot – even a simple slave like Oma would understand not wanting to throw up into your own excrement. She didn't know how she could ask for a water canteen or similar. Maybe she could say she lost the one she kept in her saddle bag and needed a new one. But that couldn't happen until tomorrow. She considered giving them the water that was left in her washing basin, surmising that something was better than nothing, but before she could act, she fell into a deep sleep.

Chapter 11

Annie sat cross-legged on her bed. The late afternoon clouds were gray and high. Outside the snow fell quickly and quietly as if hoping not to be noticed. Annie knew she should do something about the front path – if the snow came down harder it would soon be difficult to leave the house – but she couldn't muster the motivation. Not with the mystery of Samantha Weston absorbed into her every pore, allowing her to forget that she was here on borrowed time and that at any moment she might have to leave.

Laid out in front of her was everything she and Theo had collected so far – Samantha's letter to her father, the *Beckwith Station Gazette* report on Samantha's ball, the knife inscribed with the name *Elijah Fabre*, and the two lists of letters and numbers – one from the Bible, the other from Theo's barn. The only connection she could make between them were the initials SW and EF, and the date March 27, 1861.

The fact that Mont Verity and Beckwith Station were linked to her old home still seemed unreal. Could it be that Annie and Samantha Weston had walked the same paths over the Virginian landscape? She hated now that she'd not paid more attention to her surroundings – she might have passed something relevant to Samantha Weston and never even known it. It made her more homesick than ever.

Samantha's letter was the one thing Annie came back to again and again. Sometimes she would recite it before she went to sleep and sometimes, in her dreams, she would see it being written – the pen, the quill and the light from the kerosene lantern flicking over windowless walls. She had this dream several times, waking up in frustration that in the dream she hadn't thought to ask Samantha Weston any questions.

But this morning, having woken from the same dream again, Annie realized why she could not talk to Samantha in the dream:

Because it was not Samantha writing the letter. It was Annie.

I cannot tell you where I am. I do not want to endanger those around me.

We will probably never see each other again. After all that has occurred, there are many reasons why a return to my old life is impossible.

What Annie wouldn't give for a miracle whereby Samantha Weston would materialize in front of her. They would talk like old friends, she was sure.

"You have no idea how much we have in common," she'd tell her. "We're both on the run, both not knowing if we can go home again."

But what I really want you to know is that I am in love. Never did I think the love of my life would come to me in the shape and form that it has...Loving him, being able to love him – it has made me happier than I can describe.

"Who is he?" Annie wanted to ask. "Elijah Fabre? Someone else?"

And if Samantha Weston could experience such love while on the run, did that mean Annie could too?

She got off her bed and looked at her watch. Theo had said to come over anytime after school. It was nearly three o'clock.

It had been two days since she'd last seen Theo, and one thing was clear: she missed him. She missed his laugh and his energy. She missed his enthusiasm for Samantha Weston and his enjoyment of their journey thus far.

If she left now she could be there as he got off the bus. She didn't want to seem too eager, nor did she want to wait. She was starting to feel like the giddy cheerleader she used to be, without the pom-poms to hide behind.

She checked herself in the mirror and ran her fingers through her hair. It felt coarse, like it used to after straightening it, even though she hadn't seen a straightening iron since Virginia. She pulled out the contents of her pocket to see if she enough money to justify buying conditioner. All she had was the memory stick. She looked at it lying in her palm and sighed. She'd done nothing since uploading the photo in Theo's room.

Soon, she thought. *Soon.*

Annie tiptoed downstairs and past the living room door so as not to disturb her mother. She turned the corner to the kitchen and jumped at the figure standing by the stove.

"Mom?"

Her mother stared at the gas rings like they were landmines. The baggy T-shirt and sweatpants she wore were so loose Annie couldn't be sure her mother was really underneath them.

"I want to make enchiladas."

"What?"

"I want enchiladas. But I can't remember how to make them."

"I'm not sure either. I never really watched Dad when he made…"

"I taught him how to make them. He liked to pretend they were his, but they weren't. They were mine."

The last time she'd had her father's enchiladas was on the night everything changed. Her mother didn't eat them that night, which was normal. Most of the time it was Annie and her father eating all the food he made. Her mother always had salads with low-fat dressing or poached fish with steamed vegetables. Annie couldn't understand why her mother would now want something she never used to have.

"Okay," Annie said, "let's sit down and think about what we need."

She led her mother to the kitchen table and helped her into the chair. She found a piece of scrap paper and a stubby pencil.

"We need tortillas," said Annie.

Her mother stared into space. "Yes."

"Passata."

"Yes."

"Smoked paprika." Annie paused. "Actually, I'm not sure the Store at Five Corners will have that."

Her mother looked like a child whose china doll had just been smashed to smithereens.

"No, I mean, we just have to improvise," said Annie quickly. "We'll have to use regular paprika or something. It'll be the Vermont version. Vermont-a-ladas."

Annie laughed at her own joke. Her mother didn't.

"You're taking such good care of us," said her mother.

"No, I'm not."

"You are. Getting us from place to place. I couldn't have done that, not after… I don't even remember half of the places we've been."

"We've been a lot of places that aren't really worth remembering," she said, shuddering at the memory of motels with cockroaches and winged ants.

"Yes, but I don't even know what states we've been through."

"Most of them, it feels like." Annie retraced their journey. "The Carolinas, Georgia, Alabama, Mississippi, Arkansas, Kansas, Nebraska…"

"Jesus…"

"Wisconsin, Illinois, Indiana, Michigan, New York, then here."

"And you managed to avoid the ones we'd lived in when Dad was in the army."

"Yeah, it wasn't easy."

"We moved around so much when you were little." Her mother paused, staring into space. "You were all I had then."

"But then we moved to Virginia…"

"Yes. Everything changed in Virginia."

"Why weren't you happier there? We'd finally settled, like you wanted, but you still seemed so sad."

"I don't want to talk about it."

"Why not?"

"Because it doesn't matter now. None of it does. Our lives have been completely ruined. How can anything else matter?"

"I just want to go home," said Annie.

"I don't."

"Mom! How can you say that?"

"You're right. I was miserable there. And you, I didn't like what Virginia made you."

"Not this again…"

"You became a different girl once Jenna and Marcy were on the scene."

"Why can't you just accept that they were the first real friends I ever had, okay? We moved around too much before that for me to have anybody for very long. We settled down in Virginia, and Jenna and Marcy wanted to be my friends. Why does that make you so mad?"

"Because they wanted to change you. And you let them. Your father let you spend a fortune on clothes and hair and tanning. You stopped doing your homework because you were always God-knows-where with them."

"Great. You don't talk to me for months and when you do it's to have the same old argument we used to have."

"We're done." Her mother stood up and walked towards the living room.

"That's not fair. You can't start a fight and then just walk away."

"Talking changes nothing. We're here. It's better just to keep the peace."

Annie had so many things she wanted to shout. *So that's why you stopped talking? Because it's easier?* She couldn't help it – she hated her mother right then, just like she'd hated her after any of their arguments at home. Their life was upside down, yet some things were still the same.

Annie looked at the enchilada ingredients. She added cheddar and onion to the list and grabbed Theo's coat on her way out the door.

Annie lay on her stomach on Theo's bed, her feet hovering in the air, picking at the sandwich Theo insisted on making for her. She'd eaten half of it and it was amazing – artichoke, chicken and goat's cheese on olive bread. If it was possible to fall in love with a sandwich, then she had just done it.

Theo sat at his desk, entering searches into Google. In between mouthfuls Annie tried to focus on studying the two lists of numbers and letters. Trouble was, she was distracted. Theo was sitting at that perfect angle whereby she could watch him without him being aware. She watched his wrist as it operated the mouse and the roll of the sleeves on his plaid shirt. She looked at the thick, dark hair on his head and wondered what it would be like to run her fingers through it.

Get a grip, she told herself.

She forced herself to look away and fixated on the soft weave of Theo's green flannel duvet. It was so warm, so alluring – she could imagine herself underneath its feathery down, cozy and safe. She buried her head into the fabric and inhaled Theo's smell.

"Argh," said Theo.

Annie lifted her head. "What is it?"

"This is so frustrating. I can't find anything else on the Fabre family – no births, no deaths, no marriages, nothing."

"What about where you found the deb ball article? Are there other archives on there?"

"No, it was part of some weird site about cotillion history and memorabilia. If you search for *Beckwith Station Gazette* then that site is the only result worth anything."

Annie thought for a moment. "If the deb ball article came from a specialist site do you think we could ask the site's owner where she got it?"

Theo practically jumped out of his chair. "Fantastic idea." He brought up the site and clicked on *Contact me.*

"Yes!" he exclaimed, and picked up the phone on his desk.

"Who are you calling?"

"The site owner. Her number's right here."

"You're calling her house?"

"No time like the present," he said.

He dialed. Annie held her breath.

"Hello? Hi, is this the owner of southerncentral.com?" He looked at Annie and gave her a thumbs-up. "My name is Theo Mason and I got your number from your website. Sorry to bother you, but I was wondering if you could tell me where you found a particular article on your site? Yes, it's the one dated March 7, 1861 from the *Beckwith Station Gazette*. Sure, I'll hold on."

Annie scrambled to the edge of the bed. "What's she doing?" she whispered.

Theo put his hand over the receiver. "She said she's just going to double-check. Hello? Yes?" He opened his desk and pulled out a piece of paper and a ballpoint. "Okay." Annie refrained from getting up to look over his shoulder. "Okay....And are those archives online by any chance?...Okay...No, that's really helpful. I'll try it. Thank you. Thank you so much." He hung up and started typing.

"What did she say?"

Theo didn't answer. She watched his eyes flicker over the search results. He clicked the mouse onto parts of the screen that Annie couldn't see. Then she saw him open another browser window and type some more. After a few seconds he smiled and turned the screen towards her. The picture at the top of the page was a photograph of the Blue Ridge Mountains, just as Annie used to see it in the distance when driving down the highway. Annie swallowed.

"Clinton Community College Library. She got it off their archives."

Annie stood up. He was on the library's website, on the page marked *Opening Hours*. The address appeared below, and Annie put her hand over her mouth. It was a road she knew, one that was a mere ten-minute drive from her old house.

"It opens at 9am on a Saturday." He alt-tabbed to the other browser window. "According to Google Maps it's a nine-hour drive, but I reckon we can do it in seven. So, if we leave here at 2am..."

"Whoa, wait. Leave? To go where?"

"To Virginia! So if we leave..."

"We?"

"Sure. You want to know what happened to Samantha Weston, don't you? This is the best lead we've got."

"Why can't we just call there and ask them to send us what they've got?"

"No, she said it's on an old computer that's not online."

"How about we call and ask them to print it all out? Put it on a memory stick or something?"

"From what she was saying the computer it's on is so old we'd be lucky if it took floppy discs. And anyway, we don't really know exactly what we're looking for. If someone else did it they might miss something. I think we should go and do it. It's the best way."

Annie started to pace. This was not what she expected. The Samantha Weston mystery was meant to stay here and be solved here. She couldn't go to Virginia. Of course she couldn't. It was practically going home, back to where anyone might recognize her. Even worse, he might see her. If that happened, the past year would have been for nothing.

But then she considered something else: maybe being back in Virginia meant she'd see something that made sense of Samantha Weston, something she never would have thought to look for in her old life.

Could she really do this? Go home and back, undetected? It was just a library – how dangerous could that be?

"Theo, I….you want to do this tomorrow?"

"Well, sorta. More like, tonight."

Annie thought of her mother. If Annie was gone for as long as it would take to get to Virginia and back, her mother would die of panic. Angry though she was, she couldn't do that to her.

"Theo, I want to, I really do, but I… oh, this isn't fair. I can't leave my Mom. I'm really sorry, but I can't."

Theo sighed and crossed his arms. "I thought you cared about this."

"I do! I just…I can't talk about it. I'm sorry."

"Hey, here's an idea," he said. "How about you actually start trusting me."

It wasn't a question. His eyes were wide, his mouth pursed.

Annie swallowed. "I do trust you."

"I don't think you do. You're nothing but secrets. I've been going along with it so far, but now it's really starting to wear me down."

"I…I don't have secrets."

"Oh, really?" He stood up. "Then why does your mother refuse to show her face? Why don't you go to school? And why do you never talk about your father?"

It was Annie's turn to be angry. "Why don't you ever talk about your mother?"

Theo's arms fell to his sides. She watched him look at the picture on top of the chest of drawers.

"You really want to know?"

78

Annie hesitated. If hearing his secrets meant she had to divulge hers then she didn't want him to speak.

"She left," he blurted. "A year ago. Just vanished. Happy now?"

"I don't understand."

"Neither do we. We didn't think anything was wrong. She and my dad have been together since high school. They even went to Vermont College so they could stay together. They always seemed happy. And me and my brothers…okay, we're not perfect, but we're not so bad that she needed to run away."

"Maybe she didn't," Annie ventured. "Maybe something happened."

"Yes, that's possible. But we all have the same feeling, you know? Even my dad thinks she's run away. And it's probably all my fault."

"I'm sure that isn't true."

"Really?" His anger rose. "And how do you know? You don't. She and I had a fight the day she left. I wanted to try out for football, and she wouldn't let me. She said no son of hers would play a game where a group of girls in miniskirts served no purpose other than to cheer us on. She was like that sometimes. A real feminist, I guess. And I did as I was told – I didn't try out. But I stayed after school and watched the whole tryout – and saw lots of my friends wearing uniforms and getting picked. When I got home she was gone."

Annie put her hand on his arm. "I'm sorry."

Theo shook his head. "It's not your fault. I don't mean to yell at you. You don't have to tell me about your father," he said. "I should have been more understanding."

"I promise you – if ever the day comes that I can tell you everything, I will."

"Okay, I respect that."

He walked back to his desk and hit *print* on his computer.

"You're really going to go?" she said.

Theo watched the map and directions come out of the printer. "Yes, I am. I guess I just want to know that some people can be found."

Annie looked at the map of Virginia on the printer. Its familiarity sent shivers down her spine. Going would be a complete mistake. So many things could go wrong. But, she thought, it could be the best decision she ever made. They might find the answers they were looking for. Maybe it would even reveal how much longer she and her mother would have to hide. Maybe she'd see something that would signal it was finally safe for them to go home. Surely that made the risk worthwhile?

"Theo," she said, "I'm coming with you."

Chapter 12

When Samantha woke up she couldn't be sure how much time had passed. Outside it was dark, without even a glimmer of the blue light that marks the dawn. The house was quiet. Samantha jumped up and looked out the window. All the carriages were gone. The front of the house was deserted.

Her debutante ball was over.

Odus, she thought. *Amira.*

She ran to her bedroom door and pulled it open. Oma slept slumped in the chair. Samantha shook her shoulder.

"Oma, wake up."

The slave's head lolled into wakefulness. "Miss Sammy," she croaked, "you alright?"

"Oma, I think I'm going to be sick. I need an extra chamber pot."

Oma blinked and rubbed her eyes as she pushed herself out of the chair. "Yes, ma'am."

Samantha closed her door and listened to Oma's footsteps shuffling down the hall. She heard her open the door to the main cupboard and the quiet clanking of china and enamel. She was in bed by the time Oma entered her bedroom.

"Here you go, Miss Sammy." Oma looked around the room, her eyes still full of sleep. "Where your other pot, Miss Sammy?"

"Leave it for now," she said, curling into a ball and clutching her stomach. "I need more water," she said, faking a small moan. "So thirsty."

Oma reached for Samantha's pitcher.

"No," she said. "I need something else. A canteen. Like the one in my saddlebag."

Oma was now awake and indignant. "Miss Sammy, where'm I gonna find a canteen at this time of night?"

Samantha leaned over the bed and conjured a dry heave. "Just do it, Oma."

The slave left and Samantha paced the room. Downstairs, the grandfather clock chimed five o'clock. Soon the work bell would ring, summoning the kitchen slaves to make breakfast and the field slaves to work.

Samantha was so preoccupied with her thoughts that she didn't hear Oma come through the door. She clutched her stomach.

"Here," said Oma, carrying a bucket of water. "This be the best I can do." She set it next to Samantha's bed and pulled a ladle out of her apron. "You need more, you jus' holler." Oma pulled back Samantha's bed sheets. "Now, let's get you back in bed where you belong. No wonder you ill after all they put you through. You just rest here." Oma tucked Samantha in. "You want me to stay wid you, Miss Sammy?"

"No," she said. "But thank you for all you've done."

Oma let out a small laugh.

"What is it?" Samantha asked. *Has she guessed my secret? Is it obvious I'm hiding something?*

"Nothing," said Oma.

Samantha grabbed her arm. "Oma, you must tell me."

"Ain't no big deal, Miss Sammy, it just, that be the first time I ever hear you thank anyone for anything."

Oma freed herself from Samantha's grasp and closed the door behind her as she left the room.

Samantha kicked off the sheets and picked up the chamber pot and bucket. They were heavier than she was expecting and halfway across the room she realized she could only carry one at a time. What would they need more urgently – water or the pot? She picked up the bucket and went into her wardrobe with the lantern.

"I am so sorry," she said, opening the hatch. The air that seeped out of the eaves was double the temperature of her bedroom. As she crawled through, a smell she couldn't place overwhelmed the room. *Urine?* she thought. *Blood?*

The lantern light spread thinly into the space, and Samantha saw the two slaves slumped against the sloped wall. Amira lay on her side with her knees curled into her chest. Odus crawled toward Samantha, his face dripping in sweat.

"Here," she said, pushing the bucket towards him. He took the ladle and held it to Amira's lips. The girl tilted her head forward and took a small sip. Samantha looked down and saw blood stains on her skirt.

Of course, Samantha thought.

"I'll return in a moment," she said, and crawled out.

Back in her bedroom, she rustled through her chest of drawers, taking two fans in one hand and scooping up the neatly folded pile of clean blood rags in the other. She held the rags and fans under one arm, picked up the chamber pot with the other and walked clumsily through the wardrobe.

"Here," she said, handing the rags to Amira. "Next time I come I'll give you the bin for the ones you've used. For now just..." she looked around the space, "...find somewhere to put them." She handed Odus the two fans. "Do what you can to stay cool. Breakfast will be served in a couple of hours. I'll smuggle what I can and bring it to you. In the meantime, do not make a sound. And do not ever come out of here unless I tell you to, do you understand?"

Samantha didn't even wait to see if they nodded. The smell of Amira's blood made her nauseous. She pulled the hatch door closed. Once out of the wardrobe, she inhaled the fresh air and collapsed on her bed. Not only did she have two fugitive slaves to contend with, there was also the issue of her engagement and wedding. What if Eli wasn't back by then? Even if it was Eli's intention that she somehow rebel against the engagement, she didn't know how she could. She couldn't even think of a good reason to postpone it – at least, not one that her parents would believe. And as for the two slaves, how was she supposed to keep them hidden for a week? Would it mean not leaving her room for six days? She'd go mad, of that she was sure. The more her mind spun with the events of the last twelve hours, the more she wanted to scream. Instead, she curled up into the tightest ball she could manage and lulled herself back to sleep as the sun came up over the Blue Ridge Mountains.

Samantha woke up to a gentle hand shaking her shoulder.

"Miss Sammy?"

She opened her eyes. Nessie was sitting on her bed, just like she had done so many times when Samantha was a little girl.

"Time to get up, Miss Sammy." The slave opened the curtains. Samantha blinked as her eyes adjusted to the bright sunshine pouring through her window.

"What time is it?"

"It nearly lunchtime. Your daddy said we was to let you sleep until now, if that what you needed. But now you wanted downstairs. They's waiting for you."

"Who?"

"Your mama and papa. And the Fabres."

Samantha pushed herself up. "Eli?"

"No, Miss Sammy. Just Major and the Missus, and Master Royal."

Samantha sank. "Oh."

Nessie poured water into the washing basin.

"Where have you been, Nessie?"

"What you mean, Miss Sammy?"

"It feels like I haven't seen you for days. Is that right?"

"Yes and no, Miss Sammy. I mainly been helping your mama with the cotillion. But then yesterday I was called to the quarters. One of the young'uns done had a baby."

Nessie had been the plantation's midwife for as long as Samantha could remember. "Did it go well?" She didn't know why she'd asked. Even Nessie seemed surprised. Although it was well known that for every slave baby came out red and screaming another one came out blue and cold, Samantha never asked after the details. Some things were just not worth knowing.

"It okay, Miss Sammy." She wrung a washcloth in the basin and handed it to Samantha. "You wash. I'll go get your clothes."

Samantha stood up and wiped her face. Behind her, Nessie opened the door to the wardrobe and Samantha froze. *Of course she'd go in there to get my clothes. Why didn't I offer to do that for her?* Nessie disappeared into the wardrobe's recess and Samantha expected the worst.

"Good Lordy, Miss Sammy," she said, emerging with one of Samantha's best spring dresses. "You bleeding early this month or something?"

"Um…yes," she lied. "Yes, I am."

"Thought so," she said, laying the dress down on the bed. "Smells like a million blood rags in there. I'll have them washed as soon as we got you dressed."

"Actually, I've only just started," she said quickly. "You might as well leave them for now. Tomorrow is when I'm heavy, so it's probably better to wait until this afternoon to wash them."

Nessie stopped and cast a sideways glance at Samantha. "You alright, Miss Sammy?"

"Yes," she stammered. "Why?"

"You acting funny."

"I guess I'm just tired?" She didn't mean for it to come out as a question. Nessie laid the dress gently over Samantha's chaise, then picked up the corset and slid it under Samantha's arms.

Her mother, father and the Fabres were already seated at the dining table when Samantha arrived, her swaying hoop skirt skimming the door frame as she entered the room. The men stood; her mother and Missus Fabre remained seated.

"Good afternoon, Samantha," said her father.

"Father," she said. "Major Fabre. Royal." A slave pulled out her chair, and she sat down to a plate of sliced fruit.

"I trust you are well rested, Miss Samantha?" said Royal, smirking.

Samantha's eyes darted around the room to look for evidence he'd given her up. She didn't see any.

"Yes, thank you, Royal." A slave put Samantha's napkin into her lap. Iced tea was poured. Her father picked up his knife and fork, and everyone followed.

"We were just discussing last night," said her father. "We have some unfortunate news."

Samantha's fork stalled in mid-air. *Eli,* she thought.

Major Fabre cleared his throat. "My overseer, Cudgen, was killed last night transporting two of your father's slaves here."

"Oh?" said Samantha.

"Yes, it happened about a mile outside our plantation. Whoever did it tried to set fire to his body and his wagon, but only a small part of the wagon burned. Whoever killed him hit him mighty hard in the head with an axe. I've never seen that much blood come out the side of one man's head."

"Darling…" Missus Fabre warned.

Her last meeting with Eli flashed behind her eyes. She remembered the strong smell of kerosene and the blood on his shirt. "It's not my blood," he'd said. Samantha shivered so hard she had to set her fork down.

"Do they know who it was?" her voice cracked.

"We're guessing it was the slaves or someone sympathetic to their cause. It wouldn't be the first time those northern cowards come down here, interfering."

"Elijah says he's going to find the fugitives," said Missus Fabre, delicately dabbing the side of her mouth with her napkin. "That's why he's not here today."

"He is? How?"

Royal snorted in between mouthfuls. "I wouldn't hold your breath. Elijah will get as far as the Potomac and be too scared to cross."

"Royal," his mother whispered.

"I told him not to go," said Major Fabre. "We've got some of the best slave catchers in the South. But I thought I'd let him have his fun."

His fun?

"Did Eli say when he'll be back?"

"Don't you worry," said Missus Fabre. "He promised he'd be back the day before the wedding, whether he has found the slaves or not."

"Those slaves won't get very far anyway," said Royal.

"They won't?" said Samantha, her voice getting higher.

"No, the Potomac's heavily patrolled these days and they'd have to cross that to get north."

The main course was brought to the table before Samantha could ask more. Is that what Eli was doing? Having her hide the slaves so he could pretend to find them? Finally, it all made sense. But why didn't he tell her that's what he was doing? Why all this secrecy? Did he not trust her?

Freshly baked biscuits, breaded catfish and minted peas were passed around the table. Samantha checked her mother wasn't looking and took three biscuits – one she put on her plate and the other two into her napkin on her lap. She looked at Royal and their eyes met.

He'd seen the whole thing.

By the time they finished the meal Royal and Samantha's ceremony had been planned, the guest list written and the wedding breakfast decided. Samantha said nothing during these discussions. All she could focus on was getting upstairs to give the biscuits to Odus and Amira.

The men stood up, signaling to the slaves to pull out the ladies' chairs. Samantha held the napkin containing the biscuits tightly in front of her. Her father ordered mint juleps to be delivered to the terrace. Samantha edged toward the main door.

"Where are you going?" asked her mother.

Samantha turned around and hid the napkin behind her back. "Just upstairs."

"We have guests."

Samantha waited until her father and the Fabres had exited the room. She whispered to her mother. "I think I need my blood rags."

"You're not due until next week.'

"It's come early."

"What's behind your back?"

"Nothing."

Her mother held out her hand. "Now, Samantha."

Samantha brought the crumpled napkin within her mother's reach, but held it close. "Please don't touch it, Mother. I tucked it under my skirt when I felt the blood coming. I was afraid I'd stain the upholstery."

Her mother looked as though she might lose her lunch. If there was ever a topic that made her mother uncomfortable it was the subject of the human body and its functions.

"I'll just have Oma change me and then I promise I'll be back down."

"Be quick about it," she snapped, and left the room.

Samantha waited for her heart to stop pounding in her chest, then ran upstairs.

As Samantha knelt down to open the hatch to the eaves her hoop skirt billowed up to her armpits like a deflating hot air balloon. She pushed down the layers of chiffon and cursed the corset for preventing her from bending. A surge of heat followed the opening of the hatch. The smell of blood thickened the air.

"Here," she said, handing the biscuits over. "I don't have time for anything else right now. I'll be back as soon as I can."

"Miss Sammy..." Odus started, but she didn't let him finish. She pulled the hatch shut and ran back downstairs, smoothing out her skirt as she went.

Samantha struggled to ease the fluttering in her fingertips as she went out on the terrace. The men stood on one side; the two women sat in wicker chairs on the other. Out of the corner of her eye she could see her mother motioning her to sit with them, but she pretended not to see, and instead joined the three men.

"I think this set-up means we can both experiment with new methods while maintaining our current level of income," said Royal

"You mean your current level of income," said her father.

"With all due respect, sir, surely you can see this offers you the best of both worlds? You and I can implement industrialized systems for Mont Verity, as I know you want to do, while Dominion Royale will continue to bring in the revenues that will safeguard all of us in case our experiments fail."

Samantha inserted herself into their circle. "There needs to be a legal agreement that Dominion Royale will cover Mont Verity's debts if Mont Verity is to be the experimental plantation. It's only fair that Dominion Royale is the collateral if there's a threat of foreclosure on our land."

The three men looked at her. Major Fabre laughed and cast a glance at her father. "Now who told you to say that, Samantha?"

"No one has told me to say anything. I know what you're trying to do. You're trying to see if a cotton plantation can run on the kind of industrial machinery they use up north, but you don't dare make manual labor obsolete until you know the new system will yield a better profit. Dominion Royale will keep slave labor; Mont Verity will reduce ours. I just want to make sure that if it all goes belly up my plantation stays in my family."

Royal laughed nervously. "I can assure you we wouldn't have it any other way."

"Good, then you won't mind putting it in writing. And notarized."

All three men stood with their mouths open. She was afraid to look at her father, fearing she'd see his regret at letting her spend so much time in his study.

"Samantha," said Major Fabre, "why don't you go over and join the women? Their talk will be much more suitable for you."

"No, I think I'd rather stay here."

Then, from across the terrace, she heard her mother say: "We'll need to get into the eaves next to Samantha's room to fetch all of her childhood belongings, as well."

Oh no, she thought.

"Actually, I think I will. Excuse me."

As she walked away the men's conversation resumed, but in tones too low for her to hear. Her mother and Missus Fabre were both taking more mint juleps.

"Oh good," said her mother as Samantha sat down. "Tell Missus Fabre that the cradle your grandfather made would look timeless in any modern nursery."

"I don't think we need to be thinking about such things right now, Mother," she said.

Her mother pretended not to hear and continued talking. "It's all just been sitting in the eaves all these years," she said to Missus Fabre. "The cradle, the dollhouse. It will be so exciting to get them out again."

"What if it's a boy?" said Missus Fabre, her voice blunt and cold. "It's a well-known fact that Fabres only ever have boys."

"Well, I had two girls," said her mother, "so it's just as possible that Samantha will have girls."

"I hope not."

Samantha's mother's face reddened. "What is that supposed to mean?"

"Well, boys are easier aren't they? This whole issue of how to manage Mont Verity wouldn't exist if you'd had a boy."

Samantha's mother stood up. "I'm proud to have two daughters."

"Oh, sit down, Madeline. I'm just saying that boys are heartier. They last longer."

Samantha's mother let out a small cry and ran inside, leaving Samantha alone with Missus Fabre.

"You shouldn't have said that," said Samantha.

Missus Fabre took a sip of her mint julep. "I beg your pardon?"

"Making a slight like that against Georgia. That was uncalled for."

"Oh, for goodness sake," she said, waving away the criticism. "That wasn't what I meant."

"That is what it sounded like."

Missus Fabre snapped her fan open. "Your mother needs to realize that aside from her and Royal, the rest of the world stopped mourning for Georgia years ago."

Then Missus Fabre went pale. "I didn't mean that," she said.

Samantha stood up. "I dare say I think you did," she said, and left Missus Fabre sitting under the cloud of her own indiscretion.

Samantha closed the door to the dining room behind her and rested her forehead on the doorframe. *Of course*, she thought. *It all makes sense now.*

No wonder her mother couldn't separate her cotillion from Georgia's. The outcome was the same – marrying Royal Fabre.

If Georgia was still alive everything would be different. She would have married Royal and lived at his plantation. Samantha would marry Eli without any objection, surely, and be able to stay at Mont Verity.

It had never occurred to Samantha to put herself on par with her older sister or to even contemplate competing with her. It would have been an impossible height to reach. To her surprise, she found herself feeling sorry for Royal. He loved Georgia. Missus Fabre had said so. Samantha couldn't remember if he'd come calling along with all of Georgia's other suitors, simply because at that time in her life Samantha did not care. Had Georgia loved him back? For all Samantha knew, Georgia had. *And now Royal's settling for me.* She felt numb, but complacent. There was no use getting upset or depressed. It was simply how it was.

Royal's voice came from behind. "I'm sorry about my mother," he said.

Samantha turned around. "Don't be."

She was stunned to see tears welling in his eyes. "I promise you I don't think I'm settling for second best," he said.

"I wasn't asking."

He cleared his throat. Samantha thought she'd never seen a man more vulnerable than one trying not to show his emotions. "Now that I've had more time with you, I can see how you'll be the best plantation wife a southern man could ask for."

Samantha tried to hide her pleasure at the compliment. "I still don't want to live at Dominion Royale. Mont Verity will always be my home."

"I know that. If I could think of another way I would."

"You could find someone else to marry and let me marry Eli." She expected him to be shocked by her comment. But he didn't reveal even a hint of surprise.

"I can't do that."

"Why not?"

"Because even though I admit I'm marrying you so that I can merge our plantations, Eli is only marrying you so that he can have yours to himself. He won't know how to run it or make it prosper. He'll let it languish and decay until all you have left for your creditors is rubble and dried cotton stalks."

"I'd never let that happen."

Royal sighed. "You act like women have the ability to be men. You couldn't run this place. We have a hard enough time getting slaves to mind us; what makes you think they'll behave with a woman at the helm?"

"You didn't think a woman could shoot a gun and you were wrong about that."

"You missed, if memory serves."

"I missed on purpose."

Royal smiled and stepped closer, taking Samantha's hands. "You see, that's what makes me know I've chosen the right wife. Be patient, Samantha. Who knows? In time you might actually come to love me."

Samantha removed her hands from his grasp. "I'm certain that no matter how much time passes, I never will."

"Perhaps. But we have no choice but to see, do we?"

"Eli will come back and all of this will be changed."

"How can you be sure?"

Samantha realized she couldn't. Her declaration was nothing more than words she held onto because there was nothing else tangible to grasp. The longer Eli was gone, the less faith she had that any of her current circumstances would yield the result she desired.

"I should go and find Mother."

Royal stepped forward to kiss her on the cheek, but she had already turned away.

Samantha did not know how she made it through the day. The Fabres stayed for afternoon tea, and then supper. All the while Samantha was forced to endure Missus Fabre's company and listen to her plans for Samantha, Royal, and the dozens of children she predicted they would have. Once back in her room, Samantha let Oma help her out of the corset and into her nightdress. The clock on the mantelpiece chimed ten times.

"Anything I can get for you, ma'am?"

Samantha knew there was plenty she could ask for on Odus and Amira's behalf. More water for the bucket in the eaves. Food. An empty chamber pot. She could even go beyond that and see which of her old clothes might fit Amira, or if any of her riding trousers would do for Odus. But she was exhausted. She just wanted to get to sleep and be left alone.

Outside, the crickets and cicadas made their first dissonant chorus of the season. The breeze that swayed her curtains held a hint of coolness: rain was coming.

She woke up to the sound of low thunder rumbling across the fields. A figure stood over her, and a flash of lightning cut across Odus' face, Samantha opened her mouth to scream. Instead, she sat up and pulled the sheet over herself. Her gun lay in her drawer, out of reach. *He's here to kill me*, she thought.

"If you touch me I'll scream," she hissed.

Odus knelt down by her bed. "I'm so sorry, ma'am, I know you told us never to come out, but I had to. It's my sister. I think she be dying."

Chapter 13

Annie never fully let herself fall into a deep sleep. She didn't dare, for fear of what she might sleep through. Instead, she hovered between sleep and wakefulness, where dreams come furious and unrelenting in their imagery.

It was easy to stay awake for the first few hours of the journey to Virginia, high on the adrenaline of feeling free for the first time in a year. She didn't want to think of the moment when her mother would see her note and realize she was gone.

She couldn't wait to get to Virginia. Just to be there, inhale its scent and get its dust on her shoes. It would be tempting to do so many things, like go to her old high school and watch Saturday football practice or call Jenna and Marcy and have them meet her at the mall where they'd sit by the indoor water fountain and rate the boys who walked by.

Annie knew she couldn't do any of these things, but the ideas were enough to make her dizzy and thrilled.

She and Theo crossed the New York state line, where the dark outlines of the mountains descended to make way for the stars. Herds of deer lurked in the bare trees along the Taconic. Down the New York State Parkway and the lights of east Manhattan, Annie saw cherry tree blooms under pink streetlights. Before falling asleep on the New Jersey Turnpike she saw the Statue of Liberty, no bigger than an ant, but unmistakable against the backdrop of lower Manhattan.

But behind her eyes came the explosion. The fire. The police car.

"No!" she cried. "No! No! No!"

"Annie! Annie!" a voice shouted through the fire.

"But that's not my name," she heard herself say. Theo's truck hit a pothole and her eyes shot open.

"Are you okay?" Theo had one hand on her shoulder and another on the steering wheel.

Annie blinked until her eyes focused. The sky was now pale blue, the sun a mere hour from the horizon. *I'm in Theo's truck,* she thought. *Everything's okay.*

"You must have been dreaming," said Theo. "You said your name isn't Annie."

Annie faked a laugh and cleared her throat. "Where are we?"

"Nearly there, actually. We made good time. The library doesn't open for another couple of hours, so what do you say we find a place to get breakfast?"

She took a deep breath. "Sounds good."

At sunrise, they entered Virginia awash with the colors of spring. Daffodils were dotted across lawns and in clusters on the side of the highway. Coming from Vermont, where it had been snowing, Annie felt like she'd travelled forward in time. The sight of bluebells and purple rhododendrons made her feel hopeful, like new beginnings were there for the taking.

Annie was home.

It was Theo's first time in the south and Annie knew she had to pretend the same. She repeated instructions to herself to act like the place was unfamiliar, not to point in the right direction if he got lost, and to keep her head down at all times.

She also begrudgingly promised herself that when they were at the library she would somehow get onto a computer, post another photo and read the emails she'd seen in the inbox. The more she thought about it, the more she berated herself for starting those Facebook posts in the first place. They were now a burden, an irritant, a fly she wished she could swat away. Samantha Weston had seen to that. What a gift she was – not just a distraction or diversion, but a passion. It made everything else seem like a bad dream, like a long, arduous staircase that had to be climbed in order to have this reward.

And then there was Theo. She was starting to see that he might be a different gift altogether.

Theo pulled into a restaurant that promised, '*the best grits this side of the Mason-Dixon line*'. It was a place that Annie had been to a few times after home football games, famous for its BBQ pork, but where she and her family had never been. Her father didn't see the point in going out to eat something he could make at home, and her mother didn't go anywhere that didn't have a salad bar.

Head down, she thought, as they were led to their table. *Don't make eye contact with anyone.*

Annie scanned the menu, searching for the cheapest item.

"By the way," Theo said, "this is on me."

"Theo, you don't have to…"

"No, I insist. It wouldn't be half as much fun if you weren't here to keep me company. So what'll you have?"

Annie looked at the menu. The fact that Theo was buying made an even stronger case for ordering the cheapest thing. "I'll just have an English muffin," she said.

"No."

"What?"

"That's not breakfast." He pointed to the menu. "See this column here? That's nothing but side orders. Now, this column here," he ran his finger over the breakfast entrees, "that's what I'll pay for. I only support the ordering of real food."

"Theo, I…"

He held up his hand in mock protest. "No, no, not another word. I have rules, and you must obey them."

The waiter approached, his cheeks pink and round like apples. His accent was slow, southern and in no hurry. "Now what can I get y'all?"

"If these are grits," said Theo, pushing the white grains around his plate, "I'm completely failing to see what all the fuss is about."

Annie tried hard not to wolf down her Huevos Rancheros with extra chilies and jalapenos. Every mouthful made her feel guilty, but she couldn't stop – it tasted too good.

"You were smart to order recognizable food," said Theo, balking at another mouthful.

"I hate grits," she said. "Always have."

"You could have warned me," he said, putting his fork down. "I really can't eat this. I'm going to get something else." He tried to catch the waiter's attention. "When in your life were you so unfortunate that you ate grits?"

Annie stopped chewing. "Um, I don't know, a long time ago."

Theo pushed his plate to the side. "You know what? If I'd eaten these before, I'm sure I would have blocked out that memory, too."

The waiter returned and Theo ordered Corned Beef Hash.

"I didn't think you looked like a grits boy," the waiter said, and Annie and Theo laughed. Annie was starting to relax. She and Theo could be anywhere, just having breakfast, like a normal boy and girl.

"So, where to first?" he asked.

"First? I thought we were just going to the library."

"Oh come on, we can't have come all this way and not explore a little. I thought maybe we could try and find where Mont Verity was. You never know – there might be something there."

Annie did not want to explore, not in the way Theo meant. She wanted to, perhaps, accidentally drive by things that held meaning, but not intentionally seek anything out. She needed to keep this trip controlled and compact. Theo, she could see, clearly had other ideas. She was starting to think she'd made a big mistake by agreeing to come.

Hopefully all our Samantha Weston questions will be answered at the library, she thought, *and then we can go back to Vermont.*

On the way to the library Annie did nothing but look out the window. Every familiar sight made her wistful – the dance studio where she'd taken ballet lessons, the smoothie station where she, Jenna and Marcy used to go after cheerleading practice, and the book store where she and her mother went once a week until Annie stopped doing such things with her mother and went to nail bars with Jenna and Marcy instead.

She'd forgotten how flat the landscape was. They weren't far south enough to see the Blue Ridge Mountains, so all buildings and roads sat on level ground. It made her feel exposed and uncomfortable, and she suddenly missed the protection of the mountains in Vermont.

"I think we're lost," said Theo. He handed her the directions. "We're trying to find Route 102, but we might have passed it already."

Will he notice if we take a little detour?

"Left here," she said.

Annie directed Theo along the route her school bus took every day. The development where she used to live came into sight, and Annie suppressed a deep, mournful sob.

"Take a right."

"But this is residential."

"I know. We need to turn around in here."

Theo pulled the truck in and started to make a U-turn.

"No, go straight," she said.

"Why?"

"It's better to turn around down there."

"How do you know?"

"I'm just guessing. Keep going."

He drove further. "There's not really a good place to turn around. I'll have to do a three-point turn."

Annie searched for reasons to get him to keep going further. She wanted to see if her house had burned to the ground or been repaired. She wanted to see if her front door had been blown completely off or if it still clung to its hinges. As Theo turned the truck around, she craned her neck to see down her old road. Had it been a month earlier, before the trees were in bloom, she would have had a clear view to her house. As it was, rows of cherry blossoms obscured her view and no amount of stretching would allow her to see it.

Theo stopped at the exit and took the map from her.

"No offense, but directions aren't your thing," he said, checking the map before turning left."

"No," said Annie. "I guess not."

The students at Clinton Community College clearly did not study on Saturday mornings. Annie and Theo arrived at 9:30 and the campus was deserted. Stray pieces of McDonald's debris blew between concrete buildings. A spilled can of Coke reflected the sun, its sticky contents already turning to syrup in the heat.

Annie and Theo entered the revolving glass doors to the library and seemed to be the only ones there who weren't staff. Annie cast quick glances at the few people and felt relieved there was no one she knew.

As if Jenna and Marcy or anyone else I knew would be caught dead in a community college library on a Saturday, she thought.

They approached the girl sitting at the reception desk and Annie's eyes widened. The girl was bottle blonde, slathered in fake tan and heavily engrossed in applying several layers of mascara. She knew this girl. No, she knew this *kind* of girl. Her shirt was a size too small and her manicured nails a size too big. Annie guessed that underneath the desk was a skirt an inch too short above a pair of heels an inch too high.

I used to be this girl, she thought.

The girl glanced at them briefly, did a double-take to Theo, then quickly put away her make-up and batted her mascara-heavy lashes. "Well now, what can I do for you?" she said.

"Hi!" said Theo, cheerfully. Too cheerfully. "We heard through the grapevine that you were the place to go to find old newspaper archives for the area. We're looking for a newspaper called the *Beckwith Station Gazette.*"

"What's it worth to you?" she said sweetly.

Annie felt a ripple of stings across her skin.

"Excuse me?" said Theo.

"I'm kidding, sugar. Sure. Let me show you where the files are."

She emerged from behind the desk in, as Annie suspected, heels that were longer than her skirt. Annie looked down at her own flannel shirt and faded jeans. She'd forgotten what it felt like to compare herself to other girls, something she hadn't missed about high school. But she'd never experienced this – this complete lack of preparation on her part, this complete exposure without any of the old tools for her defense. High school was a battleground and everyone came dressed in uniform, ready to fight their corner. Annie realized how easily she'd let that part of her old life go and how little she missed it. And for all she knew, Theo experienced this every day. He could be swarmed by girls all day at school, and Annie would never know.

They followed the girl to the back of the library. She stopped at a long wooden table that held half a dozen computers made gray by dust that would never come off.

"How old are these?" asked Theo, as the girl brought a monochrome-green screen to life.

"Oh, honey, Clinton Community College ain't known for being high tech. I think these were made before you and I were born. Every day we turn up thinking the library will have burned down because one of these things will have spontaneously combusted."

A cursor blinked on an otherwise blank screen.

"Anyway, this here is the only computer with files for the *Beckwith Station Gazette*. Some poor soul on Work Study transcribed and typed it all in about twenty years ago, and no one can be bothered getting them off and putting them online. Now, I think all you have to do is enter in a date range – like, you know, January 2000 to December 2001 or something – and then enter in some keywords and it should give you whatever results it has."

"Thanks," said Theo.

She ran her finger over his arm. "Now if you have any questions, sugar, I'll be sitting right over there."

"Thanks for your help," said Annie through gritted teeth. The girl ignored her and left them in the wake of her flowery perfume. Annie scanned the room. Against the back wall was a row of computers, modern ones. She squinted to make out the familiar sight of a Windows log-in and vowed not to leave this building until she had access to one of them and had done what she needed to do.

They sat down, and Annie took out a folder from her backpack. It contained everything she had about Samantha Weston so far – Annie's copy of Samantha's letter, the two lists of letters and numbers copied from Annie's basement and Theo's barn, her notes on Battenkill's census, and the article on Samantha's debutante ball.

"Okay," said Theo, rubbing his hands together. "Shall we begin?"

Annie nodded, braced for the task. "The debutante ball was on March 6, 1861 and the letter was written on March 27, so how about we do that whole year and put in Samantha Weston as keywords?"

"Good thinking," said Theo, typing. They watched as only two results loaded.

Theo clicked the first one open.

"It's the debutante ball article again." Annie and Theo leaned closer to re-read what they already knew.

"Nope. Nothing we haven't seen before," she said.

Theo closed the article and clicked on the next link. Their arms nearly touched as they leaned closer to the screen, and Annie suddenly regretted all the times she'd moved away at the slightest contact.

Beckwith Station Gazette
March 14, 1861

Master and Mrs. Sanford Weston of Mont Verity are delighted to announce the engagement of their daughter, Samantha Ashton, to Evans Royal Fabre, son of Major and Mrs. Louis Fabre of Dominion Royale.

The wedding will take place Friday, March 15 at the bride's residence. The couple will take a brief honeymoon to New Orleans before settling at the Fabre plantation.

Theo sat back in his chair. "I don't get it. Who is Evans Royal Fabre?"

Annie thought about the knife in her boot. "The knife says Elijah Fabre. Do you think they're brothers? Could they be the same person?"

"I suppose they could be, but it's more likely that they're related."

"Evans Royal Fabre," said Annie. "EF."

"Do you think?"

Annie carefully opened Samantha's letter. "I don't know. It doesn't seem possible. She wouldn't be telling her father about being in love if it was with the man she was meant to marry."

"No, I suppose not. But it's worth checking out."

Theo went back to the search page and entered January 1830 to April 1861, then Evans Royal Fabre. Four results came up. Two were reports of sporting events in which he had placed first, the third was a report of the recent Plantation Owners' Society Meeting, which he had chaired, and the fourth was the engagement announcement.

"Hmmm…what about Samantha's sister, Georgia?" said Annie, flicking through her notes.

Theo typed and hit return. Two results came up.

Beckwith Station Gazette
February 20, 1858

Mr. Sanford and Mrs. Madeline Weston have announced they will be hosting a debutante ball for their eldest daughter, Georgia, on Saturday, July 4 of this year. Hold the date, bachelors and debutantes alike – this promises to be the event of the year.

Beckwith Station Gazette
June 10, 1858

Georgia Mae Weston, daughter of Mr. Sanford and Mrs. Madeline Weston of Mont Verity, has died of scarlet fever at the tender age of 16. She is survived by her parents, as well as her younger sister, Samantha. A private funeral will be held at Mont Verity this coming Wednesday. Our thoughts and prayers are with the Weston family at this most heartbreaking time.

Theo looked at the article he'd found and compared the two. "June 10. She died a month before her deb ball. Harsh."

Annie wasn't in the mood to consider Samantha's sister. "How about if we extend Samantha's search to after 1861? Maybe there'll be an article about her returning home." She gulped. "Or her obituary or something."

Theo typed *Samantha Weston* and *April 1861 – December 1900*.

Nothing came up.

He deleted *Samantha Weston* and kept the dates the same.

Still nothing came up.

"That's funny," he said.

"What is?"

"They don't have any copies of the *Beckwith Station Gazette* after April, 1861. Either the paper stopped or they just don't have anything more on record."

"I wonder why."

Theo got up. "Come on."

Annie didn't want to take Theo anywhere near the blonde at the reference desk, but she knew there wasn't a better alternative. She stood up and scanned the room. A few more people were here now, but still no one she knew.

The girl was re-painting her fingernails when Annie and Theo approached.

"Hi there," said Theo.

The girl screwed the top onto her nail polish. "Well, sugar, what can I do for you this time?"

"We've been looking through copies of the *Beckwith Station Gazette* and we can't find anything beyond April 1861. Are we doing something wrong?"

"Oh no, honey, you're not. That paper ceased to exist around the time of Fort Sumter."

"Fort what?" asked Annie, wishing she'd paid more attention in history class.

The girl rolled her eyes. "Well, you're clearly not from around here, Honey. Any nice southern girl worth her salt knows that Fort Sumter marked the start of the Civil War. April 12, 1861." She leaned in towards Theo and whispered. "That's when we southerners bombed your northern butts to bits."

"So, what happened to the paper?" said Annie. The girl glared at her as if she were barging in on the exclusive date.

"Well, I don't know. No one really does. Lots of things changed after Fort Sumter. Maybe all the men working for it got up and joined the Confederate cause. That was pretty common. Oh, and there was a slave uprising around that time, but I don't know if the two are related."

Theo turned to Annie. "The slave rebellion. We forgot about that. Remember the article we found said that Beckwith Station train station was destroyed in a slave rebellion?"

"It wasn't uncommon in the old days for them to put all their eggs in one basket," said the girl.

"Excuse me?" said Annie.

"Sometimes they'd have one building that had multiple uses. I wouldn't be surprised if the *Beckwith Station Gazette* printing press was actually in the station. It made it easier to distribute."

There is just so much I don't know, Annie thought.

"Then how did the library get any copies?"

"I don't know, but you'd be amazed at what southern people hold onto. Most of our historical stuff we get when someone dies, and their relatives bring in all the stuff that can't go to Goodwill."

"Listen," said Annie, stepping in front of Theo, "we're here because we're trying to find out what happened to a girl who lived on a plantation called Mont Verity near a place called Beckwith Station. Do you have any idea how we find out something like that?"

"Don't know. We've got some old ordnance maps on file. We could see if the plantation you're looking for is on it."

"Old maps," mumbled Annie. "Good idea."

"Don't act so surprised."

"Where do we find them?" asked Theo.

The girl leaned towards him, giving him a direct view into her cleavage. Annie looked away and let out a loud sigh. *Is this what I used to be like?* She thought. *Did I really look so fake? Or did I not realize because all the girls I hung out with were the same?*

"Come with me, sugar," said the girl. "The maps are over here." Theo started following her.

"Annie? Are you coming?"

Annie looked at the girl, then Theo. She did not want to leave them alone. But now was her only chance to do what she needed to do.

"Actually, I was going to ask you if I could get onto one of the computers? You know, one connected to the internet?"

"That's only for students," said the girl.

"Yeah, I thought you might say that," Annie mumbled. She hated what she was about to say. "But I'd really appreciate it if you could help. I only need a few minutes while you and Theo get the maps. By yourselves."

The girl raised her eyebrow at Annie and then winked. "Oh, I see." She quickly wrote something on a piece of paper. "Here, it's a generic username and password. Just don't do anything naughty."

I could say the same thing to you, Annie thought, as she watched the girl slide her arm through Theo's and disappear into the stacks. Annie sighed, then entered in the username and password the girl had given her. She checked the room again for familiar faces before opening a browser and logging into Facebook.

There were several new messages. They would have to wait. She inserted the memory stick into the USB port and uploaded the next photo with the caption:

Next time, be sure to get your good side.

She dreaded opening the inbox, but she knew she had to. To stop now would only make him think he'd won. That could not happen.

She clicked open the message and began to read.

Chapter 14

"What do you mean, dying?" Samantha asked.

"I think you need to come see," said Odus, standing and offering Samantha his hand.

"Hold on," she said, refusing his help. "Go into the eaves." She waited for him to be out of sight before pulling on her dressing gown and lighting the lantern.

"Honestly," she said, crawling through the hatch, "why you two can't..."

She stopped when the lantern's light lit Amira. Never had she seen a slave look so pale. The dark skin on her face was as gray as an overcast sky. She lay slumped against the low wall, her skirt soaked with blood.

"Jesus," Samantha whispered, kneeling down in front of the girl. She went to feel the girl's forehead, then retracted. It was not in Samantha's nature to voluntarily touch a slave.

"What's wrong with her?" she asked Odus.

"Dunno, ma'am. But I 'spect it's gots somethin' to do with the baby."

"The baby?" It was only then she noticed the swelling in Amira's stomach.

I'm going to kill Eli, she thought.

"Wait here," she said, and backed out of the eaves.

Samantha's bedroom door creaked when she opened it. Oma and Chimi were no longer guarding her door. She held her breath, waiting to see if anyone had stirred. When she decided they hadn't, she tiptoed down the hall, past the main stairwell. Never in her life had she ventured down the slaves' staircase, but she didn't dare use the main one. She opened the door into a dark, narrow stairwell and ran her fingers along the wall as she descended.

Once in the kitchen the moonlight coming through the windows guided her to the anteroom where the female house slaves slept. She opened the door and saw nothing but darkness. Nessie's voice came through the black.

"Miss Sammy? Is that you?"

Nessie fetched a bucket of water and handed towels to Samantha. "I needs you to carry these, Miss Sammy," she whispered. It was the first time Nessie had ever asked Samantha to do anything.

Odus was waiting behind the wardrobe door and took the bucket. Nessie carried the lantern and Samantha followed. There was barely enough room for all of them in the narrow space. Samantha stood near the entrance hole to get whatever fresh air was coming through and to keep guard in case she needed to quickly close the hatch.

Nessie knelt down in front of Amira and put one of the towels under her head.

"Don't worry, Nessie take good care of you." She lifted Amira's knees and put another towel under her. She slid her hands under Amira's shirt and felt around her stomach.

"You's about eight months gone," she said.

Amira nodded.

She turned to Odus. "I need you to bring the lantern over here." Odus did as he was told. Both he and Samantha turned away as Nessie lifted Amira's skirt over her belly and examined between her legs.

"The bleeding's on the outside. Good Lordy, girl, who gave you these wounds?"

Amira did not speak.

"How long you been like this, girl?"

"Since the night befo' we passed on to the auction," said Odus.

"What's going on?" Samantha asked. She was desperate for Nessie to hurry so they could get out of the eaves before someone heard them.

Nessie glared at Odus. "She talking about you, boy?"

Odus' lower lip trembled. "No, ma'am. I swear."

"It weren't him," said Amira. "It the overseer on our last plantation."

Nessie tore a rag and dipped it into the bucket. "You been ripped up something fierce." She leaned over Amira. "We's just gots to clean you up for now, and then I want you to sleep without anything on under your skirt. We need these wounds to dry out so they can start to heal. You understand me, girl?"

Amira nodded.

102

"You got any more clothes?"

The girl shook her head.

"Lemme get you somethin'." Nessie pushed her big, soft body upright and made a hunched approach towards the hatch. Samantha moved out of her way, and together they exited the wardrobe.

"Poor girl," said Nessie.

"I don't understand," said Samantha. "What happened to her?"

Nessie stood with her hands on her hips. "You want to tell me why there be two runaway Negroes in there?"

Samantha stumbled over the words. "Eli...Eli brought them to me. He said I needed to keep them for a week and that it would convince Father that he and I should marry."

"And you believed that fool of a boy?"

Samantha crossed her arms. "Yes, I did. I do. Now, what's making her ill?"

Nessie paused. "Best you don't know, Miss Sammy."

"Know what? Nessie?"

The slave shook her head.

"Nessie, I demand you tell me. Whether you approve of them being here or not I am responsible for them for the next week. I need to know what's happening to her."

Nessie spoke quietly. "Same thing that's happening to ever' female slave you ever met."

"What are you talking about?"

"Happens all the time, Miss Sammy. Why you think some of us ain't as dark as the others?"

Samantha didn't understand.

Nessie shook her head. "Why would you know, Miss Sammy. Ain't your job to know."

"For the love of God, Nessie, just tell me what's going on!"

"Keep your voice down, Miss Sammy. If I tell you this, you promise you never breathe a word of this to your mama."

Samantha crossed her heart.

"It be like this, Miss Sammy, and I'm gonna tell you plain. If a white man wants his way with us, then they ain't much we can do."

"What?"

"I said if a white man wants his way with us then they ain't much we can do."

"His way? What way?"

"Miss Sammy, I knows you have some idea of how babies are made. Sometimes we ain't got no choice in who helps us make them. You understanding me yet, Miss Sammy?"

Samantha took a step back. "No...that can't be right. Who would do...No, I don't know anyone who would do such a horrible..."

"I need to go get some things for the girl. You stay here."

"But Nessie, you can't mean what I think you mean..."

Nessie left the room before Samantha could finish.

Samantha sat on the edge of her bed, the weight of what Nessie had said bearing down on her stomach. As she stared into space, memories flooded her senses.

There was the day she and Eli sat by the river and watched four male ducks chasing one female, finally catching her when she was too tired to run anymore. All four of them took turns with her, her little head just barely above the water each time.

"That poor thing," she'd said.

"Poor thing nothing," Eli had said. "She's just doing what she's supposed to be doing. It's life."

At the time Samantha agreed.

Then there was Samantha's mother. Every week since Samantha's cycle had started two years ago, her mother made Nessie come in to check Samantha's virginity was intact, looking as Nessie inserted her finger in between Samantha's legs, awaiting Nessie's verdict. Even though Nessie did her best to be gentle, every time Samantha thought she might burst.

"Good," her mother would say every time. "Good thing you're still sensible."

She closed her eyes, but all she could see was the time one of her father's friends had cornered her on the terrace by herself and pressed himself to her. His manhood was hard and he ground it into her hip. She'd never been so frightened in her life. It was only because her mother called from inside that he stopped. She shuddered at the thought of what might have happened if he hadn't.

Nessie came back upstairs and went into the eaves. When she emerged several minutes later, Samantha was sitting on her bed, tears streaming down her face.

Nessie knelt down at Samantha's feet and put her hand to Samantha's wet cheek. "This just how life be for us, Miss Sammy."

"But...but, who? Who would do such a thing?"

Nessie hesitated, then spoke. "Round here, the overseer is the worst."

"Clement Durant? He...he...how?"

104

"He the overseer, Miss Sammy. If he comes into a cabin with his mind set on it, ain't nothing no one can do. Unless you want a beating. Or a whipping."

"But…but…has he…he hasn't done it to you?"

"He be leaving me alone the past few years. I'm too old for him now. But Oma and Chimi and mos' of the other young slaves, you can be sure he done had his way with all of us by now."

Samantha wrapped her arms around her torso, as if trying to protect herself from the truth. "Does it…hurt?"

"Well, sure it does, Miss Sammy. It's a big, hard thing going in a small, dry place. That's why poor Miss Amira is bleeding where she is. The man who had at her must have got her hard."

Nessie went back into the eaves. Samantha stayed sitting on the edge of her bed, unable to move.

Over an hour later, Samantha stood up and looked out her window. She squinted, barely making out the roofs of the slave quarters hiding beneath the moon's shadow. For every night she'd slept safely in her bed there had been a slave girl stifling her screams.

She thought of all the plantations she knew and tried to do the math in her head – how many slaves had been violated like Amira? Did her father know? It didn't matter, she decided – this was her father's plantation and his responsibility. Whether he knew about Clement Durant or not, he was complicit in the crime. *Who else?* she wondered. How many other white men thought it within their right to take such grotesque liberties? What other lies had been woven into the very fabric of her being, absorbed into her skin like sunshine?

Samantha put her palms to her temples to calm her racing mind. It was all too much. The questions were too heavy, the truth too prickled.

Something stirred in her, something she did not recognize.

She crawled quietly into the eaves and opened the hatch. Odus slumbered in the far corner. Amira slept against the wall nearest the hatch. Her breathing was deep and calm. Samantha reached up and stroked Amira's hair, running her palm over the beautifully kinked curls.

"You rest now," she whispered. "You're safe here."

Samantha crept out of the eaves and felt a cool breeze coming in from the windows. She did not pull the hatch shut, but instead left it open so cooler air could make its way in. Once back in her bed, Samantha wrapped herself into a ball and cried herself to sleep.

Chapter 15

Annie watched the long scroll of correspondence appear, starting with the first Facebook message she'd sent from the internet café in Charleston.

> **My Father's Daughter, March 31:** *I thought you might like to know two things:*
> *We survived the fire, and;*
> *I am going to make your life hell.*
> *Hope you enjoy the photo. There are lots – and I mean, LOTS – more where these came from.*

She remembered setting up the **My Father's Daughter** account and sending that initial email. She wasn't sure she'd get a response. She wasn't sure she wanted one. But she wanted him to know that he had tried to get rid of the photos – and her – and failed.

> **Rob Sanchez, March 31:** *Is this some kind of sick joke? Where did you get these photos? They are the property of Virginia State Police and you are committing a crime by having them in your possession. Give me your number immediately and turn in this evidence.*
> **My Father's Daughter, April 8:** *Stop trying to sound all official. It makes you sound like an idiot. Enjoy the next photo. I think I'll give you one a week. You know, to keep the suspense up.*
> **Rob Sanchez, April 9:** *You are only making things worse. Do yourself a favor and tell me how to find you. Trust me – you don't want me to have to come find you.*
> **My Father's Daughter, April 17:** *I'm only making things worse? THINGS COULD NOT BE ANY WORSE. YOU HAVE RUINED MY LIFE! AND NOW, I AM GOING TO RUIN*

YOURS. Hope you enjoy the new photo. I like how it's obvious a bullet is leaving your gun.

Rob Sanchez, April 18: *Ok, I didn't want to have to do this, but you give me no choice. How much do you want for the photos? Is $5000 enough? You give me a Western Union number and I'll wire it as soon as you send me the photos.*

My Father's Daughter, April 25: *You actually think this is about money? THIS IS NOT ABOUT MONEY. You are a murderer. You destroyed my life to try and cover that up. And guess what? It didn't work. You know what I've learned? That justice does not always include the law. This is my justice.*

The truth was Annie did need the money then. She could have copied the photos and sent him duplicates. That wasn't the point. She'd had no say in the course her life was now on. This was her one vestige of control and she would not let it go, especially since the more powerful she felt, the more scared he became.

Rob Sanchez, April 26: *Don't think those photos scare me. I can tell everyone they're doctored. And where will that leave you? EXACTLY WHERE YOU ARE RIGHT NOW. You can't run and you can't hide.*

My Father's Daughter, May 5: *I think it's obvious that I run and hide just fine, thank you very much. Because hey – YOU haven't been able to find us yet. What kind of cop does that make you?*

A year was a long time to be corresponding with someone you despised. The more enraged he became, the more Annie reveled in what she'd started.

Rob Sanchez, June 19: *Bet you think your funny, bitch.*

My Father's Daughter, July 3: *Ok, I didn't pay much attention in English class but even I know that that 'your' is a possessive noun used to attribute a noun to a single person, i.e. your idiocy. 'You're' is the conjunction of 'you' and 'are'; as in, 'you are a moron.'*

I'd say 'I hope this helps' but 'you're' clearly beyond help.

Rob Sanchez, July 15: *I will get these photos from you if it's the last thing I do. You think your clever. I'm here to tell you that you're not.*

My Father's Daughter, July 23:
Dear Wingnut,
Please see previous.
Hugs,
You-know-who

Every email made her feel braver, bolder, more grown-up and more in control.

Rob Sanchez, July 24: *I've found you before and I'll find you again. What makes you think I'm not going to trace where you're posting these from?*

My Father's Daughter, August 1: *Because you'd need a warrant. And for a warrant there needs to be a suspected crime. Since you are the one who committed that crime, I doubt you'll want to draw attention to the existence of this account. Then again, you might. Go for it. Because what you haven't yet realized is that I am not afraid of you. You're a coward and I hope you rot in hell.*

This was a lie – he did scare her. The beauty of email was you could hide behind everything you wished to show.

My Father's Daughter, February 3: *I am now posting one of my favorite photos from this collection. It is the one in which I can best see your cowardly face as you turn to shoot more bullets into AN UNARMED WOMAN. Bet that made you feel really big and strong, huh? Didn't your mother teach you to pick on someone your own size?*

She scrolled down to his most recent email. The date showed he'd written it after she posted the photo at Theo's house. For the first time in their correspondence, he'd included an attachment.

Rob Sanchez, March 21: *Bet you think you are the only one who has photos. I've got plenty of photos of my own.*

It was Annie, eight-years-old, sitting on his lap in her backyard. A cigarette burned in his hand. Her mother stood to the side, staring into space.

The message below the photo was simple.

I'm going to kill you.

Annie thought she might be sick.

She typed the first reply that came into her head.

My Father's Daughter, March 29: *Not if I kill you first.*

"Hey Annie!" Theo shouted a whisper from across the room. He held up a pile of Xerox copies. "I've got the maps. You ready to go?"

"Coming," she said, taking out the memory stick. She logged off Facebook, cleared the browser history, and hoped Theo wouldn't notice she was shaking.

"Hold these," said Theo, handing Annie the papers and leaning over her to take a map out of the glove compartment.

"What am I supposed to do with these?"

Theo unfolded his map of Virginia and spread it across the dashboard. He took one of the papers out of Annie's hand and set it down on the map.

"You went with Blondie to Xerox maps when you had more in your glove compartment the whole time?"

"Easy there. She had older ones."

"So?"

His eyes darted between the two maps.

"Eureka!" he shouted.

"What is it?"

"Look at this," he said, leaning over and pointing to the photocopy. "It's an ordnance map from 1840. Everything we want is on here – Mont Verity, Dominion Royale, and the actual train station for Beckwith Station. It even marks the railroad line. The best part," he said, setting the photocopy on the map, "is that it can be matched up to the current map of that area. See this road here?" Annie followed his finger along the paper. "It's on both maps. They both curve around this lake, and over here, just behind what used to be Mont Verity, are some woods and a stream. Let's just hope it's not all privately owned so we can explore without ruffling anyone's feathers."

He started the truck and revved the engine. "We're getting closer," he said, "I can feel it. The old Beckwith Station site is on the way. Let's start there first."

Annie looked at the map. Mont Verity was in the parts of Virginia where she and her family never ventured. She'd hoped she could say she'd walked where Samantha Weston had walked, that they'd climbed the same trees, even though Annie had never climbed a Virginian tree in her life. The thought made her want to cry.

Annie rolled down the window and wanted to go to sleep. Something about Sanchez's emails always left her exhausted. She didn't want to be in the truck, driving aimlessly through Virginia. The story of Samantha Weston was supposed to be revealed in that library and the fact that it wasn't made her want to scream. Why couldn't this one thing be easy?

They drove down the four-lane highway she knew so well, past multiple mini-malls, the black tarmac of their sprawling parking lots baking in the midday sun. There were no sidewalks and therefore no people – just shiny cars and bulky SUVs, most of which, Annie noticed, were carrying only one passenger. The occasional older house, ranch-style from the 1950s, sat forlorn amongst all the newness.

Annie reached down and pulled Elijah Fabre's knife out of the loop in her boot. She held it flat over her palms, being careful not to let the sharp blade near her flesh.

"Now that's what we came for," said Theo.

Annie looked up. The four-lane highway was gone; they had turned onto a two-lane road, surrounded by fields and woods. Up ahead, a mountain range rolled high over the landscape.

"The Blue Ridge Mountains," Annie said.

"They really are blue," said Theo. "And all this time I thought it was just a name."

Annie expected to be happy at such a familiar sight, but instead she felt disappointed. *The mountains in Vermont are prettier,* she thought.

"Hey!" said Theo, abruptly pulling onto the gravel at the side of the road and jumping out of the cab.

"What is it?" said Annie.

Theo stood in front of a small sign, its raised bronze letters reflecting the sun. Annie got out of the truck.

Theo read from the sign: "*Site of slave uprising on April 12, 1861 that saw the destruction of Beckwith Station. More than 100 slaves either killed or captured and executed.* When did the girl at the library say Fort Sumter was?"

"April 12, 1861. Same day."

"I wonder if the slave uprising is related to it," he wondered. "You know – maybe the slaves heard what had happened and decided to stage their own fight."

Theo reached inside the truck and pulled out a roll of paper and a piece of drawing charcoal. He held the paper onto the sign with one hand and brushed the charcoal over it with the other.

"What are you doing?" Annie asked.

"A rubbing. Now we'll have our own copy. We can do this at the cemetery, too," he said. "If we find anything, that is."

"Wow. That would never have occurred to me."

"We do them a lot at school. You know that old cemetery behind my house? Once a year the school takes a field trip there and they have us pick a grave, do a rubbing and then do some research on that person."

Annie watched as the letters on the sign appeared under the charcoal and onto the paper. "Who have you done a report on?"

Theo grinned. "I sort of cheat. Most of my family are buried in there, so I've been able to get away with doing projects on them."

"How many of your ancestors are buried there?"

"Over twenty. The first Theodore Mason died in 1801 and he had six kids, and they're all buried there, and it just keeps going. Although I tend to just stick with the Theodore Masons and their families. Makes it easier to find out what I need at home."

"But how come you knew your way around the Town Hall records? Was that just to supplement what you had at your house?"

"No." Theo paused. "I was mainly there to look for stuff on my Mom and her family."

"Oh." Annie wasn't sure how far to tread. "And did you find anything?"

"Not really. Her family seemed to move in and out of Vermont a lot. It's like they were always going to look for something they never found, because they'd always end up back in Battenkill."

"Do you know why?"

"No. That's why I went looking – to see if there were any clues as to where she'd gone or why she went. But I didn't find anything."

Like we're not finding anything now, Annie thought.

"There," said Theo, as he finished the rubbing. He rolled up the paper and wiped his charcoal-coated hand on his jeans. "Next stop, Mont Verity."

Annie said nothing as he put the rubbing into her bag.

"Hey?" said Theo. "What's wrong? I thought you'd be excited."

"It's nothing. I guess I just…I didn't think we'd be here this long."

"Look, I know things aren't going exactly as we'd hoped, but hey – you never know what might be around the corner."

"Except we do. Mont Verity isn't actually there anymore."

"I know, but aren't you excited to see where it was? To be where Samantha Weston once was?"

"I'm sorry. We've driven all this way, but maybe I should have just stayed…"

"Hey, look!" said Theo. He walked closer to the field and knelt.

Annie watched as he brushed his hand over the dirt. "What is it?" she said.

Theo smiled. "A disused railroad line."

Annie walked over and crouched down. Two lines of old track were embedded in the ground, straddling rows of cracked buffers. The line went into the field, where it disappeared amongst the tall grass. Theo got the photocopy of the old map from the truck. He stood next to Annie, the whole of his arm pressing against hers. Annie's instincts wrestled against getting closer and moving away.

"See?" he said. "There's the railroad line, and we're here. That means that Beckwith Station, the actual train station, would have been about a quarter of a mile over that field."

Annie closed her eyes and tried to imagine the outline of Beckwith Station in the field. The color behind her lids glowed red from the sun. She felt Theo's hands on her shoulders and opened her eyes. "See, I told you. We are getting closer. You just have to have faith."

She wriggled out from under his grasp. "Let's go."

Theo pulled the handle on the door of his truck. It was locked.

"Have you got my keys?"

"No. Don't you have them?"

Theo searched the graveled ground. "They must be around here somewhere."

Annie cupped her hands around her face and squinted through the truck's window. "Found them," she said.

"Where?"

"In the ignition."

Theo looked in. "Oh, great."

"It's okay," said Annie. She knew what she was about to do would raise questions, but she didn't see another alternative that wouldn't make their time in Virginia even longer or call attention to them. She put down her backpack and pulled out a twisted wire hanger and a doorstop.

Theo laughed nervously. "Most girls I know only carry lip balm and cell phones."

Annie stood at the driver-side window. "This might damage the stripping on your window a little bit, but it's better than breaking it or calling a locksmith."

"Is it?" He watched as she pushed the doorstop in between the window's glass and door frame. "I don't know whether to be impressed or scared."

She handed him the coat hanger. "This will be easier if you help me. I'm going to wedge the window open. I need you to put the hanger in and push the 'unlock' button. Ready – one, two, three!"

Theo did as he was told. Within seconds the doors unlocked. He opened the truck door.

"So you just happen to have a doorstop and a twisted coat hanger in your bag," said Theo, still confused. "Do you want to explain that?"

"My mother loses her keys a lot," she lied and got in the truck hoping Theo wouldn't ask any more questions.

The more they drove, the more the landscape resembled a Virginia that Annie had never seen. Narrow roads were canopied with trees, and gaps in the woodland along the side of the road revealed white farmhouses and fields glowing yellow in the sun.

We lived in Virginia and I've never seen this, she thought.

"This is it," said Theo, pulling over onto the shaded side of the road. As they got out of the truck Annie realized she was nervous, almost expecting that Samantha Weston would be waiting for them, in the flesh, around the corner.

Nestled in the trees and camouflaged by ivy were two stone pillars. On one was engraved *Mont Verity, 1802.* Annie slowly ran her fingers over the grooves in the stone. Shivers ran down her spine.

The two pillars straddled a gravel driveway. Theo took her hand. "Shall we?"

They walked past the pillars and down the drive. A small white gatehouse sat to the right, an old VW Beetle was parked to the side. Beyond the house sprawled a large field. Behind it lay thick woodland.

"Hey," said Theo. "What is it?"

Annie was crying.

"I don't know. Even though we knew the house wouldn't be here, I just..."

"Can I help you?" A voice came from behind. Annie and Theo turned around.

A young woman in her mid-thirties stood in the doorway of the small house. Her auburn hair was in a ponytail; her eyes sparkled behind tortoiseshell glasses. A yoga mat was slung over her shoulder and car keys rattled in her hand.

Annie froze. The woman looked familiar, but she couldn't place her.

"Hi," said Theo. He nudged Annie.

"Hi," she said.

"I don't mean to be rude," said the woman, "but this is private property."

"Oh, we're sorry," said Theo. "It's just, we drove down here from Vermont this morning to try and find out...we're looking for someone, something. Only we're not really sure what anymore."

Where do I know her from? Annie thought.

"I'm on my way to teach a class. Do you need directions or something?"

Annie and Theo exchanged glances. Annie reached into her backpack. "I have this letter that is addressed to, well, this address."

"I only just moved here," she said. "And the person who lived here before died a year ago."

"Here," said Annie, handing the woman Samantha's letter in its envelope.

She took it and studied Annie. "Have we met before?" she asked.

"Um, no. That's impossible."

"You're not from around here?"

"No, I live in Vermont," she stuttered.

The woman smiled, unsure, then read the address on the envelope. Her eyes widened.

"This is addressed to Sanford Weston," she said.

"Yes," said Annie. "Do you know anything about him?"

"No, not really, just that this gatehouse was once part of his plantation."

The woman pulled Samantha's letter out of the envelope and carefully unfolded it.

"This was written in 1861!" she exclaimed.

"Yes."

"Where did you find it?"

Annie hesitated. "In my house in Vermont. There's a concealed room in the basement and I found it in there."

Annie and Theo watched the woman read the letter. She gasped. "This is from Samantha Weston."

"You know of her?" said Theo.

"Oh my goodness. And you've brought it all the way here. Why?"

"The letter was never sent," said Theo, "and we don't know what happened to her afterwards, like if she ever came back here or saw her father again."

"I can't believe it." The woman shook her head in wonder. "Come in," she said, motioning them towards the door. "There's something in my house that I know you'll want to see."

Chapter 16

Almost everyone at Mont Verity noticed the change in Samantha.

Her mother noticed it when she showed Samantha the engagement and wedding announcement in the *Beckwith Station Gazette*. She expected a fierce confrontation, or at the very least a flurry of defiance, but Samantha, who lay on her chaise reading, only said, "Thank you, Mother."

Her mother left the room awash with relief. "Finally," her mother thought. "Finally."

Her father noticed the change in Samantha on the same day. He was in his office, meeting with Clement Durant, the slave overseer, when Samantha entered.

"What is it, Samantha?" her father asked.

Samantha had not expected to see Durant. Her father's rules meant they were rarely in the same room. But ever since Nessie told her of his forcing himself on the female slaves, the very mention of his name made her angry and ill. He was short and flaccid, with his round, soft belly hanging over his too-tight trousers. He made the whole room smell of rancid salt and chewing tobacco.

"Father, I need to speak with you."

"We're just finishing up," said her father. He nodded to Durant. "You can go, now."

"Yes, Master Weston." Durant waddled to the door. He and Samantha made brief eye contact, and Samantha felt chills run over her skin. All she could think about was poor Oma, poor Nessie, poor Chimi, the countless other slaves and the many times they'd had to endure the weight of this repulsive man. She was glad when he'd left and closed the door.

Her father came out from behind his desk and embraced his daughter. "To what do I owe this pleasure?" he said, bringing her over to the couch.

Samantha had not slept the previous night. Her head had been too full of Nessie's words and Amira's blood. She had to do something. By the time her sleepless night turned to day, she knew what that was.

"I've been thinking about everything that's happened recently – the cotillion, the engagement. And I want you to know that I think you're right. I will marry Royal."

She watched the joy spread over her father's face. Samantha still hoped Eli would return. But that was days away. Her long-term plans would have to come second to what had, overnight, become her two primary concerns: the slaves on the plantation and the care of Odus and Amira. For now, this was the only way.

"Samantha, that's wonderful," he said. "I'm sure you know it means a great deal to your mother and I…"

"Papa, if I'm to marry Royal there are some things I need to know first."

Her father shifted in his seat. "Um… perhaps it would be better if you had this conversation with your mother."

Samantha blushed. "No, no, not that conversation. What I mean is, when I marry Royal I will become lady of the house. Of two houses, in fact. And I believe it's essential that I learn how a house is run. I want to spend some time this week with the house slaves so I can find out more about their duties and how they're assigned and organized."

"Samantha, there's no need…"

"I promise I won't get in the way. Please, Father. Surely you agree I can't arrive at Dominion Royale with nothing to offer. Please."

She felt her father's hesitance and readied herself for more debate. But he softened, and smiled.

"I'm proud of you, Samantha. Let's go round up the house slaves and let them know you'll be observing and asking questions this week."

Samantha threw her arms around him. "Thank you, Father," she said. "Thank you."

The house slaves also noticed the change in their young mistress. It was as if the girl they'd known for 17 years had gone to bed a caterpillar and woken up a butterfly. She passed the whole morning in the sweltering kitchen asking what the slaves thought about their situation and what could be done to make it better. Most were too scared to offer any suggestions, just in case their comments were one day used against them. But even spending one morning in the kitchen, Samantha could see clearly what needed to change.

"It's madness to allow them only one task," she said to her father over lunch. "The poor girl that's stuck washing the dishes all day – have you seen her hands? I'm surprised she has any skin left. They should be on a rota – perhaps one for the breakfast dishes, then another for the lunch wash. And it's far too hot in there. There should be at least two slaves on fanning duty, and installing a larger window on the north side would let cooler air in."

Her father nodded repeatedly to hide his bemusement and promised Samantha that he and her mother would look into the practicality of her suggestions. He didn't notice her slipping parts of her lunch into a napkin, food destined for Odus and Amira.

The last person to notice the change in Samantha Weston that day was Clement Durant. It was the end of the day and he was in Samantha's father's office to give him a report of the day's work. At the end of their meeting he emerged into the darkened hallway, and the last thing he expected was to have a pistol pressed into his back.

Samantha's voice came from over his shoulder. "I'm only going to say this to you once, Mr. Durant. If I ever again hear of you forcing yourself on one of the slaves, I'll personally tie you to the whipping tree and let every single girl you've raped have a turn with the whip. Do you understand?"

Durant thought it was a joke. He turned to laugh. Samantha twisted his arm and pushed him against the wall.

"Do you understand?" she repeated.

The answer stuck in his throat. "Yes, Miss Weston," he whispered.

Samantha pushed him away and did not move until he was out of sight.

Only Nessie knew the real reason behind Samantha's transformation. But even she was not prepared for the change. When Samantha wasn't leaving one of the house slaves wide mouthed over her sudden concern for their welfare, she was doing everything she could to help Odus and Amira. She brought them food five times that day. She commissioned new work clothes for some of the house slaves so that their old clothes could be passed to Odus and Amira. She did the same with bedding so that Odus and Amira each had a blanket to sleep on and a pillow under their heads.

The only one not surprised by the change was Samantha herself. She didn't even notice. She had found a purpose so strong that it was hard to conceive she might have once been any different.

But Nessie was completely unprepared for Samantha's insistence that Odus and Amira be let out of the eaves at night.

"The air just doesn't move in there," she said. "I'm surprised either of them can breathe."

Her instructions were that between the hours of 10pm and 6am, Nessie would guard Samantha's door and tap the floor three times if someone approached. If her parents asked why their daughter needed a slave outside her door she would say that she was bleeding particularly hard that week and would need extra help in the night if either she or her bedding needed a change of linen.

On the first night of Samantha's new regime, Nessie assumed her position outside Samantha's door. All was quiet and still in the house until the grandfather clock struck twelve, and then she heard hushed voices behind Samantha's door.

Miss Amira, she thought. *She's bleeding again.*

Nessie carefully opened the door into Samantha's dark room. First, she saw Amira, curled up on Samantha's bed, sound asleep. Then she saw Samantha and Odus, sitting by Samantha's open window, their backs to the door. Both were hunched over a dimly lit lantern.

"Miss Sammy," she whispered. "Everything okay?"

"It's fine, Nessie," Samantha whispered back. Nessie saw an open book on the floor between Samantha and Odus, and a small stack on the windowsill.

Nessie thought she might melt into the floor. *She's teaching him to read,* she thought. "You take care not to be too loud now."

"We will, Miss Nessie," said Odus.

Nessie closed the door and mumbled to herself, "I's an old woman and I seen lots in my time, but I ain't ever expected I'd see anything like that."

"We'd better stop now," said Samantha, closing the book. "But take the books and the lantern. It will give you something to do while you're in the eaves." She handed them to him and smiled. "You're a fast learner."

Odus looked at Samantha in the moonlight. "Why's you doing all this, Miss Sammy?"

"What do you mean?"

"Being so nice, teaching me."

Samantha looked over at Amira asleep on her bed. "I don't know how to explain it. I guess I always thought – or was always taught – that you, Negroes, I mean – were animals, of the devil, not human. Something about seeing Amira last night…I just want her to be where she'll never be hurt like that again."

"You know," said Odus, "when Mister Eli promised us our freedom, I thought it couldn't be for real. I thought there be no way a white man would promise such a thing. But now, being here, meetin' you, I's starting to think some white folks might not be so bad after all."

Samantha put her hand on Odus' arm. "Eli promised you he'd free you?"

Odus hesitated, certain he'd said the wrong thing. "Well, yes ma'am. He say, that's why he come when Cudgen taking us here to be slaves. He say, if we can do as we told for a week he gonna go find a way fo' us to get north. He said, your daddy didn't really believe in slavery anyway. He say, something about some kind of railroad that can take us where we don't have to be slaves no more."

"But I don't understand. It doesn't make sense. He said what he was doing was going to convince my parents that he and I…" She looked at Amira sleeping on the bed. "Of course, why didn't I think of that before? He knows Father wants to cut back on slave labor. He wants to show him he's serious about it too. But why didn't he tell me? Was he afraid I'd tell Father? He should have trusted me. Why didn't he trust me?"

Odus had no answer for the questions that poured out.

"That doesn't matter now. What matters is that he's taking you north. He's taking you north. Oh, I am so relieved! I didn't know how I could protect you."

"What do you mean?"

"I thought perhaps his intention was to pretend he'd been looking for you all week and deliver you back to my father. But…no, that can't happen."

"Why not?"

"Because I've only just realized what will happen when he does. Someone has to hang for Cudgen's death and it's easier to blame a black man." She was ashamed of the words that left her mouth even though she no longer believed them. "And Amira. This is the best way to make sure no one ever hurts her like that again. I've been raking my brains trying to think of a way to protect her and now it's here. This is how it should be. You should be free." She stood. "We need to do something. We need to get you ready. You'll need food, water, a travel pack, some blankets…"

"Miss Sammy, now don't you go getting yourself into trouble over this…"

Samantha didn't hear him. "He said he'd be back in a week. That means we've got less than four days to get you ready." She nodded to herself. "That should be enough time to gather everything without drawing attention to ourselves. I'll tell Nessie in the morning. She'll help. We can do this. I know we can."

In the corner, Amira sighed in her sleep.

Odus put his gentle hand on Samantha's face. His skin was cool, yet his touch filled her with warmth. She'd never been touched by a Negro man before. To her complete bewilderment, it felt safe.

"Thank you, Miss Sammy," he said. "Thank you."

Chapter 17

"I'm Kate, by the way," said the woman as Annie and Theo followed her into the house.

The front door led into an open, sunlit room with wooden floors and wainscoted walls. Brightly colored cushions rested on worn, wooden furniture.

One wall was occupied by floor-to-ceiling shelves, which held paperbacks, structured pieces of blue glass and an array of colored photographs. On the middle shelf was a picture of a school class. There were about thirty children, all young enough to be in kindergarten. Kate stood amongst the children, holding a sign that said *Clinton Elementary School, 2011.*

My old school. Annie squinted, as if the picture was too bright. Then she remembered her own kindergarten glass with Mrs. Richards, and a student teacher called Ms. Jotowski. Could Kate be her?

Kate set Samantha's letter down on the table and walked to the back wall. Annie and Theo watched as she took down a large, rectangular black and white picture and laid it on the table.

"Have a look," she said.

Annie and Theo leant over the photograph. Over 100 people stood in rows in front of a large white house. The men were all in old-fashioned suits and cravats; the woman in hoop skirts and ruffled sleeves. At the bottom of the photo in faded brown ink read, *Samantha's debutante ball, March 6, 1861.*

Annie let out a shriek. "Oh my God! This is her cotillion! Which one is she?"

"I don't know for sure," said Kate, "but I'm guessing she's this one. She's in the front, center position on the photo and if you compare her to the rest of the women she's definitely the best dressed."

Theo reached into Annie's backpack and gave the woman his printout from the *Beckwith Station Gazette.*

"March 7, 1861," she read. "This past Saturday, Samantha Ashton Weston, only daughter of Sanford and Madeline (nee Jacobs) Weston, was introduced to society. Oh, my heart."

Annie stared at the picture and the image that gazed back at her. Samantha's face was soft and round, her dark hair pulled up into a feast of ringlets. Annie wanted to touch her, just to see if Samantha Weston could be felt.

"Do you know anything about the family?" Theo asked.

"Not much. The realtor told me that the original plantation burned down just before the war. Sanford Weston lived here in the gate house until he died. This photo has been here ever since. When I moved in I found some very old wooden crates in the attic, but I haven't had time to go through them. It would be incredible if there was something in there. Can you come back later?"

Annie and Theo exchanged helpless glances. "We need to get back to Vermont tonight," he said.

The woman handed him a piece of paper and a pencil. "Here, write down your number and email address. If I find anything of interest I'll let you know."

Annie watched Theo's left hand move across the paper, and then he gave it to the woman. She ripped it in half and wrote down her own details: *Kate Jotowski,*

It was her.

"Well, this has been just incredible," she said, leading them out the door. "I really wish I didn't have to go. Where are you off to now?"

"Back to Vermont," said Annie.

"Unless," said Theo, "there's somewhere you'd recommend? You know, someplace we haven't thought of that might give us more information?"

Kate thought for a moment. "The old cemetery is just the other side of those woods." She pointed to the trees in the distance. "You can walk there. Go through the woods until you get to a stream – that's the property marker. Turn left and follow it for about half a mile. I'd love to know what you find."

"Great," said Theo. "And thanks for your help."

Kate got into her car. Annie and Theo waved. Halfway down the drive, the car stopped.

"Wait a minute," Kate said and ran back toward the house.

She's recognized me, Annie thought. *She's going to call the police.* A whirlwind of possibilities swirled – she could try and lie her way out of it, deny every accusation, or take Theo's truck and drive it off into the mountains.

Instead, Kate returned with the photo of the cotillion and handed it to Annie. "You should have this."

"Really? Are you sure?"

"Consider it a loan," Kate smiled. "You can give it back when you find out what happened to Samantha Weston. Something tells me you're closer to her than you think." She got back into her car and drove away.

"Well," said Theo, "care to walk through Samantha's fields?"

Annie couldn't speak. She just nodded and let Theo lead her through the coarse, yellow grass.

The sun was high as Annie and Theo walked across the field. When they entered the woods, the change in temperature was so marked that Annie trembled against the chill.

"I can hear the stream," she said, moving toward the sound of water bubbling over stones, not looking to see how closely Theo ambled behind her. The louder the sound, the faster Annie walked until finally she found herself running toward the water.

Standing over it, she could feel its coolness. She took off her boots and stepped in. The water that swelled around her ankles was biting, as if ice lay in between the rocks and stones, but Annie did not care. She closed her eyes. She heard Theo arrive behind her.

"What are you doing?" he asked.

"Soaking it all in," she said. 'Soaking her in. It's almost like she should be here, like she is here."

Theo took off his shoes and waded in beside her. "Good Lordy, this is cold."

Annie opened her eyes. "Thank you for bringing me here. Sorry I've been so up and down."

Theo sat down on a large, flat rock at the edge of the stream. "It's okay. I can imagine it's all a bit emotional, being here."

"Why would being in Virginia make me emotional?" she snapped.

"Well," he said, "you're away from your mom, which as far as I can tell is a big deal."

Annie sat down next to him. She picked up a flat, oval stone and dried it on her jeans. She could feel Theo's eyes bearing into her skin.

"It must be lonely, where you are. Not going to school. Don't you ever just want to, I don't know, be a part of something?"

"Every day," said Annie, putting the stone in her pocket.

Theo moved closer.

"Annie," he said, pulling her chin towards him. "You can trust me."

It would have been so easy to kiss him. The very thought made her want to melt into the water and rush away with the stream. Maybe that's not what he wanted, maybe this was just a gesture. But she had to stop this now. Being so close to home, reading Sanchez's emails, worrying that Kate had recognized her – it brought her back to reality. There was no point getting closer to Theo, or to anyone.

She stood abruptly and almost fell over. "I can't," she said, stepping out of the stream and wiping her feet with her hands. "I'm sorry, Theo." She slid her damp feet into her boots and walked briskly towards the cemetery, not knowing if Theo would follow and too scared to turn around and find out.

The wrought iron gates that marked the entrance to the cemetery creaked when Annie pushed them open. Large, old trees loomed so high they seemed to be competing with the sun. Annie walked past moss-covered graves that looked as if they would soon become one with the grass on which they sat. Many engravings had been worn by years of wind and weather. She heard the gates creak behind her; Theo had arrived. Would he even speak to her now? She saw him out of the corner of her eye, meandering through the cemetery and reading the stones as he passed. Annie stopped in front of a grave for a baby girl who had died on the same day she was born and wanted to cry at all this little girl never had the chance to become.

"I found it!" Theo shouted.

Annie saw him standing by a large, stone monument.

"Look," he said.

Annie ran to his side and read the engraved lettering.

WESTON
Here lies
Sanford Emmanuel Weston
b. August 11, 1813
d. January 8, 1910
His devoted wife
Madeline Jacobs
b. October 30, 1820
d. June 11, 1861

and their cherished daughter
Georgia May
b. February 28, 1839
d. May 11, 1856

"Mrs. Weston died not long after Fort Sumter," said Theo. "Kate mentioned that Mont Verity burned down just before the Civil War started. I hope they're not related."

There was nothing in Theo's tone to suggest that he was angry with her. Somehow, that made Annie even more irritated.

"Where is she? Where's Samantha? Why isn't she here?"

"Well, maybe she never made it back. She did say in the letter that she was never coming back. Or maybe she wasn't buried with her family." Theo's voice broke. "Maybe she got married and is buried with her husband."

"Theo, what is it?"

"Nothing."

Annie took his hand, almost without realizing. "Are you sure?"

"It's just…this is my first time out of Vermont since my mother left. It feels weird. Like she could be around every corner, because she could be anywhere. She could have been eating breakfast at the diner or sitting at a desk in the library. Even walking around here I half expect to come across her grave."

"I'm sorry, Theo."

"It's not your fault."

"No, but I'm sorry for being so wrapped up in my own stuff that I haven't noticed you're not finding this easy either."

"Oh well," he said, shrugging away her hand. "Let's have a look around and see if we find any Samanthas."

He walked away, his head bowed as he read the gravestones. Annie stood where he left her, unsure of where to go.

"Over here," Theo shouted, pointing to a small house made of stone slabs. "It's the Fabres!" Annie ran over.

FABRE
Major Louis Fabre
b. March 6, 1810
d. April 12, 1861
Beloved wife
Narcescsa Millet
b. December 20, 1818

126

d. July 12, 1899

Noble son
Evans Royal
b. May 16, 1833
d. May 10, 1901

His devoted wife
Olivia Bradford
b. February 25, 1848
d. November 12, 1885

Theo pulled the rubbing out of Annie's bag and studied it. "Every time we find something new I just get more confused."

"What do you mean?"

"Samantha didn't marry Evans Royal Fabre. And look. The slave uprising was on April 12, 1861. Fort Sumter was April 12, 1861. And now we know that's also the day that Elijah Fabre's father died. The worst part is that we know there's no *Beckwith Station Gazette* copy to tell us how and why he died."

"Elijah Fabre's not here," said Annie.

Theo scanned the ground. "Yes, he is," he said, leaning down over a tall, thin gravestone.

Elijah Fabre
Brought into this life
October 1, 1843
And tragically taken from it
On March 13, 1861
Justice not gained in life
Is assured in the sweet hereafter

"Elijah Fabre died in March, 1861?" said Theo. "And what do they mean by 'tragically'?"

Annie reached into her backpack and checked the date of Samantha's debutante ball.

"He died exactly a week after the cotillion. Look – the ball was on March 6 and he died on the 13th."

Theo checked the lists of letters and numbers. "If he died on March 13, then he can't be the one who made the EF markings in the Bible, and he can't be the one Samantha said she was in love with."

Annie pulled the knife out of her boot and looked at Elijah Fabre's name engraved into the blade.

"If he's not EF," said Theo, "then how did his knife get all the way up to Vermont?"

"Maybe he gave it to Samantha before he died. Maybe Royal is EF, and he was given it as a keepsake. I don't know."

"But if Royal was EF then why didn't he and Samantha get married?"

Annie studied the gravestone. "I don't get what 'tragically' means. Was he in an accident or something?"

"I don't know." Theo clapped his hands over his face. "We're idiots!"

"What?"

"We didn't look him up when we were at the library. Maybe there's an article on him that we completely missed."

He grabbed her hand and together, they ran back to his truck.

Theo sped back to the library and tore into the parking lot.

"Afternoon," said Theo as he pulled Annie past the library desk. The blonde was no longer there.

Theo rushed straight to the computer with the *Beckwith Station Gazette* files and didn't even bother sitting down. He just leaned over and typed: *Elijah Fabre, January 1861 – March 1861.*

One result came up. Theo clicked it open. He read the headline and sank into the chair behind him. "Whoa," he said.

"Oh my God," said Annie.

They both sat silenced by the words before them.

"I wasn't expecting that."

"Me neither."

They stared, reading and re-reading what was in front them, unsure whether or not to believe it. After several minutes, Theo leaned over and hit *print*. He and Annie watched as the words on the screen appeared as ink on paper.

Theo picked it up and read it one last time.

"Well, now we know what happened to Elijah Fabre."

"Yes," said Annie, blinking in disbelief. "Now we know."

Chapter 18

"Miss Sammy," said Nessie, "you gots to calm down."

It was Wednesday morning, a week after Samantha's cotillion, and the sun shone down from a cloudless sky. She was due to meet Eli in the woods that night and all she'd collected for Odus and Amira lay on her bed: two blankets, a canteen, an extra dress for Amira, bandages, hard tack and dried beef.

"It's not enough," she said. "They won't even get halfway to the Potomac with this little food."

"Too much, and poor Odus'll struggle to carry it. Don't you worry, what I hear about this whole Underground Railroad is that they'll be taken care of ev'ry time they're taken in."

"Go find Oma. Tell her to go to the kitchen and get at least four biscuits. I can smell them from here."

"Are you sure, Miss Sammy?"

"Yes. Now please go."

The past week had flown by. The days were spent smuggling food into the eaves while feigning interest in the wedding preparations. The nights passed with Amira asleep on Samantha's bed while she and Odus huddled by the window as she taught him how to read. He'd learned so much and could now read three-letter words. This was one of the many reasons she would be sorry to see him go. She had so much more to teach him.

She hardly thought of Eli. Only as the day to meet him arrived and she prepared to say goodbye to Odus and Amira did the questions come. When he was done taking Odus and Amira north, how soon would he come back? Were there other slaves he intended to free? Should they put their wedding plans on hold? Should they even get married at all? Surely they would achieve more if she married Royal and had two plantations under her control? But was this even his plan? Was freeing Odus and Amira just a one-time effort? Did he still want to marry her and live at Mont Verity?

She would just have to wait and find out.

Nessie returned to find Samantha still standing over all she'd gathered. She began rubbing Samantha's back, just as she had done when Samantha was a colicky baby refusing to go to sleep. "Miss Sammy, you done enough."

"What if they don't make it, Nessie? It'll be all my fault."

"Miss Sammy, you already done more than I ever thought you could do. God bless you."

Samantha began putting the rations into a canvas sack. There was a knock at the door. Nessie cracked it open.

"I gots six biscuits," she heard Oma say.

"Did anyone see you?" Nessie asked.

"I don't think so."

"Well done, Oma," said Samantha. "Here – you keep one."

"Thanks, Miss Sammy," she said, putting it into the pocket of her apron.

Once Nessie had closed the door Samantha went into the wardrobe. A blast of heat from the eaves hit her as soon as she opened the hatch. Amira lay feebly slumped against the wall, her face ashen and dull. Odus fanned her with two of Samantha's fans. Samantha crawled through the hole and looked around the darkened space.

"Not much longer now. Here," she said, handing them the biscuits. "Oma got these for you."

"Thank you, Miss Sammy."

The water bucket was empty.

"This needs filling. I'll be right back."

She backed out of the hole and begrudgingly closed the hatch. Nessie met her at the wardrobe door.

"Miss Sammy, you's gots to come quick."

Samantha came out of the wardrobe. Chimi stood at the window, out of breath. She pointed out the window. "Miss Sammy, look!"

Samantha looked out and saw Oma being led across the drive by Clement Durant.

"He coming out of Master Weston's office, and Cook tell him that Oma been stealing."

"What?"

"Yes, Cook noticed biscuits missing and said she seen Oma leaving right before she noticed they gone. When they find one in her pocket the overseer say he taking her to the whipping tree."

Samantha ran out of her bedroom and down the stairs.

"Miss Sammy!" called Nessie. "Where you going?"

But Samantha did not answer.

Samantha barged in to her father's office, throwing open both doors. It was empty. She ran to the front door, where Charles, the doorman, sweltered in his wool suit.

"Charles, have you seen Father?"

"He done left this morning, Miss Sammy."

"Left? Where?"

"I think he off to the Fabres, Miss Sammy. Don't think he be back until late."

Samantha flew down the front steps and ran towards the slave quarters. It was almost noon and unseasonably temperate. Her eyes squinted against the brightness, and her dress felt like a weight holding her down. But she did not stop.

A crowd had already gathered by the whipping tree.

"Let me through," she panted, pushing her way past the slaves. "You have...to let...me through."

Oma's hands were tied to the lowest branch and as Samantha broke through the crowd, a collective gasp erupted as Durant tore off Oma's shirt with one hand, bearing her breasts to the sun and the crowd. In his other hand was the whip.

"Stop!" Samantha yelled.

Durant's eyes widened at the sight of his master's daughter. Then anger pinched his face. She had humiliated him only a few days ago, pointing a gun at his back and telling him what he could or couldn't do with his slaves.

"You have no business being here, ma'am," he hissed.

"I have every right to be here," she said, catching her breath. "I am ordering you to let her go."

"Can't do that, ma'am. She was caught stealing. Rules is rules."

"She wasn't stealing. She was doing as I asked. I wanted those biscuits."

Durant paused. Then a horrible grin spread across his face as he picked up the whip and walked slowly towards her.

"I don't think I believe you, ma'am. I think you'd say anything to protect these niggers. You've gone soft over them over the past few days and everyone here has noticed."

Samantha put herself between Durant and Oma. "Let her go or so help me I will see to it that you are relieved of your position as soon as Father gets home."

Durant stood so close his words spat in her face. "I've worked for your father my whole life, and my father worked for his father. You think a word from his little missy is going to mean anything? I know your father better than anyone and he has the spine of a jellyfish."

Samantha slapped him as hard as she could. He raised his fist.

"Go ahead," she said, her jaw clenched.

Durant's hand fell to one side. "Fine. I'll let her go."

"Thank you," said Samantha. As she turned and reached for Oma's torn shirt lying in the dirt, Durant pushed her to the ground and raised the whip. The crowd gasped.

"No!" Samantha yelled. She jumped to her feet and lunged for Oma, throwing her arms around the girl just as the whip came down.

Several of the women screamed, including Oma. Some of the male slaves jumped, wanting to intervene, until well-ingrained fear held them in place.

Durant lowered the whip, then dropped it to the ground. He took a few steps back, not wanting to believe the sight in front of him.

The whip had gone straight down Samantha's back, searing through the fabric of her dress and cutting a line through her skin. She clung onto Oma, afraid to let go. She was in the worst pain of her life, even more than when she broke her arm falling off the palomino two years ago, even more than the worst of her blood cycle cramps. It was as if lightning had struck and split her back in two.

"Miss Sammy," whispered Oma, tears falling down her face. Samantha released her clasp on Oma long enough to untie the rope holding Oma's hands. She kept her arms over Oma's shoulders, afraid to let go.

"Please take me back to the house," Samantha managed to whisper, and she and Oma hobbled toward the crowd.

"Wait," said Samantha, leaning down to pick up Oma's shirt in the dirt. "Put this on first." She let go of Oma and started to sway. Two of the field slaves ran forward to catch her.

"I'm alright," she said. "Thank you." She summoned one of them closer. "I need you to spread the word amongst the slaves that Mother and Father are not to find out about this. Make sure Durant knows it, too."

"Yes, Miss Sammy," said the slave.

No one spoke as Samantha and Oma limped back to the house, and no one moved until Durant walked humbly, shamefully, back to his cabin.

Samantha let Nessie dress the whipping wound on her back, and then insisted that she stop fussing. "I'm alright," she said. "We've got more important things to do."

Odus and Amira came out of the eaves at 10 o'clock. They sat with Samantha on the floor, holding onto the packs she had prepared. Nessie kept watch at the door. Samantha looked out the window. It was a clear, cold night, which made Samantha nervous. The brighter the moonlight, the greater the chance of being seen. None of them said a word; they simply sat in silence and waited for the clock to chime quarter to twelve.

Samantha dared not admit her anxiety to Odus and Amira. So many things could go wrong. They could be caught at any point: sneaking out the window, shimmying down the pillar, making their way across the moonlit field to the woods. What if Eli wasn't there?

The clock chimed. It was time to move.

They made it out the window and down the pillar without a hitch, both Odus and Samantha working together to help Amira. They all held hands as they ran across the horse paddock, with Samantha carrying Amira's pack. The moon shone so brightly that their shadows ran alongside them. Amira started to wheeze.

"Almost there," said Samantha.

They leapt into the dark woods and followed the sound to the stream. Once they reached it, Samantha took the canteen out of Amira's pack and brought it to the girl's lips.

"You did really well," said Samantha, stroking the girl's hair. "You rest now."

Odus stood by the stream, looking into the dark.

"You take good care of her," she said.

"Yes, ma'am," he said softly. Their eyes met, and Samantha looked away. There was so much she wanted to say to him. It wasn't even as if she knew him or much about him. Odus and Amira were, to her, two of the most beautiful human beings she'd ever met. They'd both endured so much, and yet they remained kind and gentle.

She scanned the dark woods, looking for signs of Eli. Part of her was desperate for him to arrive, and another part didn't want to see him at all. His coming would change everything: Odus and Amira would be taken away, and she would begin a new and very different life.

Eli and his horse emerged from the dark. Samantha gasped. She wasn't sure it was him, at first. His clothes were dirty and his trousers were torn at the knee. He dismounted and didn't bother holding the reins of his tired horse. He took a step towards her and winced – that was when Samantha noticed his feet were bare and his face had a trace of stubble.

She walked towards him and held out her arms, unsure of what was expected. Eli responded with a loose embrace. It didn't feel quite right, as if over the past week they'd both changed shape and no longer fit. He smelled of rotting hay and mulch.

"It's so good to see you," she said. Her words were disingenuous, and she knew it. She hoped he didn't notice. "We have so much to talk about."

Eli looked at Odus and Amira. "You've still got them. Good."

"They're as ready as I can make them," said Samantha, leading Eli towards them. "They've got food, water and blankets. They've been well fed this week, so hopefully they're fortified for the journey."

"Journey? What journey?"

"North. They told me you were going to take them north."

Eli spoke low in Samantha's ear. "Samantha, I only told them that so they wouldn't run. I'm taking them back to your father."

Samantha stepped back. "What?"

"What did you think I was going to do? The plan all along was to take them back. I'll tell him I've spent this week tracking them down. Don't you see? This is how I'll convince your father that I'm the only one you should marry. While two of his slaves have been on the run all week, I'm the one that's been doing something about it. Royal's just been sitting on his haunches."

Samantha put her hands over her ears and shook her head as if to block out all Eli had just said. "Eli, you told them you were going to free them. You promised."

"No one ever tells a nigger the truth. There'd be slave rebellions all the way down to the Delta if they knew half of what we know."

"This can't be happening," she whispered.

"Go home," said Eli. "I'll take it from here." He pulled out his pistol and aimed it at Odus. "Okay, nigger. Start walking."

Neither Odus nor Amira moved.

"I said walk!" he shouted.

Samantha stood in front of Eli.

"I can't let you take them."

"Samantha, what is wrong with you? This is what you wanted! After tonight we can be married and you can stay at Mont Verity forever."

"No," said Samantha. "Not this way."

"Now you're just talking nonsense. I've known you all your life, Samantha, and I know you're a girl who only ever wanted two things. Ride her horse and stay at her daddy's house."

"I've changed."

Eli rolled his eyes. "It's past your bedtime. You're tired and not thinking straight. Go home. Go to bed. We'll talk in the morning after I've brought these niggers to your father."

"No, Eli. We won't."

"What are you talking about?"

"I won't see you tomorrow. And I'll never marry you. I thought you were noble. I thought for the first time in your life you were taking a brave stance. That you actually believed in something. But Royal was right. You only care about yourself."

"Shut up," he said.

"You're a child. And a liar. And a coward."

Eli pushed Samantha to the ground and she cried out as the wound on her back split in two. Eli raised his hand. His fist came down, until it was halted in midair.

Samantha looked up. Odus held Eli's wrist.

"You leave Miss Sammy alone," Odus said.

Samantha watched the rage flash across Eli's eyes. He shook himself free from Odus' grip and stepped back. Then he laughed.

"You know what? As long as your father gets these niggers back, he won't care if they're dead or alive." He raised his gun and pointed it at Odus' chest.

Amira screamed as a shot rang through the night sky, echoing through the trees and floating up to the stars.

Blood splattered over Odus' face, but he did not move. Instead, he watched as Eli came slowly to his knees. Samantha's bullet had gone straight through his back to his chest. He slumped onto the ground, rolled onto his side and then Elijah Fabre took his last living breath.

"Miss Sammy," Amira whispered. "What have you done?"

Samantha walked over to Eli's body and knelt down. His eyes were still open. She closed them. She pulled Eli's fingers to extract his gun, got up and walked over to his horse, feeling like her body moved of its own volition. She opened Eli's pack and dumped the contents onto the ground. All that came out was a canteen and the knife Samantha had given him a mere two weeks ago. She saw traces of blood on the blade, then the engraving caught the moonshine: *To Elijah Fabre, With Love from Samantha Weston, 1861.* She cleared her tightened throat.

Later, Samantha would replay the scene over and over in her head, trying to imagine a scenario in which shooting Eli had been an accident. She'd meant to fire a shot to distract him. She'd meant to shoot the gun out of his hand.

No. Nothing could replace the fact that Eli had died because she had deliberately shot him.

She handed Odus the gun. "Odus, please put Eli's things into our pack. Amira, come here."

Samantha cupped her hands together and hoisted Amira into Eli's saddle.

"Miss Sammy?" said Odus.

Samantha looked towards the direction of the house, her house, her home. She then gazed up at the sky. Through the trees, the North Star burned brightly.

"You were promised your freedom," she said, taking the reins of Eli's horse. "And that's exactly what you're going to get."

Chapter 19

Theo drove along the highway towards Maryland. Annie sat in the passenger seat. Their last printout from the library lay on her lap. Annie retrieved the flat stone she'd found at Samantha's stream from her pocket and began absentmindedly sharpening the blade of Elijah Fabre's knife.

"Read it again," said Theo.

Annie cleared her throat.

Beckwith Station Gazette
March 16, 1861

Elijah Fabre Shot Dead; Escaped Slaves Suspected

Elijah Fabre, son of Major Louis Fabre of Dominion Royale, was found dead in the early hours of Thursday morning. The body was discovered on the property border between Dominion Royale and Mont Verity, home of the Weston family. Master Fabre died of a single gunshot wound to the heart. According to his father, he had been traveling the previous week but did not inform them of his exact whereabouts.

Master Fabre had no personal effects on his person upon discovery. His father told this paper that his son would have traveled with his horse, pistol and travel pack. It is also believed that he was carrying a knife that had his name engraved on the blade. At the time we went to press, these items were considered stolen and a potential motive.

As to the suspects, it is believed that Elijah Fabre had been seeking out two fugitive slaves, belonging to Sanford Weston. The only story to have reached this reporter is an account by one Septimus Woodfield, a sharecropper who resides near the Potomac, who reported seeing a white woman, two Negroes and a horse on the edge of his property on Friday morning.

Early reports that the bullet which killed Elijah Fabre came from a gun belonging to the Weston family have not yet been verified.

The wedding that was to take place at Mont Verity this past Friday has been postponed.

"I can't believe he was murdered," said Theo.

"Me neither."

"How could Samantha have had that knife in Vermont a week later?"

137

Annie couldn't think anymore. "I'm starting to wonder if maybe she was never really there. That letter could have been written anywhere. Anyone could have left it in that room."

"No, she was there. Her initials are in the Bible."

"It might not be her."

"Come on, Annie, don't do that."

"Even when I first found it I didn't think it was real. It felt like a joke, like it wasn't possible it could have been down there all that time."

"You and I both know it's her," he said, definitely. "I can feel it. Can't you?"

Annie scraped the stone across the blade. The sound reminded of her of nails running down a chalkboard. "Maybe one of the slaves who murdered him stole the knife and used it to kidnap her. Maybe he forced her to take him north."

"That doesn't make sense either. In her letter she sounds so happy. I can't imagine she'd been kidnapped."

"Maybe she was, but then escaped, and that's why she was hiding. Although it doesn't explain why she didn't think she could ever go back home to Virginia."

"I'm so confused," said Theo.

"Me too," said Annie, sighing.

"But hey, Kate said she'd look through her attic tonight. Who knows what she might find? And that blonde girl at the library seemed to know a lot about Southern history. Maybe we could call there and see what she makes of it all."

"Not that you're looking for an excuse to call her or anything."

"What's that supposed to mean?"

"Nothing. She just seemed to like you, that's all."

"Is that a problem?" he asked.

"Nope," she said, putting the knife on her lap and crossing her arms. "No problem, at all. If blonde and bulimic is what you go for."

She didn't know where the spite came from or why she was throwing it in Theo's face. As soon as she said it she was sorry.

Theo pursed his lips. "Guess I have a thing for brunette anorexics instead."

It took Annie a minute to realize he was talking about her. "You don't know what you're talking about."

"Yes, I do."

"I'm not anorexic."

"Yes, you are."

"Theo, stop it."

"Last year a girl at school was sent to hospital because she wasn't eating. It wasn't even a hospital, actually – it was like a rehabilitation center. She still isn't back yet. The school did a whole educational thing about anorexia and bulimia after that and I'm telling you, you are everything I learned that day."

"I've never made myself throw up."

"You don't need to. You never put enough in."

"I ate breakfast today," she said.

"And you've had nothing since."

"I haven't had the chance."

"Fine. Will you eat if we stop somewhere?"

"We need to get back."

"See? You're making excuses."

"No, I'm not."

"Yes, you are."

"I don't want to talk about this." She crossed her arms. "I'm fine."

Theo shook his head. "You've got all the symptoms. You're always cold because you don't have enough body fat to keep you warm."

"I blame Vermont weather for why I'm cold all the time."

"All I'm saying is that you don't eat enough. And you're going to make yourself really sick if you don't get a grip on it."

She knew she couldn't tell Theo the real reason she ate so little. And even if she did, she wasn't sure he'd believe her.

"Going quiet isn't going to shut me up," he said.

"Theo, why can't you just let this go?"

"Because I care about you!" he yelled. "There, I said it."

In spite of herself, Annie couldn't help but smile. "Look, it's just… complicated."

"Always is," he said under his breath.

"What's that supposed to mean?"

"Just that it's typical. Girls never say what they mean. They talk around what they mean and when we ask for a clear-cut explanation, we're told it's 'complicated'."

"My set-up is not typical."

"And how would I know that?" said Theo.

"What do you want from me?" she yelled.

"I want to be with you," he yelled back. "There, I said it."

Silence fell between them. Annie closed her eyes.

But what I really want you to know is that I am in love. Never did I think the love of my life would come in the shape and form that it has. I do not know what will become of this love, but just to know that there exists in this world someone so kind, so strong, so extraordinary – that is enough for me.

"I can't…" Annie started.

"Yeah, yeah, I know. But can you at least tell me this – is it because you can't, or because you don't want to? Because I'll be honest, Annie, there's something about you that drives me crazy. Maybe it's because there's so much mystery around you, but I don't think that's it. I like you. I like that you're so different, but without trying to be different. You're interesting, and you're interested. I don't know any other girl at school who would react so passionately to finding a letter like Samantha's in her basement. And no matter what you think, that girl at the library wasn't my type." He took a deep breath. "So which is it – because you can't or because you won't?"

If Annie wasn't certain of the laws of gravity then she was sure she could float above the roof of Theo's truck and watch the girl below play out a scene from the movies. She'd never had a boy tell her he liked her. It was thrilling, titillating, something she'd always hoped would happen, yet certain it never would. But this couldn't have come at a more hopeless time.

"It's because I can't," she mumbled. "I'm sorry."

Theo half smiled. "So if you could, you would?"

Annie pressed her knees together. For the first time, she wanted Theo to hear the truth. "Yes, if I could, I would."

"So," he said grinning, "you like me then?"

More than you'll ever know, she thought.

"Maybe," she smiled.

Theo gently punched her arm.

"Hey, careful," she teased. "I've got a knife, you know."

"Yeah, I noticed. It was sharp enough already. Be careful. You don't want to hurt someone."

"You're right. I don't."

Annie put the knife back in her boot.

"I really don't know where we go from here," he said.

"Home," said Annie. "We go home."

Annie knew there was no way around it: they were on their way back to her house, back to her mother, back to being on the run. Maybe one day she could tell Theo the truth. But there was also a chance this would never be over and she, like Samantha Weston, would have to be content knowing that the love of her life existed somewhere else in the world.

"Uh oh," said Theo.

"What's wrong?"

"There's a police car behind us."

"What?"

"His lights are flashing. I'll just pull over." Theo signaled and brought the truck to the side of the road, keeping his eyes in his rear-view mirror. "Yep, it's me he's pulling over. Oh, great – it's a state trooper. Those guys are known for being brutal. My dad is going to kill me. Annie?"

Annie had grabbed the dashboard and was struggling to breathe, inhaling and exhaling as if she'd just come out from too long underwater.

"It's okay," said Theo, turning off the ignition. "I'll probably just get a ticket."

She grabbed the door handle, ready to pull. Theo reached over and put his hand on her arm. "Annie, you can't get out."

Theo saw something in Annie's eyes that he'd never seen before. Annie was scared to death.

He held her hand and took deep inhalations of his own. "Breathe with me. It will be okay. I'm here."

She began to cry. "I'm sorry, Theo."

"Hey, come here." He pulled her in and held her. "Everything is going to be alright."

A state police trooper appeared at the driver-side window and tapped. Theo rolled it down.

"License and registration, please."

Theo let go of Annie so he could get the papers from the glove compartment. He handed them to the officer.

"Any idea why I pulled you over?"

"I was going too fast."

"Bingo." Then he noticed Annie. "This your girlfriend?"

"Yes."

"Look at me, young lady."

Annie clenched her fists, then did as she was told. The officer noticed her tears.

"You okay?"

She nodded.

"You approve of your boyfriend driving like a speed demon?"

She shook her head.

He stared at her for too long, then checked Theo's license. "You two are a long way from Vermont."

"Yes," said Theo. "We're just heading back now."

He looked at Theo's license. "To Battenkill?"

"Yes, sir."

"How old are you, young lady?"

"17."

"Have you got any kind of identification?"

Annie hugged her backpack. "No."

"Well, then, that's a problem. You're a minor and a heck of a long way from home with another minor. Did you know we have rules about under-18s coming in from out-of-state?"

"We didn't know," said Theo.

"Yeah, I bet you didn't. Now if you can't produce any kind of ID, young lady, I'm going to have to bring you in."

"I'm not from out-of-state," she said.

"No?"

"No. I'm from Virginia. I have a Virginia learner's permit."

"You do?" said Theo.

"I still need to see some ID, young lady."

Annie slowly unzipped her backpack. She still had the learner's permit she'd got on her 16th birthday, a week before the night everything changed. She'd left Virginia before she had time to get her license. For all the times she'd stolen a car, she'd never been stopped because she drove perfectly, never crossing lines and obeying all traffic signals.

And now it has all been for nothing, she thought.

She passed the permit over, keeping her hand over her name to prevent Theo from seeing it.

"I'm going to have to run this through. You two stay here."

Annie watched in the side-view mirror as he walked back to his car.

"So," said Theo, slowly, "you're from Virginia."

Annie dug her fingernails into the seat. "Theo, drive."

"What?"

"Go. Drive."

"Annie, I can't. That cop has my license. He knows where I live."

"You can outrun him."

"No, I can't! You're not thinking straight."

"If you don't drive right now I'm as good as dead!" she shouted.

Theo undid his seatbelt and leaned towards her. "You need to start leveling with me. What the heck is going on?"

"I can't tell you."

"Then I can't drive."

"Theo, you don't understand."

"How could I? I only just found out you're from Virginia! What else don't I know? Have you known where we were going this whole time?"

"Theo, I…"

The state trooper reappeared at the window, full of smiles. "Righty-ho, kids, looks like this is your lucky day." He returned Theo's license. "I'm going to let you off with a warning. But we state troopers talk to guys from other states. If I hear of your truck speeding again I'll tell them to show no mercy."

"Yes, sir."

"As for you, Miss Wright, I need to confiscate this learner's permit. It expired over a month ago. You need to apply for a new one."

Please don't say my first name, she begged. *Please don't say my first name.*

"Now you two have a good day," he said. He leaned into the cab. "And Miss Wright? You tell your boyfriend to slow down."

She didn't even nod. Theo waited for the trooper to get back in his car and drive away before pulling into the slow lane.

"Are you okay?" he said.

She nodded.

"You want to tell me what that was all about?"

She shook her head.

Theo pulled the truck back onto the highway and drove, slowly.

Neither of them spoke the whole way back to Vermont.

It was dark when Theo pulled in front of Annie's house.

"Come by the store tomorrow. I think we could both use some sleep. Let's clear our heads and try again. And let me make you a sandwich," he grinned.

"Sure," she said, even though she knew she wouldn't. By tomorrow, she would be gone. "Thank you so much for doing this today. Really, it's been great."

Theo shrugged. "Yeah, well, believe it or not, I'm interested in finding out what happened to Samantha Weston. And I like you."

Annie shivered. "I like you, too."

Theo leaned towards her. "I suppose I can't kiss you goodbye."

I can't, she thought. *There's no use pretending that I can. It will only make him more confused once he realizes I'm gone.*

"I have to go," she said and closed the door behind her before he could respond. She stopped at the door and waved, but it was too dark to see if he had waved back.

"Goodbye, Theo," she said.

She paused at the front door.

I've ruined everything, Annie thought. *I never should have gone to Virginia.*

This was the end. A Virginia state trooper had her name and the location of the town where she now lived. Annie knew she and her mother would have to leave, tonight. She wasn't sure where they'd go. They had already made it from one side of the country to the other. They were running out of places to hide. Once they reached the coast Annie feared they'd be left with little choice but to swim.

She thought of Theo. Even he knew too much now.

Maybe one day they would meet again. Maybe once she'd found a new place for her and her mother and enough time had passed, she could get in touch. With any luck, by then he would have found out what happened to Samantha Weston. But it was something he would have to do on his own.

We can't keep doing this, she thought. *I have to do something. Emails and photos aren't enough. He will kill us, unless I kill him first.*

Something had to be done. She just didn't know what.

She opened the door, dreading having to tell her mother that they had to move.

As soon as she walked into the house she could tell something had changed in her absence. The house was eerily quiet. The television had been turned off. The lamp burned in the living room, and she could hear her mother's voice. It sounded strange, different, like for the first time in months she had something to say.

Annie walked slowly towards the living room. The first thing she saw was her mother, on the couch. She was sitting up, her legs relaxed in front of her. The blanket she lived under still sat on her lap, but it was folded neatly instead of crumpled. As she stepped into the room, what she saw next nearly made her scream.

It was a man, both familiar and a stranger. He was bearded and tired, bedraggled and rough. He stood up and opened his arms.

"Dad!"

Chapter 20

Samantha did not dare admit to Odus and Amira that she did not know where they were going.

They followed the North Star that night and avoided all signs of life – a barking dog, a neighing horse, a chimney emitting smoke into the night sky. She wasn't certain how far they'd gone by the time the sun poked over the horizon, calling an end to their traveling for the night. They found a fallen tree overgrown with brambles. Samantha and Odus added to the cover with dead branches and brush. No sooner had they crawled into their makeshift cave than Amira fell asleep on the leaves. Samantha covered her with a blanket.

"You stay here," she said to Odus. "I'm going to see if there's anything worth foraging."

She didn't wait for Odus to reply, but burst out into the sunlight and looked around the vacant woods. She didn't know where to begin. Despite the warmth of the past week, the forest's plants were still in hibernation. She scraped her foot over the ground under a chestnut tree; the few nuts she found were already halfway to becoming one with the earth.

Behind her, there was rustling. Samantha pulled out her pistol and aimed, sighing with relief when she saw it was only a rabbit. She paused. The rabbit was an easy shot. It would provide just enough meat for the three of them, but she risked the shot being heard. Then she remembered Eli's knife sitting inside her boot. As quietly as she could, she pulled it out, drew back her hand and threw. The knife sailed through the air, but the rabbit ran before it landed.

Samantha fell to her knees.

"What have I done?"

Eli was dead. She had fired her gun at his heart. *He would have killed Odus,* she thought. *He never intended to free them.* How could she not have seen who he really was all this time? Perhaps because Samantha herself had been an altogether different person, with different dreams and ideals. Odus and Amira had changed all that.

She couldn't begin to think about all she'd left. Her father. Her mother. Her home. It was too painful to contemplate.

They stayed in the shelter while the sun forged its path from east to west, all three of them falling in and out of sleep. When they emerged at nightfall, Samantha looked up to find an overcast sky. There was nothing to guide them. The clouds were too thick.

"This way," she said, helping Amira onto Eli's horse, avoiding Odus' eyes for fear he'd see that she did not know which way to go.

They walked for what felt like hours, waiting for the woods around them to change, to reveal something that would point them in the right direction. Samantha could feel blisters forming on her feet and hunger taking over her body. She was about to suggest they rest when she noticed the air felt damp.

"The river," she said and accelerated her speed, swatting away branches with one hand and pulling Eli's horse with the other. Behind her, Odus' footsteps quickened to match her pace.

Then she heard it: the sound of water.

"The Potomac," she said.

They emerged from the woods and into tall, thick grass.

"Stay here," she said, and left Odus and Amira standing on the edge of the woods.

Her feet sank into the watery ground. The Potomac River came into view. Even at night, it appeared to own the land, cutting through it in one wide swathe. Samantha reckoned it was at least a quarter of a mile across.

"Now what?" she said. No one answered.

A high-pitched whistle pierced the air, and Samantha threw herself to the ground, peering through the grass to see where the sound had come from. A few yards in front was a figure, a man holding a rifle and walking along where the grass met the riverbank. The whistling came again and the man stopped. Shouting came from across the river and a gun was fired. Samantha covered her eyes and tried not to cry.

Next time she looked, the man was gone. As she scrambled back towards the woods, she saw more figures on the riverbank. A man was on the ground, a slave. Two white men with rifles kicked him. She felt for her pistol. Two shots would be needed, but she had no way of knowing how many more men were there nor should she draw attention to herself. She hit the ground with her fist. There was nothing she could do.

146

"Miss Sammy," whispered Odus when she was back in the woods. "What do we do?"

"I don't know."

Rustling from behind made them all turn. Samantha pulled her pistol and pointed it in the dark. A shadow approached, and Samantha squinted. It was a man, about 50 years old, wearing a wide-brimmed hat and high leather boots covered in marsh mud. His hands were in the air.

"Come any closer and I'll shoot," said Samantha.

The man continued his approach.

"I mean it. I'm a good shot."

The man spoke so quietly Samantha had to strain forward to hear. "We need to move you farther along," he said.

"What?"

"There's a bit of river to the west where we've got our men patrolling, except our men are Moses' men."

Samantha did not understand.

"You're trying to get north," said the man.

Samantha hesitated. "Yes."

"Then come with me."

Samantha looked at Odus and shrugged.

Odus took the reins of Eli's horse. "We've got nothing to lose, Miss Sammy."

We've got everything to lose, she thought.

The man led them to a dry path. Minutes felt like hours. The woods spilled over into a deep bank.

"You're gonna have to leave the horse here," he said, his voice gentle and calm.

"She's pregnant,' said Samantha, motioning to Amira.

"Sorry, ma'am. To be honest, having an animal like that in tow will only increase the risk of getting caught. Once they're across, it's only five miles to the next station."

"Station?"

"You can go home now," he said. "I'll take them from here."

"No. I'm going with them."

"It's not necessary for conductors to go over the Potomac. We've got it pretty well covered once they make their crossing."

"It's not necessary for what?"

The man studied Samantha. "Is your name Weston?"

Samantha froze. "Yes."

"There was a man here earlier looking for you."

"A man?" *Father?* she thought. "Did he say what his name was?"

"No, ma'am. Said he needed to keep it quiet, but said it was important that they find you. Said they thought you'd been kidnapped, although looking at you now I'm guessing you ain't standing here against your will."

"No, sir."

"Well, then all I can say is you'd best stay low and you'd best move fast. It don't sound like you're going to be getting away easily."

He helped Samantha onto the raft, extinguished the lantern, then picked up a long stick from the ground and used it to push the raft off. Samantha watched as Eli's horse got smaller and smaller, until she could no longer see it on the bank.

"Next stop is a log cabin to the northwest," said the man. "Stick to the woods. Follow the sawdust. If you hit the railway tracks you've gone too far. If you get lost, wait until the next nightfall, then try again. All else fails, just stay out of sight and keep heading north."

"How do we know you ain't goin' turn us in?" said Odus. Samantha was struck by the panic in his voice. It hadn't occurred to her that he might be scared, too.

The man smiled as he continued to push the raft towards the shore. "Young man, if I were truly in the business of turning in escaped slaves you'd know it by now."

They walked well into the night. Samantha tried to ignore the sores on her feet, the rumbling in her stomach and the chafing of her dress against the whipping wound on her back. She ached for her bed, for the ability to fall into a deep, deep sleep under a soft blanket, to have Oma and Chimi take off her dress and put her into a bath full of steaming water. She thought back to the smells of the kitchen: the bread, the beef, the rice. It all felt so far away.

Who was looking for her? Her father? Royal? They already realized she was missing, but she could not be sure they'd found Eli's body and connected the two events. What she couldn't gauge was if they knew she'd run off with the slaves Eli meant to return.

Only if Nessie told them, Samantha thought. As far as Nessie knew, Eli was meant to take the slaves to freedom, not Samantha. With Eli dead, Nessie must have grasped that this was what Samantha had done. What she wouldn't conceive was how Eli had lied and given Samantha no other course. Part of her wanted to find a way to explain everything to her father so that he would know, so that he would understand. But she knew she couldn't just yet. She would have to wait until they were all safe in the north. Then she would write a letter, to her father, explaining everything. Whether or not he'd accept or forgive were questions Samantha found too excruciating to consider.

"Miss Sammy?" said Odus. "I think Amira be needing to rest."

Samantha did not want to stop. She wanted to keep going until they'd found the cabin. She wanted to feel like they'd gotten somewhere, like they weren't just walking into nothing.

"Alright," she conceded, sitting on a stump and opening up the pack. She gave Amira and Odus the last of the hard tack and dried beef.

In the distance, a train blew its whistle. "If you hit the tracks you've gone too far," the man had said.

"We can't be that far off," said Samantha. "We have to keep going."

Amira excused herself and disappeared into the woods. Odus sat next to Samantha on the stump.

"We over the Potomac now, Miss Sammy, you done enough. S'time you start making your way back home."

"I couldn't go home if I wanted to. I've killed a man. If I go back I'll hang."

"You's can always tell 'em it was me who shot Mistah Eli."

"No, I can't. They'll know it was my gun."

"You can say I stole it from you."

"No, I killed Eli. Someday, I'll have to face up to that. But that day is not today. And if you're wanted for the murder of a white man you'll never be free, no matter where you are."

Odus smiled. "Then I guess we all fugitives now."

Samantha leaned her head onto his shoulder and closed her eyes. "Yes, I guess we are."

They'd been walking for an hour when Samantha noticed that the ground under her feet felt different. She stopped and crouched down, running her hands over the shards of wood.

"What's wrong, Miss Sammy?"

Samantha smelled the dust on her hand. "Sawdust. He said to follow the sawdust."

The grains on the ground got thicker. The smell of sawdust became stronger. Then, up ahead, a clearing, and in it, a single lantern drawing the darkened outline of a small cabin and a barn.

They stood on the edge of the clearing, looking in.

"Are you sure this is the right one, Miss Sammy?"

Samantha was sure of nothing. "There's only one way to find out."

As soon as they took a step into a clearing the front door of the cabin opened. A short, thick man bounded down the steps and extinguished the lantern. In the dark, he motioned for Samantha, Odus and Amira to make their way to the barn, around the edge of the clearing.

"What's he doing, Miss Sammy?"

"He wants us to stay in the woods. We need to get to the barn without going into the clearing."

"But why?"

"I think he wants to make sure we aren't seen."

Their eyes readjusted to the dark as they walked the perimeter of the wood. When they got to the back of the barn, the ground near it moved. Samantha stifled a scream as the man came up from a hole in the ground that had been covered with wooden planks and foliage.

"Down here," he said.

Samantha jumped first, then Odus helped lower Amira in. They crawled under the back wall and then climbed a small ladder into the barn.

"First thing you need to know," said the man. "This here is my bird whistle and it makes this sound." He blew into it. "You hear that, you crawl into this hole and stay there until I come and get you out. Understand?" His voice was stern, but kind.

"Yes, sir," said Samantha. Then she noticed another slave, a male with a mass of gray hair curled tightly to his head, sitting against the back of a horse stall.

"This here's Wool," said the man. "You can call me Jem. No doubt you're tired and hungry, so I'll go get some blankets and some food. Then you rest. You've got a long day tomorrow."

"Tomorrow?" asked Samantha.

"Moses be coming tomorrow," said Wool.

"Moses?" said Odus.

"That's right," said Jem. "Moses is comin' to take you to freedom."

Jem came back with soft wool blankets, plates of biscuits and gravy, and a bucket of tepid water for them to wash their face and hands. Clean and fed, they made their beds in the horse stall – Wool and Odus in one, Samantha and Amira in the other. The night had become chilly, and Wool, Odus and Samantha hovered around the lantern, warming their hands while Amira slept.

"How long you been on the run, Wool?" asked Odus.

"A long time, my friend," said Wool, "but that ain't nothin' compared to a long life in chains. I come up from Georgia. I born there and ain't never been anywhere else until now."

"How did you escape?" Samantha asked.

"Well, as you can see I ain't a young'un anymore. I done passed out in the field too many times, and they's looking to sell me on. Day before I s'posed to be goin', I pass out again, but this time, they don't know I's pretendin'. They put me in the sick house and that's when I go." He laughed. "I bet they think old Wool didn't have it in him to run. What about you three? I have to admit I's surprised to see a white woman runnin'. Usually they's the one we runnin' away from."

Samantha laughed, then told him about Eli's promising Odus and Amira their freedom and what happened the night Eli tried to turn them in.

"Well, that's mighty good of you, ma'am," said Wool. "Mighty good. And what about you, boy?" he asked Odus. "Where was you before you on the run?"

"Mississippi. Tobacco plantation. Then 'fore that me and Amira were in South Carolina. And before that we at home. In my village, with my mama, my father and my family. Three brothers and two sisters. Amira here's one of 'em. Then one day, we sleeping, and these men come into the village with guns, burn everything. They kill my father, sayin' he too old to be any good. But they take my mama, and the rest of us. Mama died on the boat, couldn't have been more than a day after they done put us on it. My littlest brother, Zeke, he sick the whole way, and one day they just throw him over. That leave just me, Amira, our other sister and two brothers. Soon as we land, they lock us in chains and put us on wagons. Amira and me, we together. The rest of my family, I don't know where they gone."

"How old was you?"

"I ain't sure. I guess me and Amira was three or four. We share our mama's belly, you see."

"And how old is you now?"

"Don't know. Probably 'bout the same as Miss Sammy."

He looked at Samantha and saw she was crying. Her tears came as if they had a mind of their own, bursting out of her eyes and soaking her cheeks.

Odus put his hand on her shoulder. "It's alright, Miss Sammy," he said. "It ain't your fault."

But Samantha couldn't speak. All she could do was put her face into her hands and let her tears for Odus come.

151

Samantha awoke to the sound of the barn door creaking. She opened her eyes and saw a red and purple sky. She didn't know if the sun was setting or rising.

"Time for y'all to get ready," said Jem. "Moses'll be here any minute to take you on."

They all stood up. Jem pulled a penknife from his pocket. "Fore you go, what's your full name, ma'am?"

Samantha didn't think to hesitate. "Samantha Weston."

Jem opened the hatch door to the barn's concealed entrance and knelt down. Samantha looked over his shoulder as he carved SW, 3/24/61 - M. It was just one of a long line of initials and dates, the first one going back as early as 1841.

"What is this 'M' for?" she asked.

"For Moses. She like to keep track of how many come through, how many make it on and who it was that helped them."

"I don't understand."

"We all do this, all of us conductors, I mean. We log who's been here and when. It's the only record we keep." He turned to Odus. "What's your name, boy?"

"Exodus," he replied.

"Exodus, what?"

"Just Exodus, sah."

"What was the name of your last owner?"

"Smith, sah, but he ain't my owner no more. Next it was supposed to be Samantha's daddy, but I guess I never got to be his slave."

"Well then," said Jem, smiling, "that makes you a free man. Sounds to me like your name has to be Freeman."

Odus smiled. "Yes, sah," he said, as Jem carved EF into the beam.

Samantha leaned into Odus. "I didn't realise your name was Exodus."

"Exodus Freeman now, Miss Sammy."

Samantha smiled, feeling the heat from his arm. "Exodus Freeman. What a beautiful name."

Chapter 21

On the night everything changed, Annie's day had started like any other Saturday. She'd slept late, gone to the mall with Jenna, and came home wondering where to hide the credit card receipt for items she did not need, but most certainly did want, especially the red leather belt that matched the cowboy boots her father had given her for her 16th birthday.

Not long after she got back from the mall, she and her mother had a fight because Annie wanted to turn her bedroom ceiling into a starry night sky. Her mother vetoed the idea before Annie could barely state her case. She nearly argued that her mother should let her simply because it wasn't Jenna or Marcy's idea – it was Annie's. "I thought you wanted me to start thinking for myself, to stop doing the things they told me to do. I'm trying to do that and you won't let me." But she didn't because that would have only sparked a different argument.

If they hadn't fought over that, they would have fought over something else: Annie's recklessness with the credit card, Annie's attitude, Annie's complete indifference to the education at her disposal. There was always something her mother found to criticize, and therefore always something for Annie to hate her mother for.

The truth was her mother was angry all the time. Even when Annie had done nothing, her mother seemed angry – angry that Annie no longer listened to her advice, that she preferred the company of her friends, that it was raining on a day she wanted sun or that there were other cars sharing the road. It was the kind of anger that had no rhyme or reason and no identifiable source.

Annie's only consolation was that it wasn't all directed at her. Annie's mother was angry with her father as well – for working too much, for ignoring her needs, and for the amount of time he spent with a state policeman named Robert Sanchez.

Her father met Sanchez in the army. They were stationed at the same army

153

base in Arizona. Sanchez was there the night Annie's parents met at a bar in Tempe where her mother was working to pay her way through college. After her parents got married and moved from base-to-base, it felt like wherever they were, Sanchez managed to follow.

It was Sanchez's idea that Annie and her family move to Virginia. He had been discharged from the army a year earlier and retrained with the state police. Annie's family relocated for what her father promised would be the last time. He set up a security firm that catered to the number of technology companies sprouting up all over the Beltway and, for the first time in his life, leaned heavily on Sanchez for advice. Her mother was drafted in to look after accounts and manage the office, even though she hated math and organizing other people.

For as long as Annie could remember, no matter where they lived, Sanchez was there. He would turn up at their house at least once a week and help himself to her father's enchiladas and the beer in the fridge. Annie never liked it when he was around. He insisted she sit on his lap and she hated how her clothes always smelled of cigarette smoke afterwards.

It also annoyed Annie that he always acted like their home was his. He had habits that she loathed. No matter what time of year – winter or summer – he'd come in and crack open the window, letting out either heat or air conditioning. She asked her father once why he did it and her father didn't know. "He's full of weird routines like that," he said. "I just don't ask."

Her mother had always despised Sanchez, but this hatred intensified now they'd all settled in the same place with no prospect of moving on. She said more than once, "If a creep like Sanchez is a cop, then no one is safe."

Even her father didn't seem to have much time for him. "You have to understand," he'd say, "we're army brothers. They're your friends for life."

A few months before the night everything changed, Annie's father poked fun at his upcoming midlife crisis and playfully warned that he was trying hard to find alternatives to the clichéd purchase of a red sports car.

He did find alternatives. He came home with hiking and camping equipment and seemed surprised when Annie and her mother refused to use them.

"We live within driving distance of the best hiking and camping in the state. Look," he said, pointing out the window. "The Blue Ridge Mountains are right on our doorstep and we've not hiked them once."

"I prefer plumbing and electricity, thank you very much," said her mother.

Annie wanted to go. She loved the idea of being outdoors with her father, just the two of them. But she couldn't afford to spend a weekend away from Jenna and Marcy. Any time spent away would give Jenna and Marcy chance to dissect her faults and make assumptions about her thoughts and actions. Absences would be marked and give others the opportunity to replace her. She'd seen it happen to other girls.

It was futile trying to explain this to her father. He wouldn't understand.

So he went by himself, sometimes hiking for the day, sometimes staying all weekend. He bought a high-end digital camera and started combining hiking with photography. On Sunday nights he would come down from the mountain and disappear into the computer room with the memory card and print his photos.

Rob Sanchez started to join him. Her father would joke that, for an ex-army policeman, Sanchez was a slow hiking companion, preferring to look into crevices and down ravines instead of enjoying the beauty of the landscape and sky. One night he came home and said he and Sanchez had found a set of caves. Her father joked that if you wanted to hide a dead body then that was the place to do it.

On the night everything changed, Annie and Jenna were eating enchiladas and watching a re-run of *Gossip Girl* before going to a party hosted by Jenna's latest crush. Annie's mother was at Jenna's house, no doubt drinking wine and complaining to Jenna's mother about Annie's father. Annie heard her father's truck pull into the driveway and awaited his tales of views captured and sights seen.

He appeared in the doorway, as white as a cloud. Annie noticed his ripped cargo pants and the bloody scratches on his shins.

"Jenna, you need to go home."

"Why?" said Annie. "We're just about to go out."

"I'm sorry, Jenna. You've done nothing wrong. I just need to talk to my daughter in private. She'll meet you at your house when we're finished."

Jenna gave Annie a look that said, "I don't know what you've done, but it looks like you're in big trouble for something." Annie saw Jenna to the door, then found her father in his office, turning on the computer. She crossed her arms, bracing to find out what crime she'd unknowingly committed.

Instead he said: "I just witnessed a murder."

He'd been coming down the mountain. Having misjudged the timing of sundown and forgetting to pack extra batteries for his flashlight, he felt his way to the bottom in the dark. He realized he'd gone too far west and had overshot his truck by at least half a mile, so doubled back. But he got that wrong, too, and had a few moments of panic. Then he heard voices. He walked towards them, hoping that whoever it was would give directions to the parking lot. As he got closer, he recognized the caves he and Sanchez had found the previous week. In front of one was a four-wheeler with a trailer, its light shining on a man and a woman. He was about to shout out to them when he saw the man raise a gun. The woman began crying, saying words in Spanish that her father couldn't understand. A shot was fired, the woman swayed, but did not fall. Her father reached for his camera and started taking a rapid succession of photos, too shaken to take his time and too frightened to do anything but hit the shutter over and over and over. The man fired the gun again and the woman finally fell to the ground.

Then Annie's father ran, not thinking to gather his camping pack and hiking equipment. He just held his camera and ran as fast as he could, tripping over stumps and plowing through brambles. Once he reached his truck, he dropped the keys twice. On the frantic ride home, he ran three red lights.

Annie watched her father extract the memory card from the camera and insert it into the computer's USB drive. The photos began to appear, first her father's usual snapshots of birds and raccoons, close-ups on wild rhododendrons, and rivers reflecting the sky above. Then came another set, showing dark, shadowy photographs of a poorly lit figure.

"I don't have time to go through these," he said, rifling through his desk drawer, "so I need you to do something for me." He handed her three memory sticks.

"Copy all the photos onto each of these. Put two in your pocket. Hide the other one, in one of the plants by the pool or something. Somewhere they won't find it, but that will be easy for me to get. Then I need you to erase them off my camera card and my hard-drive. Can you do that?"

"Dad, I don't understand. Why am I doing this?"

"Because," her father said, his eyes squinting at the computer screen, "of that."

He pointed to one of the dark photos and his finger landed on the round patch on the figure's arm. Annie watched as her father zoomed in.

The letters that appeared were fuzzy, but unmistakable: *Robert Sanchez, Virginia State Police.*

"Where's your mother?"

"At Jenna's."

"Once you're done copying the photos I want you to go there too. Tell your mother that I need you two to stay there until I get back. And please, please don't tell her anything yet."

"Dad, you're scaring me."

"I'm sorry, sweetheart. I'm sure it's all a big mistake. I need to go to the police station. And then I have to talk to Rob."

She followed him to the front door, then watched his truck pull away, all the while trying to ignore the feeling that, somehow, their life would never be the same again.

"What do you mean we can't be in the house?" said her mother.

"Just until he gets back," said Annie.

"Where did he go?"

"I'm not really sure."

"It's not a problem," said Jenna's mother. "If he's not back by 11, why don't you two stay here?"

Annie slept on the floor in Jenna's room, ignoring Jenna sulking that their plans for the evening had been thwarted. It was two in the morning when Annie heard a car outside. She got up and peered out the window expecting to see her father's truck. Instead, it was a state police car. Annie held onto the windowsill for support as she watched a lone police officer enter her house, smoking a cigarette and carrying a small duffle bag. He emerged five minutes later with nothing. As soon as his car was out of sight, she ran to the guest room and shook her mother awake.

"Mom, something's wrong."

She pulled her groggy mother down the stairs and out of the Jennna's house just as her father's truck pulled in the driveway.

"What are you two doing?" he said, jumping out of the cab.

"Where the hell have you been?" her mother yelled.

"Dad, a policeman was just here. He went into the house."

"Did you see his face?"

"No, it was too dark. But Dad, I'm pretty sure it was him."

"Did he come out with anything?"

"No, I don't think so. I did everything you said."

"What are you talking about?" her mother said.

"I knew something wasn't right," said her father. "They kept me there too long."

"Who did?"

"The police." He approached the house. "I want you two to wait in my truck."

"What are you going to do?" said Annie.

"I'm going to see what that bastard's done to our house."

Annie pulled her mother into the truck. They watched her father enter the house and disappear into its darkness.

"What the hell is going on?" her mother said.

"I don't know."

"If he's not back in ten minutes I'm going in. I'll be useless tomorrow if I don't get at least six hours sleep."

"Mom, I don't think..." Annie started, but did not finish. Her father had thrown open the door and run out carrying his old brown suitcase. He was barely clear when the house behind him erupted into flames and he was thrust to the ground. Annie and her mother screamed. He scrambled to his feet, threw the suitcase in the truck and screeched out of their driveway.

"Oh my God! Oh my God!" her mother screeched. "Our house! What just happened to our house?"

"Dad?" said Annie, trying not to cry.

Her father concentrated on the road as he sped out of their neighborhood and raced down the highway towards the Blue Ridge Mountains.

Her mother grew hysterical. "You tell me what's going on right now or so help me I will divorce you as sure as the sun rises."

"I knew I couldn't trust them," he finally said.

"Where are we going?" Annie asked.

Her father didn't answer. He just kept his eyes on the road.

Half an hour later he pulled into the parking lot at the base of the mountain. A single street lamp burned above a pay phone. Her father jumped out of the truck. Annie watched him pull a piece of paper out of his front pocket and copy something off the pay phone.

"Here," he said, handing it to Annie through the window.

"What the hell is that?" said her mother.

"This is the safest way to reach me. I can't promise I'll always answer it, but it's the only thing I can think of right now."

"What do you mean, reach you? Where are you going?"

He motioned to the mountains.

"All my camping stuff is still up there. I'm going to lay low for a while until I can figure out what the hell is going on. Then I'm going to nail this son of a bitch and everyone in the police force who's helping him."

"And what about us?" her mother screamed. "Our house just exploded right in front of us. Where the hell do you expect us to go?"

"I need you to drive," he said. "Drive until you run out of gas, then abandon the truck. Travel by bus, train, whatever, but stay low and keep your heads down. I'll let you know when it's safe to come back."

"To come back? I'm not going anywhere. This is our home. This is our life and I'll be damned if..."

"Don't you get it? Sanchez killed someone tonight. He knows I have photographic evidence. That's why he just tried to kill us. It's not safe for any of us to be anywhere near here."

"But..." her mother started.

"He'll figure out soon enough that none of us were in the house when it caught fire and then he'll come after us. Now, I need you to do as I say and get the hell out of here. There's over $10,000 in the brown suitcase. That should last a while if you're careful. Sweetheart, do you have the memory stick?"

Annie reached into her pocket and handed it to him. "The second one is where you told me to put it. What do I do with the third one?"

"Keep it. Just in case."

"In case of what?"

He looked at Annie and her mother. His voice cracked as he spoke. "Take good care of each other. I love you both. And I'm so, so sorry."

He disappeared into the woods.

That was the last time Annie saw him. Until today.

Annie hugged him tight. He felt thin and weary, and looked ten years older than when she'd last seen him. But he was still unmistakably her father.

"I don't understand," she said. "What are you doing here? How did you get here?"

He held her arms tight. Too tight. "I'm here because I had no choice. How could you run off like that? Your mother and I were worried sick."

Annie looked at her mother. She did not meet Annie's eyes. "I didn't run off. And I left a note."

Her father held the piece of paper in his hand and read from it. "'Be back tonight. Promise.' What kind of an explanation is that?"

"Look, I had something I had to do. And I am back."

159

Her father threw his hands into the air. "Your mother thought he'd got you. That's why she called me. She took a big risk tracking me down, and I've taken a huge risk coming here."

Annie crossed her arms. "Well, he didn't get me. I left a note. What else do you want from me?"

"You should know better. Now where were you?"

"None of your business."

"It is my business! You know Sanchez's network is all over the country. I need to know where you were so I can have some kind of idea if he knows we're here."

Annie felt her neck muscles clenching around her throat. "He might."

Her father pursed his lips. "Tell me."

Annie looked at her mother for help. She provided none.

"I went to Virginia."

For the first time in her life, she thought her father might hit her.

"Why the hell would you do that?"

"I'm trying to find out more about a girl who wrote a letter in 1861 and never sent it."

"What?" said her father.

"I found it in the basement. The bottom two steps of the basement stairs are actually an entrance to a small room. The letter was in there."

"What?" said her mother, sitting forward.

"Not now," said her father. "You expect me to believe that any of this justifies what you've done?"

"Go downstairs and have a look for yourself."

"That is not the point! Going anywhere for any reason, not least of all Virginia, was incredibly irresponsible of you."

She knew he was right, but the rage directed at her felt wrong. No one ever asked her to be responsible, yet she'd been nothing but over the past year. She had moved when she was told, never mind all she'd done without being told. She kept herself and her mother hidden, and alive – all while torturing the man who'd ruined their lives. She did it because she knew if he was edgy, he'd be more likely to slip up. No one thanked her for any of this.

"You want to talk about responsibility, Dad? Who do you think has been taking care of Mom all this time?"

Her father waved the idea away. "Your mother doesn't need taking care of."

"Look at her, Dad! She never gets off that couch! I'm the one who packs up every time we have to move. I'm the one who makes sure we get to wherever we end up and unpacks when we get there. I clean the house. I don't go to school because someone has to stay here and keep an eye on her."

"It's true," her mother whispered.

Her father collapsed into the chair behind him. "Look, it won't be like this forever. We're almost there." He pulled a large manila folder out from behind the couch. "Here are all of my photos. See for yourself. I've almost got enough."

"I don't understand."

"I found a clean contact at the FBI. I was about to send him everything I've got when your mother phoned me in complete hysterics."

"So now this is my fault?"

"No, it's not your fault, honey." Her father sighed. "I promise, this will soon be over."

Annie had lost count of how many times this promise had been made. "I don't believe you," she said.

"Well, that's your problem."

"You don't know anything…" she started. Then she stopped. No one but she and Sanchez knew about the emails. It was best to keep it that way. But her parents needed to know about the state trooper in Virginia. They needed to know he'd taken her learner's permit, and that it was only a matter of time before Sanchez knew they were hiding in Battenkill. It wouldn't take long. They needed to leave here, now.

Samantha's words appeared in her head. *I have changed, Father. I am certain you would not like what you would see if you were here. I have had my eyes opened to the real workings of the world, in all its cruelty and wonder.*

No, Annie decided. *I'm not leaving Battenkill.*

She turned towards the door. Her father stood.

"Where are you going?"

"I need to clear my head."

He grabbed her arm. "You know you can't leave."

"Let me go."

"It's not safe for you here anymore. We're leaving tomorrow."

"I actually like it here. I didn't think I'd like anywhere that wasn't Virginia, but here is different. I've met someone and I'm not leaving him. I'm staying."

"Dammit, it's not up to you."

Annie kicked him square in the shin with the steel toe of her cowboy boots. He doubled over in pain. Before he had time to recover, Annie bolted out the door and ran as fast as she could down the dark road.

All the windows at the Store at Five Corners were dark except for Theo's bedroom on the top floor. Annie rang the doorbell and tried to calm her breathing.

Theo answered the door. His plaid shirt was untucked and his feet were bare. A relaxed sleepiness had settled on his face. He seemed surprised to see her. She was surprised to be there.

"Is your father here?" she asked.

"No."

"Your brothers?"

"No."

"Good." She stepped across the threshold and closed the door. Then she kissed Theo with a passion and urgency that made her forget everything she should or shouldn't do.

Chapter 22

Samantha could not feel her toes. Her arm had fallen asleep an hour ago. The muscles on the right side of her neck were pulled so taut she feared they might snap. For three hours she and Amira lay crammed into a small compartment embedded in the undercarriage of a delivery wagon. Odus and Wool were in a similar compartment in the wagon behind. It was impossible to move, and Samantha could do nothing but ignore the itch on her foot, the aches in her sides, and the sweat as it trespassed down her face and soaked her undergarments. Her throat was so dry she couldn't clear it, not that she would have anyway: Moses had impressed upon them the absolute need for silence.

"I been caught enough times I could tell you tales that would make your skin crawl," she'd said. "You think they bad to slaves on the plantation? That ain't nothin' compared to what they do to you if they catch you."

How many hours had they been traveling? Without a view to the sun and its movements, Samantha couldn't be sure of the time of day or the distance they'd covered. All she could hear were the creaking wheels of the wagon and Moses singing. "I sing when we okay. If I stop, we ain't."

They'd left Jem's cabin that morning in a whirl of confusion. When Moses had opened the compartment and instructed them to get inside, Samantha waited for Jem to help her into the wagon seat.

"Sorry, Miss Weston," he said, "but I'm afraid you're going to have to ride in the compartment with Amira."

"I don't understand?"

"I heard of you before I got here," said Moses. "You as wanted as Odus and Amira."

"Why?" she said, even though she knew the answer.

"Depends on who's talking. Some say you wanted for running with two fugitives. Another say you kidnapped. Someone else said you wanted for murder. Now, I don't need to know which one it is, but I do need you to ride hidden."

Moses told them they would be convoying for at least ten days, maybe more. She wanted to reach a station just over the border from Massachusetts. "If we lucky," she'd said. There she would leave them to continue their journey with another conductor.

On their first day of travel, they stopped once for food, water and a chance to release tired muscles. All except for Amira stood and stretched; Amira sat against the trunk of a large oak tree. Samantha heard her take a sharp, quick breath. She knelt down.

"What is it?" Samantha whispered.

"It nothing, Miss Sammy..." she said. No sooner had she spoken when her face winced in pain.

Samantha called Moses over.

"There's a blanket under my seat," said Moses. "I need you to get it for me."

As Samantha got the blanket, she saw Odus and Wool standing by their wagon. Odus' eyes caught hers, and she blushed before looking away.

"Boys?" said Moses. "I need you to put your backs to us for a while. Here, girl," she said, easing the blanket under Amira. "I jus' need you to relax so I's can have a quick look at you."

Moses put her hands under Amira's skirt, and Samantha looked away.

"No point hiding from it," said Moses. "This here girl's having a baby soon, and you're probably gon' be there to help deliver it."

Samantha shot around. "She's having the baby now?"

Moses put her hands on Amira's rounded stomach. "No, not yet. They done now, ain't they?" she asked. The girl nodded. "That was' jus' her body practicing for the real thing. But it's a sign that this baby be thinkin' about coming out. So we gots to keep moving."

Samantha closed her eyes. She found it made her feel less sick. Everything in her body hurt – her legs from being bent, her neck from being stretched, her arm from bearing the weight of her body as it endured every jolt and divot in the road. It was their second day of traveling. Moses said they'd lost time yesterday, so they would need to move faster. She wanted to reach Pennsylvania by nightfall. To Samantha, in private, she'd whispered, "We gots to get Amira as far north as we can 'fore that baby comes."

The days wore on. The further north they went, the colder it got. They'd spent nights huddled around a weak fire and nothing Samantha did relieved the chill from her bones. In the compartment, she was grateful for the warmth of Amira's back pressed into her stomach, but the rest of her body felt as if she were in ice-cold water. She thought of Mont Verity, where – even in the dead of winter – she had never been cold. Well-tended fireplaces ensured her comfort in every part of the house.

It was the tenth day of their journey and Samantha could not stop the tears from streaming down her face. Since her arms were pinned, she was unable to wipe them away. Instead they clung to her skin, drawing in the cool air even more.

Through the cracks in the compartment she could see the sky getting darker. She could smell dampness and mud: *a river,* she thought. The ground became uneven, throwing Samantha and Amira about the compartment, despite the limited space.

"Miss Sammy," whispered Amira, "I don't think I can do this no more."

"Hang on, Amira," said Samantha. "We must be stopping soon."

After a series of jolts, the horses stopped. Samantha heard water lapping against a low bank.

Samantha heard voices, and a rustling in Odus and Wool's wagon.

"This here is the Hudson," she heard Moses say. "It's about a fifty miles to Troy. On foot you can expect it take you about two days. Take this."

"Oh, Miss Moses, ma'am, I can't take no more from you. You done so much already." It was Wool.

"Please. Take it. And good luck finding your family."

"Thank you, ma'am. And God bless you."

She heard footsteps on a gravel road as Moses' weight bore down on the wagon's seat. The horses started again.

"We makin' good time," said Moses. "We might make it by tomorrow night if we don't come across no trouble."

Samantha heard the words, but couldn't take them in.

She was asleep by the time they stopped for the night. Moses and Odus helped Amira and Samantha out of the compartment. Odus held Samantha's hands as he lifted her to the ground and Samantha did not want him to let go. Then she noticed their surroundings and her mouth fell open.

A large fire burned in the middle of a small clearing in the woods. Several people sat around it – some sitting, some singing, some dancing, some playing flutes and drums. They wore a mixture of cotton and hide. The smell of meat filled the air and, as they got closer to the fire, Samantha could see a wild boar carcass roasting over embers. Some of the woman sat with babies, their breasts exposed to the night air as the babies suckled. The men's heads were devoid of hair, except for a small square centered on the back of their skulls.

"Indians," Samantha said. *Savages,* she heard her mother say.

"The Negro's best friend," said Moses.

Moses made her way towards the fire, where she was fervently greeted by a man who wore a tall headdress made of feathers. Moses pointed towards Samantha, Odus and Amira, talking in a language Samantha could not understand. A woman with gray braided hair and a face lined with kindness approached them.

"You," she said to Amira, putting a gentle hand on Amira's belly. "We can take care of you over here."

Samantha could not hide her surprise at how well the woman spoke English. She watched as the woman led Amira into a house that was three times longer than it was wide. Sheets of thin wood covered the arched frame. Moses approached with two plates of stew.

"Here," she said. "Take this into that longhouse over there and eat. Then I want you to get some sleep. We gots another long day tomorrow."

Odus and Samantha did as they were told. The longhouse they entered had a fire burning in its center, surrounded by log stumps for sitting. Four beds made of canvas and hay lined the perimeter, each covered with thick bear hide. Odus and Amira ate their stew in silence.

"I'll take them plates back, Miss Sammy," said Odus when they'd finished. Samantha knew he was leaving so she could get undressed for bed, but she did not want him to go. She readied herself for sleep, washing her face and hands in the wooden basin to the side, and crawled under the bear hide. She hoped to still be awake by the time Odus returned. It was the first time she'd been alone with him since they left Virginia. Not that she knew what she'd say or do. All she knew was that a space felt differently when he was in it, and when he was gone, it felt like nothing could ever feel right again.

Samantha woke to a woman bringing in wood for the fire. Sun streamed in through the longhouse door. Smells of roasting meat and grass drifted in with sounds of morning laughter. Two of the three beds in the room had been slept in, but were now empty. If Odus had been here, she'd missed him.

The woman pointed out the door and handed Samantha a breechcloth made of deerskin, like the other women in the tribe wore. "You, go to river. Bathe. Then come back for food." The woman picked up Samantha's riding dress. Its whiteness was now replaced by brown dirt and gray clay. "I will wash this."

Samantha waited for the woman to leave before crawling out from under the hide and putting on the breechcloth. Once out of the longhouse, she took in the sight around her.

It was a beautiful, warm day. The river below sparkled in the sunshine, cutting a curved line through a small mountain range that was reflected in the river's wide expanse. Behind her, women and men went quietly about their business. The younger women suckled babies and toddlers; the older ones cooked, swept out the longhouses and gathered wood. There were few men on the site; Samantha could only guess they'd already ventured out on a morning hunt.

She walked along the river's edge looking for a secluded place in which to bathe. She did not have to go far – the woods and the river held each other close, creating several sheltered coves. She slithered down the bank and let the wet silt ooze in between her toes. Ahead she saw a patch of flat bank and decided she would undress there.

Moses appeared at the top of the bank, wearing a breechcloth like the one Samantha had been given. Her hair, which had been hidden under a hat since the day they met, was still wet, although already starting to curl. In the tunic, her womanly shape was unmistakable.

How does a woman like Moses end up helping escaped slaves? Samantha thought. *Had she been a slave once herself? How many slaves has she helped?* Samantha's head flooded with questions she feared she'd never have the chance to ask.

"Go on in, girl," said Moses. "The water is mighty fine this morning."

Samantha made her way towards the flattened part of the lower bank. Once there, she sat on a low rock and began to pull her arms out of the breechcloth's sleeves. Then, out of the corner of her eye, she saw a head bobbing in the river about 50 feet away. It was Odus, swimming toward the bank farther along the river. He had not seen Samantha, but she felt the blood rushing faster through her veins.

She watched as he swam towards the shore. He reached the shallow part of the river and stood up. Samantha gasped and covered her mouth.

She'd never seen a man naked before and knew she should turn away or shield her eyes, but she couldn't. Instead she watched as he waded to the bank, his long, sinewy limbs glistening in the sun. He stepped out at the bank and brushed himself dry before pulling trousers over his damp skin. He climbed up the steep bank and walked towards the camp.

He's coming this way. He's bound to see me now. She put her arms back in the sleeves and hid under the bank's ledge. After a few minutes, she emerged, sure he would be gone.

"Good morning, Miss Sammy." Samantha jumped. Odus stood above her on the bank.

"Oh! Hello! I didn't know you were here. I was just about to have a wash. Have you had a wash?" The words came out frantically, nervously, and Samantha found she had no control over her body's movements. Her hands went from her hips to crossed in front of her, her weight shifting like a pendulum. She dared not look at his face.

Odus grinned. "Yes, Miss Sammy. I've had a wash." He walked away. *He knows I saw him,* she thought. *Oh, God – what must he think of me?*

She waited until he was out of sight before pulling off the breechcloth and jumping into the cold water, wishing the river could wash away the flittering sensation that came every time Odus was near.

After a breakfast of cornbread, rabbit stew and dried fruit, Samantha, Moses, Odus and Amira gathered by the wagons. Samantha wore her riding dress, freshly washed and dried over the fire. Two of the younger men loaded parcels of food and extra canvas. Samantha watched the kindly woman from the previous evening give Amira a parcel wrapped in a muslin cloth. "If you feel baby coming in wagon, eat this. Baby will stop coming, but only for little while."

"Thank you, ma'am," said Amira.

"We hoping to make Battenkill by nightfall," Samantha heard Moses say to the head of the tribe. "Then I coming back down to make another run. I see you then. Thank you for all you do."

The chief smiled and bowed. Odus helped Amira into the compartment. Amira struggled to curl tight so Samantha could fit in the compartment.

Moses made her way towards the wagon. Samantha approached her and spoke in a low voice. "Amira isn't going to last much longer."

"I know. I jus' need us to get to Five Corners. She be able to stay there long enough to have the baby."

Samantha felt her toes curl inside her boots. "I think she should have her own compartment until we get there. She'll be more comfortable that way."

Moses looked at Samantha with wide, surprised eyes. "What you sayin', Miss Sammy?"

"I think I should travel in the other compartment. It will give Amira more space."

Moses looked over at Odus with a glint in her eye. "You know that means sharing with Odus, don't you, Miss Sammy?"

Samantha's stomach was on fire. "Yes, I do. But it will only be for one day. And if it means Amira is more comfortable then I'm willing to make that sacrifice." She quickly turned to the second wagon, deliberately avoiding Moses' knowing smile.

Odus couldn't believe what was happening. Samantha had explained it so quickly. Something about Amira and her size and how it made perfect sense that she ride with him for the rest of the journey. Before he could even respond and offer to ride with Amira himself, Samantha had crawled into the compartment and pressed herself against the back to make room for him.

Odus knew a great many things, one of the most important being that a black man was never to look at a white woman, let alone share a hidden compartment with one. Surely there had been some mistake?

"Well, come on, boy, we don't got all day." Moses' voice bounced across the river and back. Odus shrugged, mainly to himself, and nervously got in.

When Samantha had shared with Amira, her only possible arrangement was to be sandwiched against the girl's body in the compartment; there was simply no room for it to be any other way. Odus, however, managed to press himself against the other side of the compartment so tightly that Samantha could hardly feel him at all. Even as Moses started the horses and the wagon began its now-familiar rocking and rolling, he stayed as far away from her as he could get, given their circumstances.

He doesn't want to touch me, she thought. *Is that because he knows he's not meant to, or because he doesn't want to?*

Fine, she resolved. *I suppose that tells me all I need to know.*

She fell asleep. When she woke up, something was different. Something felt wrong.

Then she realized: Moses had stopped singing.

"Whoa," she said, and the wagons were brought to an abrupt stop. The sound of horse's hooves approached.

"Mornin', ma'am. Where do you think you're going?"

"Vermont, sah. Gots me a delivery I's making to the Negro settlement up there."

Samantha heard footsteps walk the perimeter of the wagon.

"I need you to unload it all," he said.

We're dead, Samantha thought.

"Sah?" said Moses.

"You heard me."

The wagon shifted as Moses got down. Samantha heard her pull the canvas back.

She couldn't be sure how long it took for Moses to unload the two wagons. She did know she did it by herself; the white man, whoever he was, didn't help. For what felt like hours the wagon's suspension creaked with relief as the contents were emptied onto the ground.

"What's this here?" the man said.

"Case of whisky, sah," said Moses.

"Open it."

Moses did as she was told.

"Well, I can't let you move on with this,' said the man. 'A bunch of Negroes drunk on whisky just sounds like a recipe for trouble, if you ask me.'

"Yes, sah."

"What else you got in here?"

"Dried beef, corn meal…"

"Give it to me."

Moses again did what she was told.

"I suppose that'll do. You can load it back in now."

Samantha heard the man get back on his horse, the whisky bottles clattering in his side packs as he galloped away.

"He gone now," said Moses, as she lugged the first crate back onto the wagon. "He gone."

Samantha let out the breath she'd been holding while the man had searched the wagon. Only then did she notice that Odus had been holding her the whole time. As she exhaled he eased the grip his arm had around her torso. Before he could remove it, Samantha grabbed his hand, pulled it in, and did not let it go.

When the wagon finally came to a stop, Samantha was asleep, her hand still holding tight to Odus. The latch to the compartment opened and Samantha was surprised to see not Moses, but a white man with weathered skin and green eyes.

"Give me your hand," he said, his voice soft and reassuring. Samantha did as she was told and was pulled into the cool, night air. She looked up at the stars, then at the mountainous horizon that curved and rolled just like the Blue Ridge Mountains in Virginia. As Odus crawled out, she turned and saw a two-story building, standing on its own in the corner of a four-way crossroads. The painted sign read *Store at Five Corners*.

"Well, now," he said, "not often we see a white woman in here."

"This one's special," said Moses, as he helped her down from the wagon.

The man put his arm around Moses' shoulder like she was an old friend. "Nice to have you safely back in these parts."

Moses laughed. "Theodore Mason. It's mighty good to see you."

What Moses, Theodore Mason, Samantha, Odus and Amira did not see was the man who had pulled the wagon over earlier that day, watching them from the woods on the opposite side of the crossroads. A simple man, cruel, and always out for a quick buck. He had heard about a reward for finding a particular white woman with two slaves, and even though he saw nothing to suggest that the round black woman whose goods he'd stolen had anything to do with it, he was willing to put in the time to make sure.

Sipping at the whisky he'd claimed hours earlier, he saw two black women being taken into the store. The white woman and the black man were put back into the compartment that he had completely failed to notice earlier.

A figure emerged from the building, someone who had not been there when the wagons arrived. A pastor. Or at least, someone dressed as one. The man in the woods watched as the pastor climbed into the wagon's seat and took the reins. When the wagon was out of sight, the man mounted his own horse and rode fast in the opposite direction.

Chapter 23

Annie sat in the darkened kitchen of the Store at Five Corners, her hands cupped around a mug of steaming hot chocolate. It was her second, and every sip was a palliative comfort. An empty plate graced the table, holding the remnants of a grilled cheese sandwich. Theo poured hot chicken noodle soup into a large bowl and set it on the table. Annie took a mouthful and, even though it burned her throat, it tasted too good to wait.

"How much more do you want to know?" she asked.

"Everything," he said. "I want to know everything."

Annie blew on the soup, inhaled, then picked up where she'd left off.

We did what Dad said that night and drove for eight hours, until the truck ran out of gas. By then it was morning and we were about an hour outside of Charleston, South Carolina. We left the truck in a parking lot near the beach. Before we left I took off the license plates and threw them into the trash. We caught a bus into downtown and found a small bed and breakfast where the lady let us pay cash.

We stayed in Charleston for three days. We didn't have any clothes – no pajamas, no tooth brushes, nothing. On the second day I finally went out to get things we needed, like shampoo and underwear. There was a Wal-Mart a few blocks away, but I only got as far as the front door. A camera scanned faces at the entrance, and I was too scared to risk being caught. Instead, I found a Goodwill and bought us some clothes and sweats to sleep in. I tried to find things we wouldn't have worn in Virginia so we'd be harder to recognize.

That's when I cut my hair. It used to be down to my waist. I got up at six every morning to straighten it. Every four weeks I had it highlighted blonde. It felt like straw. But it was what all the other girls did and, I'm a little ashamed to say, that really mattered.

In Charleston, Mom wouldn't even go downstairs for breakfast. She just stayed in bed, watching the television and eating M&Ms. I guess she was just too numb from the shock. Or at least, that's the excuse I've come up with. I don't know how else to explain why she's completely shut down.

There's so much about her I don't understand. It used to be that she'd get angry with me for just about anything. Now she'll barely talk to me. She told me a few weeks ago that she doesn't even want to go home to Virginia, but wouldn't tell me why. I feel like I don't know her at all.

Anyway, after a few days in Charleston I spent a whole day trying to get in touch with Dad. I just wanted to make sure he was okay and let him know we were, too. When he finally answered that payphone and I told him where we were, he started screaming that we needed to get farther away, that Sanchez had an APB on us. I told him we'd leave first thing in the morning.

"No," he said. "Now."

So I got Mom dressed and dragged her downstairs. The landlady stood in the doorway. "You're not leaving now, are you?" she said.

I can still see her standing there, offering to let us stay for dinner. I knew she was trying to get us to stay. I told her we had a bus to catch. She asked where we were going and I made up something about cousins in Florida.

I pulled Mom out the door and around the corner. We stayed there for a few minutes. Sure enough, a Virginia State Police car pulled up in front of the bed and breakfast. I saw him get out of the car, smoking a cigarette like he always did. He'd just missed us.

That was the first time I stole a car. It was pretty easy. I hid Mom in an alley behind McDonald's while I went into the ladies room. A woman was washing her hands and her purse was on the edge of the sink. When she wasn't looking I knocked it over and everything came out. I said I was really sorry and helped her put things back in. She didn't notice that I'd taken her keys.

The car had a full tank of gas, and it got us as far as Alabama. We stopped in Huntsville and found a little motel that had a row of efficiency apartments in the back.

It was summer by then and we completely melted in there without air conditioning. It didn't have a kitchen or a microwave, so we only ate cereal bars and apples. That was when I realized I had to keep a tight grip on the money and I decided not to spend more than $1.50 a day on food. Then I noticed how much weight I was losing, and it became all I thought about. Every waking moment was centered around when I would let myself eat, and how much it would cost us when it did. It was almost like I had something to prove. I suppose I've proven it now.

I talked to Dad only once while we were in Huntsville. He was still living on the mountain, but coming down at night and trying to track

Sanchez. He was sure he'd slip up again and do something Dad could catch. He still had the photos from the night of the murder, but he didn't know who he could trust with them. So he wasn't just spying on Sanchez, but the whole police force. He took pictures of everything and everyone.

Every time we talked – about once every two weeks – he had a new number to call him on. I don't know if they were pay phones or cell phones – I didn't ask.

After two months in Huntsville, Sanchez found us. God, I still hate saying his name. We were asleep, not that I sleep well anymore. A flea could hiccup and it would wake me. I heard the police car pull up and went to the window. It was too dark to see what it said on the side of the car, but I just knew.

"Mom, we've got to go," I said, and pulled her up. We didn't even sleep in pajamas anymore – it was easier to sleep in our clothes. There were always things we left behind and had to replace later – toothbrushes, socks and magazines. But I always grabbed Dad's briefcase of money. We'd have been dead without that.

There was a forest behind the motel and we ran into that. He chased us for at least a mile, but we finally lost him.

After that we went all over the country using stolen cars. That's why I had the doorstop and hanger in my backpack. What else could I do? I had no way of buying a car and it wasn't safe taking the train or a plane. You know now that I don't have a license, but I was careful. I never gave anyone any reason to pull me over.

We lived in motels all through fall and into winter. We were staying in one in Troy when I saw the classified ad for the house we're in now. I called the realtor from a pay phone and she said its ownership was currently under some kind of probate, but that if we were happy without a lease then we could have it for practically nothing. I said yes, provided we could pay in cash. She said fine.

So that's how we ended up in Battenkill. Seeing that one classified ad changed everything for me. It brought me here, to Samantha Weston.

And to you.

Sanchez hasn't found us since Huntsville. I was starting to think he never would, and then you and I went to Virginia. That trooper knows my name, and he knows where I live. It's not safe for us here anymore.

But Dad's got an idea now of who was murdered that night and why. He thinks Sanchez is running some kind of prostitution and child trafficking ring. It starts in Arizona, where the State Police guard the border with Mexico. They take women and girls who have managed to *sneak in and sell them. If they try to talk or show any sign that they're trying to escape, they're killed. And because they've been taken before anyone has a record of them, it's easy to make them disappear. Those girls are being sold in every state.*

The one thing he hasn't been able to get proof of is Sanchez killing one of them again. How awful is that? He has to wait for some other innocent girl to be killed before we can have our lives back. There's a way in which I hope that doesn't happen. I don't think I could be happy getting my own life back knowing that someone had to die for it.

What makes us all sick is that he was someone we knew, someone we let into our lives even though there was something about him that made us all feel we couldn't trust him. Looking back, I think we were all on edge when he was around. My parents fought more. When I got older I just hid in my room whenever he came over. If I get to go back to my old life that is something I will take with me – life is too short to spend with people who don't bring out the best in you.

And anyway, I'm not sure I even want my old life back anymore.

Going back to my old life means leaving you.

She looked at Theo, whose face was covered in disbelief. Her soup had cooled, so she ate it, waiting for Theo to speak.

"You are so brave," he said finally. "I knew you had secrets, but I couldn't have imagined…I can't believe you've been through all that and are still sitting here."

Annie blushed. "I did what anyone else would have done."

"No, you did better. You've kept you and your mom going all this time. How can you not see how incredible that is? I can't think of a single girl at school who could have done what you've done. They would have crumbled a long time ago, but you…you're something else."

He stood up and paced the kitchen. "There has to be some way to end all this," he said, "without someone else getting hurt."

He knelt by Annie's chair. "I wish I could fix it. I wish I knew how to make it all go away." He took her hands. "There's so much I can't promise you, but I can at least promise you one thing."

"What's that?"

"For tonight, at least, you are safe."

Annie smiled. "I know."

Theo led Annie to his third-floor bedroom and lit a candle before pulling down his window shades. She watched him fold back his rumpled quilt

175

and stand over his bed, shifting his weight. The ease they felt in each other's company minutes before had been replaced by squirming and nerves.

Now what? Annie thought.

"Do you, um, want to borrow some PJs?" he asked.

"Yes, please."

He fumbled through his drawers and handed her a worn white T-shirt and a pair of plaid boxers. He stood on the other side of the room, unsure of where to look.

"Um, should I get changed in the bathroom?"

"Oh, no. You don't have to do that. I'll just step out for a minute." He backed towards the door and misjudged when to turn, banging the side of his face against the doorframe.

Annie stifled a giggle.

"Back in a minute," he said.

Annie undressed quickly, folding her jeans and scrunching up her shirt. She pushed them underneath the bed with her cowboy boots and Elijah Fabre's knife.

Annie was sitting up in his bed, Theo's quilt pulled over her legs, when he returned with two glasses of water.

"In case you get thirsty."

"Thanks."

Annie tried to focus on the greens and blues of the patchwork quilt while Theo pulled his shirt over his head and pushed his jeans to the floor. She couldn't help but steal a glimpse of the outline of his shoulders and the muscles in his back.

He swung his legs under the quilt and Annie pressed her knees together.

She had never been here before, with Theo or with anyone else.

Theo switched off the bedside lamp and pulled the covers over them. She felt his body heat through the bed sheets.

"So," he said slowly, "I guess we should go to sleep."

"I guess so."

Silence fell, marred only by the pounding of Annie's heart.

"Can I tell you something?" said Theo.

"Anything."

"I'm in this with you now. No matter what happens. Sanchez could come here tomorrow, and I'd still be in this."

Annie inched closer. "All this time I've been missing Virginia, missing home. Going back there today made me realize that I've changed.

I wore a mask every day when I was there. Now I'm without it, I don't think I want it back. I don't need it anymore."

She slid her hand over Theo's soft, bare skin.

"It's all because of you, Theo."

Theo put his hand to her face.

"I love you, Annie."

"I love you, too, Theo."

They began to kiss, and Annie knew what it must feel like to fly.

She woke up wrapped in Theo's arms, exactly where she'd fallen asleep hours earlier. Early morning sunlight shone determinedly around the edges of the window shade. She looked at the clock on Theo's bedside table: it was just past eight o'clock.

She watched him sleep. Gently, carefully, she stroked his head, running her fingers over his hair.

She knew last night was their first and their only. She contemplated trying to sneak out while he was still asleep. It would be easier than saying goodbye.

Her parents would be going crazy with worry, that much she knew. Angry as she was, it wasn't right to keep them in the dark. They hadn't asked for this either. The best they could do was stick together.

The phone next to Theo's bed rang. Annie started, and Theo was jolted out of sleep.

"What the heck?" said Theo, reaching over Annie to pick up the receiver. "Who calls this early on a Sunday?"

"Hello?" he said. "Hi!" He sat up and pulled Annie upright. "It's Kate," he said, holding the receiver between them. Annie leaned in to hear.

"I'm sorry to call so early," said Kate. "I've wanted to call all night. I actually haven't slept because I didn't want to miss the chance to call you as soon as possible."

"What have you found out?" said Theo.

"Well, I spent all last night going through the wooden crates that were upstairs. Oh, I wish you'd been here! You would have been as amazed as I was. Basically, as I told you, it looks like Sanford Weston, Samantha's father, lived here after the war. Most of what is here is dated after 1861. That matches up with reports that the main house burned down right around the time the war started. The picture of the cotillion seems to be the only thing here that pre-dates the war. But everything in those crates belonged to him. It doesn't look like he married or had any more children. I think he lived here alone until he died."

"That makes sense," said Theo. "We found the family grave. Madeline Weston died in June, 1861."

"The real reason I'm calling..." Kate's hesitated.

"What it is?" Annie said.

"In the crates he had a small collection of newspapers."

"The *Beckwith Station Gazette?*" said Annie.

"Yes. A few copies dated before the war started."

Kate paused.

"What?" said Theo.

"I've just finished scanning them into my computer. I'm emailing them to you now. I think you need to see these for yourself."

Theo reached over and turned on his computer.

Annie crossed her arms to control the fluttering in her stomach. "Tell me what they say."

Kate took a deep breath. "I know what happened to Samantha Weston. And I'm afraid to say it's not the happy ending we were hoping for."

Chapter 24

Neither Samantha nor Odus expected the journey from the Store at Five Corners to the next stop to be so short. They'd crawled back into the wagon compartment as instructed, expecting another several hours of proximity. But a mere 15 minutes later, a man in a pastor's suit opened the compartment and let them out in the woods behind a small farmhouse.

"This way," the pastor whispered. "And stay low.'"

They followed him towards the house and its welcoming light. He tapped in rhythm on the back door. A plump woman with white hair opened it. They entered a scullery where the smell of beef stew and biscuits made Samantha swoon.

"I believe you are Odus and Samantha. I'm Reverend Jennings," said the pastor, "and this is my wife."

Mrs. Jennings looked at her husband. "I thought there'd be three."

"The other young lady is staying at Five Corners. She is with child and Moses reckons the baby will come by next nightfall. Moses will stay with her until that happens."

Mrs. Jennings ladled the beef into two bowls and laid biscuits on top to soak in the sauce. "You'd best send him down," she said to her husband, handing the bowls to Samantha and Odus.

"Actually, they're both going down," said the Reverend.

Mrs. Jennings nearly dropped her ladle.

"This is a special circumstance," he said. "Samantha is just as much on the run as Odus."

"We've never had a white woman stay under…"

"I'm sorry,' he said. "But it is for everyone's safety."

Mrs. Jennings shook her head and went back to the stove.

Reverend Jennings opened a door and led them down wooden stairs to the basement. There was no railing. Samantha ran her hand along the wall.

"Sorry we can't let you stay upstairs," said Reverend Jennings. "Usually we can at least let the conductors stay if they're white, but it's too risky in this instance, especially with you, Miss Weston."

Samantha forgot all manners and desperately pushed a biscuit into her mouth.

He continued. "There's a bounty on your head now. You're wanted for murder and kidnapping. Usually they just send slave catchers after fugitives, but because of you there's a small Virginian army headed this way. Stand over here, please."

Reverend Jennings knelt at the bottom of the stairs. Samantha and Odus watched with wonderment as the bottom two steps moved under the Reverend's hands.

"We'll be moving you on before first light tomorrow, but in the meantime I need you both in here."

Samantha handed her bowl of stew to Odus, then Samantha took the Reverend's hand and let him ease her through the gap. She panicked briefly, unsure of how far she needed to go before her feet reached the ground, but was relieved to find it was only a four-foot drop. The Reverend handed her the lantern and the small space was revealed. Above her the underside of the stairs ascended. The room was no more than six feet long and four feet wide. A small cotton pillow and a wool blanket lay on a rectangular piece of canvas. Samantha set the lantern down on a small wooden crate, next to a copy of the Bible.

"As I said, we don't usually put the white folk in here, but this is an extenuating circumstance," said Reverend Jennings. He put his hand on Odus' shoulder. "Can I trust you to be honorable with this here lady?"

"Yes, sir," said Odus, just as Samantha said, "He can be trusted."

Odus slipped through the gap.

"Reverend?" said Samantha.

"Yes?"

"I hope this isn't too much to ask, but I was wondering if I could have paper and a quill?"

"What for?"

"I need to write to my father. I need to let him know that I'm alright."

"That's pretty risky, Miss Weston, all things considered. The letter's postmark will put him on your trail just when we need to be throwing him off."

"I know. I don't mind if you wait a few days before posting it. Or perhaps give it to Moses, and she can send it from somewhere further south so that it's harder to trace. Please, it will kill him not to know."

Reverend Jennings sighed. "Alright."

Samantha and Odus finished their meal in silence. Reverend Jennings returned with an envelope, quill, inkwell and paper. Odus handed him the empty bowls.

"I need to shut you in now," said Reverend Jennings. "When you're finished with your letter, just tuck it into the Bible. I'll post it once I'm back from taking you on. When you're finished with your letter, I need you to leave your marks. Have you done that before?"

"Yes," said Samantha.

"I have my passengers leave them on the inside of the back flap in the Bible." He smiled. "And if you end up reading a passage or two, then all the better."

"Yes, sir," said Odus.

"You do your best to get some rest," said Reverend Jennings. "I'll let you out before dawn. God bless," he added.

Samantha and Odus watched as the two steps were slotted back in at the bottom of the stairs and secured into place.

Samantha set the paper onto the wooden crate and dipped the quill into the well. As she began to write, the board that ran across the middle of the crate cracked under the weight of her arm.

"Darn it," she whispered.

She reached into her boot and pulled out Eli's knife. Its blade caught the lantern light. Samantha tried not to look at the engraving. Instead, she lifted the crate and pushed the knife so it sat horizontally under the broken board and embedded the tip into the crate's side. She pressed down on the broken board – the knife underneath held it firmly in place. She turned the crate upright and again began to write:

Dearest Papa,
There is so much I want to tell you that I don't know where to
begin...

"I'm finished," she said, folding the letter and putting it in the envelope. Odus handed her the Bible and she secured the letter in its binding. She opened the back flap and wrote *SW 3/27/61* and *EF 3/27/61*.

"I suppose I should extinguish the lantern," she said.

"I s'pose so," said Odus, handing her the blanket.

She turned the key and they were plunged into darkness. She could feel Odus near her and heard only the sound of his breathing. Her stomach felt as if a thousand lightning bugs danced within it.

"Miss Sammy?" he said quietly.

"Yes, Odus?"

"Can I ask you something?"

"Of course."

"In your letter to your father you told him that you in love. That true?"

She hadn't noticed Odus reading over her shoulder. Then she realized something else. "Odus, can you read?"

"Yes, ma'am."

"Why didn't you say so? Why did you sit through me teaching you what you already know?"

Odus paused. "I guess I jus' wanted to be next to you," he said.

Samantha wondered if he could hear her smiling in the dark.

"Well," she said, "you're next to me now."

"Yes," he said.

"Please would you do something for me?"

"Anything, Miss Sammy."

"Please would you be next to me always?"

"I'd love nothing better, Miss Sammy."

"Samantha," she said. "Call me Samantha."

She felt Odus' strong arms wrap around her waist.

"Very well. Samantha."

A loud noise shook Samantha awake. Or was it a gunshot? She was too sleepy to know. Then, she heard the door to the basement burst open. Two sets of hurried footsteps bounded down the stairs. The bottom two steps were pulled from their place. The lantern-lit figures of Reverend Jennings and Theodore Mason came into view.

"We've got to go," said Reverend Jennings, reaching his hand through the gap.

"What is it?" said Samantha, wiping the sleep from her eyes.

The sound of gunfire echoed down the stairs and made them all jump.

"We know you're in there!" came a voice that Samantha recognized but could not place. "Come out or we'll smoke you out."

Mason and Reverend Jennings looked at each other, their faces pale.

"They've come for me," said Samantha.

"They've come for all of you," said Mason.

"Have they got Amira?"

"No," he said. "They rode straight past the store. Didn't look once."

"So Amira is safe," she said, to no one in particular.

She took Odus' hand and looked into his eyes. "I need you to stay here."

"No, Samantha. We in this together."

"I need you to understand something. If you go out there, you are a dead man. If I go out there, we have a chance. They'll take me down south and then I'll come back. I'll find you. You need to keep going north where you can be free." She stroked his face. "And then we can be together."

She prayed to God that Odus could not know that these things would never happen.

"This is your last warning!" the voice bellowed.

"You're not going out there without me," said Odus.

"Yes, I am," she reached for Reverend Jennings' hand.

"No!" yelled Odus and pulled her back in.

"Help me," said Samantha to Mason.

The Reverend pulled Samantha out while Mason struggled to keep Odus inside.

"Please, Odus," she said, "stay here."

"No," he said, and tried to clamber out of the gap. Mason pushed him back in and he fell to the ground.

"Put the steps back in, quickly!" said Mason.

"There's a divot you can slot it in that makes it near impossible for the person to get out," said the Reverend, heaving from his efforts. Together they jammed the stairs while Odus pounded at them from the other side.

"Will they hear him?" she asked Reverend Jennings.

"Let's pray not."

Samantha briefly put her hand on the wooden steps, saying goodbye, flinching at the sound of Odus pounding and screaming. Then she ran up the stairs. Reverend Jennings and Mason hurried behind her.

"Miss Weston, do you have any idea what you're doing?"

"They might be satisfied just to have me. They don't need to know Odus and Amira made it this far," she said. "I need you to make sure Odus gets north. Promise me you will take him on after I'm gone."

He nodded.

She walked towards the Jennings' front door. Light glowed from outside, highlighting a stained-glass window above the front door and throwing its colors over the floor on which she walked. She put her hand on the doorknob and caught sight of herself in the mirror hanging on the wall. Even she was surprised by the determination in her face.

Mr. Jennings put his hand on her arm. "Miss Weston, are you sure?"

Samantha squeezed the door handle.

"I've never been more sure of anything in my whole life," she said.

When she emerged from the house she saw it wasn't the sun lighting the sky, but more than half a dozen torches blazing against the darkness. She blinked as her eyes adjusted, and figures and their features came into focus.

The first wave of recognition hit, and she gasped.

Clement Durant stood a few feet away from the front porch. At the center of the group, unshaven and worn, was Royal Fabre. He opened his mouth to speak.

"Samantha," he started, then stopped.

Clement Durant's horrible voice came through the night. "Samantha Weston, on behalf of your father, Sanford Weston, and the sovereign state of Virginia, you are hereby under arrest for the murder of Elijah…"

"Shut up, Durant," said Royal. "Samantha," he said, taking tentative steps towards her on the porch. "Samantha, my brother was shot and killed on our property border over two weeks ago. The bullet came from a gun like yours. I need to know if you know what happened."

"I do."

"It is believed that you killed him. But I believe that the slaves my brother sought somehow got a hold of your gun and killed him. What I don't know is how or why."

"Royal, it was me. I did it."

Royal became unsteady on his feet. "No, you didn't."

"Yes, I did."

"Why?"

Samantha saw Durant and the smirk on his face. If she had her pistol she would have blown his head off.

"Because he was going to kill someone very dear to me."

"Who?" said Royal, confusion spreading across his face.

"His name is Exodus Freeman. And now that's exactly what he is, a free man."

"I knew it!" said Durant. "I told you she'd become a nigger lover…"

"Shut up!" Royal yelled. He and Samantha stood face to face. "Are you admitting that you killed my brother because of some…slave?"

Samantha met his red eyes. "Eli would have killed him," she whispered.

A primal scream came out of Royal's mouth as he raised his hand and hit her across the face. Reverend Jennings rushed to her, but one of Durant's men pushed him back.

Stars circled her peripheral vision. Royal grabbed her arms and shook her upright. "How could you?" he whispered through his tears. "I could have loved you. I thought you might have one day loved me, too. But now, it's ruined. You killed Eli, and you've ruined everything."

He pushed her back and she fell against Reverend Jennings.

"I'm sorry," she whispered.

Royal wiped his eyes and raised his voice. "She's all yours, Durant."

Durant approached the porch, his lips unable to hide his rotting teeth. The men with torches gathered behind him.

"Now, Miss Weston," he said, rubbing his hands together, "there's a small matter of two niggers you helped to escape. Where are they?"

"Long gone. Probably even as far as Canada by now."

Durant sniggered.

"You think I'm going to buy that?"

"It's the truth. Isn't it Reverend Jennings?"

"Yes, Miss Weston."

"So you expect me to believe that two stupid niggers managed to get from Virginia to Canada in just fourteen days?"

"I don't expect an ignoramus like you to believe much of anything."

"Put her in the wagon," Durant yelled. "We'll take her back to Virginia. You," he said, pointing to two of the men, "keep on searching. Those niggers have to be around here somewhere. Where are you keeping them, Reverend?"

"Miss Weston told you they're not here," he said, "and I resent you making such a baseless charge."

"Don't be a fool, Reverend. How do you think we found you? We have a witness, a man of honor who saw you transporting Miss Weston and a fugitive in a wagon just like the one you've got over there." Durant pointed to Moses' wagon. Reverend Jennings went pale. "So, how about we just do a little search of the place?" said Durant. "Shouldn't take too long."

"This is private property, gentlemen. You have no right."

"Well maybe you, Reverend, need to be thinking about a little something called the Fugitive Slave Act. It's a crime for anyone to be hiding something that does not belong to them. What do you say we put you in the wagon too and you can stand trial alongside Miss Weston here?"

"No!" Samantha yelled.

"Or maybe we could just burn this house down. Smoke them out."

Royal pulled Durant by the scruff of his neck. "We're not thugs. And we are not the law. We are here for Miss Weston."

"But the two nig…"

"Sanford Weston's slaves are not my concern. Now shut up and put Miss Weston in the wagon. We're going home."

Durant scowled and grabbed Samantha by the arm. She shot a look at Reverend Jennings. He nodded, solemnly.

Durant dragged her to a small wagon, enclosed except for two barred windows. He sat her down on the step and tied her hands together with coarse rope. Samantha winced at his stench. He put his hands on her bent knees and leaned in.

"I'm going to enjoy this, Miss Weston. First, we're going to go back to Virginia. Then we're going to put you in jail. After that you're going on trial. And you know what happens then? You're going to hang. If not for murder, then for being a nigger lover. And when the day comes, I'll make sure I'm the one who puts that noose around your pretty little neck."

"My father will never let that happen."

"Your father can't do a thing to save you now, little missy."

Samantha spat in his face, hitting him square in the eye.

"Why you little…"

"Durant!" Royal yelled, mounting his horse. "It's time to go."

Durant wiped his face. "Just you wait," he scowled. "Just you wait."

Chapter 25

Annie and Theo watched as Kate's scanned copies of the *Beckwith Station Gazette* appeared on Theo's computer screen.

Beckwith Station Gazette
April 6, 1861

Samantha Weston Found; Arrested For Murder of Elijah Fabre

    Samantha Weston, daughter of Sanford Weston of Mont Verity, missing since the night of March 13 was found after a two-week search involving law enforcement up and down the eastern seaboard. Miss Weston, it is alleged, had been hiding in the home of Reverend Zachariah Jennings of Battenkill, Vermont, who – this reporter has been informed – is a known abolitionist and slave sympathizer.
    It is believed that the two slaves Miss Weston helped to escape have not yet been found, despite an extensive search of Mr. Jennings' property and the surrounding area. They have possibly already made a successful crossing into Canada. Miss Weston is currently being detained at the Beckwith County Courthouse, where she awaits trial for the murder of Elijah Fabre of Dominion Royale. She is also charged with theft under the Fugitive Slave Act, although it is expected her father – who owns the slaves in question – will testify that he will not seek damages or retribution for the loss of his property.

Beckwith Station Gazette
Special Edition
April 9, 1861

Trial of Samantha Weston Commences

    The trial of Samantha Weston, who is charged with the murder of Elijah Fabre of Dominion Royale, began in earnest yesterday at the Beckwith County Courthouse.
    Among those giving testimony were her father, Sanford Weston, her former fiancé, Royal Fabre, and her father's overseer, Clement Durant.
    Master Weston testified that it was his wife who, upon summoning her daughter for breakfast, raised concern about Miss Weston's whereabouts on the morning of Thursday, March 14.

Master Weston then summoned the help of Royal Fabre to help him with his search, as it was originally believed she may have arranged to meet Elijah Fabre, who – this reporter has been told, in confidence – she desired to marry. Elijah Fabre's exact whereabouts the previous week are unknown, although it has been confirmed that he had been in valiant pursuit of two escaped slaves belonging to Master Weston.

Master Weston told the judge that upon finding the body of Elijah Fabre, they at first believed him to be asleep. It was when trying to wake him that they first noticed the gunshot wound, which Royal Fabre testified had been made at close range.

Until the trial, there had been a number of theories about the events of the evening. One theory was that one of the fugitive slaves had stolen Miss Weston's pistol, used it to kill Elijah Fabre, then forced Miss Weston to travel north at gunpoint, but in their respective testimonies, both Royal Fabre and Clement Durant told the court how Miss Weston confessed to both the murder and the slaves' escape upon her capture.

Clement Durant spent a great deal of time in the witness seat, explaining to the court how, in the week before she disappeared, Miss Weston had developed what he called "a fondness for niggers." He said, "She went all soft on 'em, and was interfering with my methods of keeping them in line. I wouldn't have been surprised if she weren't planning to free every last one of 'em."

Miss Weston's mother, Madeline Weston, was not present at the trial.

Beckwith Station Gazette
Special Edition
April 10, 1861

Samantha Weston Found Guilty of Murder of Elijah Fabre

It has taken our Beckwith County judge a mere one day of testimony and deliberation to conclude that Samantha Weston, daughter of Sanford Weston of Mont Verity, is guilty of the murder of Elijah Fabre. The sentence is death by hanging.

In his verdict, the judge said, "This is a clear-cut case with a clear-cut outcome. While charges have not been brought against Miss Weston for the theft of her father's property, the murder she committed was in support of that theft. In this current political climate, it is more important than ever that those who aid and abet fugitive slaves are punished severely, and held up as an example of the consequences of doing so."

It has been reported that Royal Fabre left in the middle of the judge's sentencing.

Clement Durant began to cheer while the judge read his sentence and was escorted from the courtroom.

Neither of Miss Weston's parents was present at the verdict.

The date of Miss Weston's hanging was not available at the time we went to press.

Beckwith Station Gazette
Special Edition
April 11, 1861

Samantha Weston, daughter of Sanford Weston of Mont Verity and convicted murderer, is to hang in front of the Beckwith Station Courthouse tomorrow, April 12.

Rather unusually for the hanging of a woman, the judge who convicted Miss Weston has announced that all residents and slaves within a five-mile radius be present.

"Now more than ever," he said, "it is essential that whites and negroes alike understand that aiding and abetting fugitive slaves will have the most severe consequences. That Miss Weston is female and from a prominent family just goes to show that no one is exempt from the penalties for assisting runaways."

Although Miss Weston's family lives less than five miles from the courthouse, it is rumored that they will not be present at the hanging. Clement Durant, Master Weston's trusted overseer, will bring Master Weston's slaves to the site.

"Where's the rest?" said Annie.

Theo scrolled down.

"That's it. That's the end."

"No, that can't be it. There has to be more."

Theo checked Kate's email. "No. Just four attachments. That's all there is."

Annie bashed her fists against Theo's desk. "No. No! This isn't right. She can't have died this way."

"Annie, calm down."

"I won't! I can't! Don't you see? If there's no hope for her then there's no hope for me."

"That's not true."

"It is! You want to know the real reason why I've wanted to know what happened to her so badly? Because she and I are more alike than you realize."

"Annie, I know…"

"No, you don't know. You think you do, but you don't."

Annie grabbed her jeans from under the bed.

"What are you doing?"

"I'm going home."

"Why?"

"There's nothing else for me to do here. We wanted to know what happened to her, and now we do. We're done."

"Listen for a minute. Maybe this is all Kate had, but there has to be something we're missing."

"We're not missing anything. The girl at the library said the paper probably stopped after Fort Sumter because all the men went to fight for the south. That was April 12, the day Samantha was hung. There's nothing more." She pulled on her boots and rushed to the door.

"Wait, Annie," said Theo. "Don't go."

Annie paused and rested her forehead on Theo's doorframe. She feared if she turned to face him she would never leave.

"I have to," she said. "We both know what has to happen now. My family and I will leave here today."

"You can't go. You just can't. We've only just...I care too much just to let you go."

"If Samantha Weston didn't get a happy ending then there's no reason why I should either." She opened the door and walked down the stairs. Theo quickly pulled on his jeans and grabbed his coat.

"At least let me walk you home."

"Why?"

"Because," he said, "if you really are leaving then I'm staying with you until you do."

Annie held Theo's hand as they walked down the road to her house for the last time. His grasp calmed her and she decided to walk slowly. Most of the times she'd travelled this road had been rushed – her head down and her focus on getting from one place to the other quickly. This time, she took in everything around her – the icy puddles reflecting the sun and the small cracks in the pavement as they went over the bridge. She looked up at the mountains, the beautiful mountains, just as sparkling snow began to fall from the sky.

"Does it ever stop snowing here?" Annie half-joked.

"Eventually," said Theo. "Although we have been known to get dumped with a few feet in May."

"When it snows in Virginia everything shuts down. Schools get canceled, even the Metro into DC won't run. That's one of my first memories of moving to Virginia, actually. I'd been promised a trip to the National Zoo to see the new panda, but then it snowed and my mother refused to drive to the Metro stop."

"Sounds traumatic," he said, squeezing her hand.

Small talk felt futile, but Annie did not want to stop. She wanted to take in everything he had to offer, so she could take it with her wherever she went.

"What's your first childhood memory?"

"My mom telling me that under no circumstances was I allowed in her study. I don't think I even asked or tried – it was just a rule for all of us that she instilled early. Her study was sacred. I guess because it was the one room in the house where she could escape all the testosterone."

"What did she do in there?"

"I'm not really sure. She read a lot, and wrote sometimes. She kept diaries – you know, journals and things. But I think mainly it was just a refuge."

"So did you stay out?"

"Mostly. I went in there a few times, but only when I knew everyone was out of the house."

"What's in it?"

"A desk. Mementos, I guess – stuff she's collected over the years. Mostly shelves crammed with books I've never heard of. I never touched them, but I would always get a crick in my neck looking at the titles."

"Have you been in there since she…"

"No. Not yet. I'm almost afraid to. Like going in there might explain why she left and sometimes I'm not sure I want to know."

"I understand."

Theo stopped and held both her hands. "Do you want to know what I'm going to miss most about you? The fact that you really do understand. I know things haven't changed for me as drastically as they have for you, but Mom's leaving still feels like a big deal."

"That's because it is."

"And now you're leaving, too."

They resumed their walk.

"Where do you think you'll go next?" said Theo.

"I really don't know," said Annie. "We don't tend to plan these things in advance."

Theo half laughed. "Yeah, I guess that makes sense. Do you think your father will go with you?"

"I don't know," she sighed. "I kinda left before he could tell me much."

"It's not going to be the same here without you."

"Nah, you'll go back to high school tomorrow and be around all those girls, and you'll soon forget I was ever here."

Theo put his hand around her waist. "I can't see myself ever settling for someone who isn't you."

"Thank you," she said, kissing his cheek. "For everything."

"And I'm not giving up on Samantha Weston either. Maybe that was all Kate found, but I'm sure we're missing something."

"Maybe you're right."

"You have to promise me something."

"What?"

"When all of this is finished, when you finally get a normal life back, you have to let me know. Facebook, phone, whatever. Just let me know when you're okay."

"I will. I promise."

"I know it's no joke. You're in real danger. And I'm going to be worried sick until you tell me it's over."

"I promise. You'll be the first to know."

"So," he said, as they rounded the corner, "do I get to meet your parents?"

Annie laughed. "I don't see why not. As long as you remember to forget us."

"Your parents, yes. You, never."

Her house came into view. Annie stopped dead in her tracks.

"Annie?" said Theo.

In front of her house, bright as day, was a police car. A Virginia State Police car.

"Oh no," she whispered. "He found us."

Chapter 26

Samantha Weston sat in her cell, the same cell into which she'd been deposited after the journey back from Vermont. From the hard wooden bench on which she'd slept over the past week, she looked out the barred window at the hanging platform. Two men secured the noose that would go around her neck and then checked the trap door that would disappear under her feet. The yard in which it sat was surrounded by a tall, thick wooden fence. Behind it, Samantha could hear the sounds of the crowd. In the time Samantha had been in her cell, there had always been a crowd outside the fence. They threw rotten food. They yelled "nigger lover" and "murderer." And today they would watch her hang.

She'd already been granted her final wish for a washtub, warm water and soap. She'd scrubbed the dirt from behind her ears and untangled the knots in her hair. She'd washed her dress and petticoats, the same clothes that had taken her on the most extraordinary journey of her life.

She was not afraid to die. If dying meant Odus might live, then she would happily put the noose around her neck. But was he safe? She would never know. She could only hope that he'd stayed hidden as she'd instructed, then continued his journey north. At the very least, she hadn't heard he'd been caught. On this last day of her life, she decided, that would have to be enough.

She thought about her parents. Her father had testified at her trial, only to confirm that his slaves had in fact disappeared on the night of Samantha's cotillion, and that he and Royal had found Eli's body. If he'd tried to meet his daughter's eye while in the witness stand, Samantha did not know; she simply couldn't bring herself to look at him. It was only when he stepped down from the stand and exited the courthouse that Samantha looked up to catch a glimpse of him, but by then he was gone.

As the sun rose higher, the voices on the other side of the fence became louder and thicker. She knew that this would be a public hanging, that she was to be an example to both whites and blacks.

She was happy to be that example.

The guard came to her cell. She had been his sole charge over the past week, and Samantha felt that he wasn't quite sure what to do with her. In here, she was a prisoner, guilty of two of the worst crimes one could commit. In the real world, she was a lady, a plantation owner's daughter. He spoke to her with a mixture of respect and repulsion, never sure whether it was right for him to be kind or cruel.

"Miss Weston," he said, "it's time."

Samantha rose and clasped her hands together so he could bind her wrists. He took her by the elbow and led her down the corridor. At the entrance to the yard, another guard stopped them.

"You need to wait here," he said. "They just opened the gate to let people into the square. It could take a while."

The two guards stood awkwardly, unsure of where to look. Samantha stared at the ground, until she found it easier to lean against the brick wall of the corridor and close her eyes.

She remembered Odus' arm around her while they lay in the compartment of Moses' wagon, how he'd held her tight during the danger and beyond. She conjured the sensation of his body against hers on their last night together, hidden underneath Mr. Jennings' stairs. She pictured his face when she told him to stay in the hidden room, his eyes dark and deep like the woods in which they'd first met. What she'd give just to see his face once more, to tell him that she loved him and that there was no one else on this earth for whom she would more willingly die.

"Miss Weston?" said the guard.

Samantha opened her eyes and let him lead her into the square. The sun temporarily blinded her as she emerged into daylight. Her eyes adjusted, and she was stunned by what she saw.

People. Hundreds of people. Whites at the front, blacks at the back. The loud rumble of voices waned as Samantha was led onto the platform. The guard let her walk up the ramp first, her feet unsteady as she navigated its creaks and grooves.

Once on the platform, she was awed by her view of the crowd. Not by the dozen or so rows of whites, mainly farmers, but by the throng of slaves behind them, hundreds of faces receding into the back of the square so far that Samantha could not make out their features. There were too many to fit into the courthouse yard, so instead they surrounded the fence to the courthouse, and even the courthouse itself. She'd never seen so many people in her life.

The guard positioned her over the trapdoor.

She thought of the trapdoor in Jem's barn, how it was so well hidden and how it led her to safety that night.

How very different to the trapdoor on which she now stood.

Clement Durant approached. The front of the crowd cheered. True to his promise, he slipped the noose around her neck.

"I hope you rot in hell," he said.

"I look forward to seeing you there."

Durant jumped off the platform. The judge ascended the stairs.

"Have you any last words, Miss Weston?" he shouted.

Samantha scanned the crowd. If her parents were there, she could not see them. At the back of the rows of whites, she saw Royal Fabre, his tired eyes sunk deep into his once flawless face. She stood tall and spoke clearly.

"I am not ashamed of what I have done. If my actions have ensured the freedom of just one slave, then the consequences have been worth it."

The whites began to boo and hiss. The air was heavy. The judge stepped off the platform, and the guard took the lever in his hand. Samantha waited for the floor beneath her feet to disappear. A pastor stood in front, his hand in the air, praying for her absolution. Samantha prayed only that it would be over quickly.

Everything came to a halt as a man came out of the courthouse and ran to the judge. Samantha could not hear what was said, but judge bounded up the stairs and held up his hands. The crowd quietened.

"Good people of Virginia!" he shouted. "I have news! In the early hours of this morning our brave Southern Army fired on the Yankee post at Fort Sumter. Word is that it has been completely destroyed."

The whites erupted into applause and cheer, hugging and patting each other on the back. The blacks behind them were still and silent. The judge held up his hands to quiet the crowd.

"Let this be a day where clear messages are sent. To the North we say, leave us alone! Let us live our lives as we have for centuries! To those who want an end to slavery, let them look at the hanging body of Samantha Weston and know the consequences of their interference!"

The crowd cheered again, and Samantha noticed that in their revelry two black figures pushed their way through the throng of jubilant whites. Samantha blinked, convinced her eyes were playing tricks. Making their way into the center of the crowd, plain as day, were Odus and Moses. Samantha gasped.

The trapdoor moved under her feet, and the noose tightened around her neck.

Chapter 27

"He's here," Annie cried. "Sanchez is here. He's going to kill them. Theo, he's going to kill my parents. I have to do something."

She lurched, and Theo grabbed her arm. "Wait! What are you doing?"

"I have to save them."

"Annie, are you crazy? From what you've told me, we can't go anywhere near this guy. Let's run back to the store and call the cops."

"We can't!" She wrestled her arm out of Theo's grasp. "I have to go in there before it's too late."

"You can't go in there by yourself."

"What, and you're going to come in? This isn't a game, Theo. He'll kill you."

Theo's eyes darted around the landscape. "We need to find out if there's anyone else in there besides Sanchez."

"But, Theo…"

He pulled her towards the house. They stayed low until they reached the side window to the living room, then got on their knees. The smell of cigarette smoke drifted out the window, followed by the sound of Sanchez's horrible voice.

He's opened the window, she thought, *just like he used to at home.*

"You think I don't know what he's been doing?" He hissed. "Spying, taking pictures. You're going to tell me where he's keeping it all." His words were followed by a hard thump. Annie heard her mother groan. Where was her father? Had Sanchez killed him already? It took all Annie's willpower to not stand up and look through the window.

"Theo," she whispered, "my mother…"

"Where's your father?"

"I don't know."

Theo looked at Sanchez's police car. "I'm going to lure him out of the house."

"How?" He began rifling through her backpack.

196

"Just trust me. Stay here and wait for my signal."

"What signal?"

"You'll know it when you hear it. Then I need you to get into the house and free your mom. I'll hold him off as long as I can."

"Theo, you don't know what…"

"Annie, please." He kissed her quickly and ran toward the front of the house.

Annie waited. With every passing second she expected to hear a gunshot ring out, either at Theo or at her mother's fragile heart. Still on her knees, she peered around the corner of the house. She saw Theo run to the side of Sanchez's police car, out of view.

She looked down into her open backpack and saw what Theo had taken: the doorstop and hanger.

Theo squatted beside the driver-side door and willed himself to get a grip. All his life, he had never felt he was a guy with much to offer. For what did he know? He knew that the best bread to have with Provolone was sourdough, that the Red Sox weren't going to win the World Series, and that he would never get into an Ivy League college unless it offered a major in *World of Warcraft*. Then Annie walked into his family's store, confident and reticent at the same time, with three lifetimes already lived. She embodied everything he now knew really mattered: bravery, curiosity and the infinite rewards for daring to look in corners and under stairs. He steeled himself, squeezed the two objects he held in his hands, and remembered something else she'd taught him.

How to break into a car.

Annie's mother could not see straight. No amount of blinking brought even the nearest of objects into focus. Her head throbbed in three different places from where Sanchez had hit her with his gun. The skin on her wrists and ankles chafed against the ropes that tied her to the chair.

She was experiencing what she could only assume was her life flashing before her eyes. She saw her parents' tiny house in Arizona, the history library at Arizona State, and the bar where she'd worked to pay her way through college. She saw the night she met her husband, a shining beacon in a sea of army uniforms. She saw the ream of sleepless nights she'd endured when Annie was a baby, the monotony of the dozen army bases where they'd lived, and the fury at her husband for all he'd never let her become. How could she have done it differently? Sitting in this chair, about to die, she knew what she'd failed to do: speak up.

197

Sanchez circled the chair, a cigarette burning in his hand.

"You gonna start talking?"

"I told you," she said wearily. "I haven't seen him since the night you burned our house down."

"But you've talked to him?"

"No."

Thump. She groaned.

"And what about that little slut of a daughter? Where is she?"

"I don't know."

Thump. "I know she lives here. One of my comrades saw her, in Virginia. And while she was there she sent me a little email."

She looked at Sanchez with widened eyes.

He laughed in amazement. "Didn't she tell you? Little missy has been trying to taunt me with photos. I kept on telling her to knock it off, that she was only making it worse. But she wouldn't listen."

He leant over and blew smoke into her face. "She'll come back eventually. And I'm really looking forward to when she does." He raised his gun to hit her again but was stopped by the sound of a siren.

Annie covered her ears as the siren pierced her eardrums. She craned her neck: where was Theo? Sanchez's footsteps came out the front door and down the porch stairs. Annie wished she had the tools to kill him. She watched him run towards Theo. What was he going to do to him?

She knew she didn't have time to find out. She shoved the window open, then threw her backpack in before lifting herself through the gap. Her mother was in the center of the room, slumped and bound to a chair.

"Mom," she yelled over the noise of the siren. "Are you okay? Where's Dad?"

Her mother's words came slowly through her swollen mouth. Annie struggled to hear.

"He went...He's gone."

Annie pulled Elijah Fabre's knife from her boot and cut the ties.

"Come on." She pulled her mother up.

"But..."

"Listen. Sanchez will be back in here soon. We need to be ready when he does."

"What the hell have you done?" Sanchez yelled, one hand on his gun.

Theo held his hands in the air. Sanchez punched him in the face. As Theo fell to the ground he felt his jaw might come through his skin.

Sanchez pulled his gun, yelling over the siren. "Who the hell are you?"

"Sorry," Theo shouted, even though it was agony to speak. "I was just looking and it went off."

"You're where you shouldn't be. Now get the hell out of here!"

"Yes, sir," Theo said, and got up. Sanchez reached into the car and turned off the noise. Silence surrounded them.

"You don't have to pull a gun on me," said Theo, rubbing his face. "It's just, we don't get many Virginia State Police cars around here. You visiting my friends?"

Sanchez lowered the gun. "You know the girl who lives here?"

"Sure. She was going into my family's store as I was coming out. You want me to take you there?"

Sanchez paused, unsure of which way to go. "No. Tell her...tell her..." He shook his head. "Just do as I say and go." He hurried towards the porch.

Theo had failed. He had to do something else to prevent Sanchez from going back into the house.

"By the way," he yelled. Sanchez stopped on the porch and turned. "You look just like your photos."

Sanchez raised his gun and fired.

"Theo!" Annie screamed when she heard the shot. She ran to the front window. Sanchez chased Theo around the police car, a schoolboy's game in which Theo was faster on his feet. She had to get Sanchez away from Theo, and fast. She grabbed the Bible out of her backpack, pulled the memory stick out of her pocket and threw the front window open.

"Hey, Sanchez!" she yelled. He stopped. Theo ducked behind the car. She waved the memory stick in the air like a lighter.

"You want Dad's pictures? They're all right here on this memory stick." She cupped her hand around the Bible and held it up. "If you shoot him, this iPhone can make my little Facebook page public right now."

Sanchez shot at the window, splintering the frame. He pointed the gun at Theo and opened the back door of the car.

"In here, you son of a bitch. Now!" Theo did as he was told. Sanchez slammed the door. Annie grabbed her father's manila folder out from behind the couch and left a trail of photos behind her as she and her mother went downstairs.

Sanchez burst through the front door with his gun drawn. "Where are you, you little bitch?" he bellowed. He looked down.

Underneath his feet were dozens of photos. He was in every single one. There was one of him in a coffee shop in Alexandria, handing a brown bag of money over to one of his contacts at Border Patrol. There was one of him standing beside the white van that he used to transport the girls from state to state. Another picture showed him emerging from one of their base houses in Richmond, adjusting his belt.

"I'll kill him. All of them."

The photos were strewn everywhere. They thinned out at the back of the room and he walked over them slowly.

Then he saw the door to the basement. It creaked in its hinges as he opened it. A photo had been placed on each stair.

Who to kill first, he thought, the mother or the daughter? Both looked down on him, like he was no better than the dirt beneath their feet. All he wanted was a place where he felt at home. He'd never had one as a boy, not with his mother letting the boyfriend of the moment bankrupt them and force them to move. The army was the first place he felt like he belonged and he clung to his army buddies like a leech. Shame only a few of them knew the meaning of family.

Sanchez made slow, deliberate steps down the stairs. He stopped on the second from the bottom, where the memory stick sat crushed on top of the pile of photos.

"Why has she…"

Sanchez had no time to think. All he knew was that he was losing his balance as the stairs on which he stood were pushed out from under his feet.

Annie's father was nearly home. Or rather, nearly back at what his wife and daughter had called home for the past few weeks. It was Sunday and if one thing was obvious as he walked through the quiet streets of Battenkill, it was that this was not a town that operated on the Lord's Day. He had tried – and failed – to get in touch with his contact at the FBI on the one payphone he found in town. He got his messaging service. He left a lengthy explanation as to why he couldn't give him the evidence yet and told him he'd try again once he and his family had left Battenkill and found somewhere else to hide.

The next most pressing need was to find his daughter. He'd waited up for her all night. She couldn't have gone far. He'd half hoped he'd find her in town, but it did not happen. His wife mentioned a boy from the store down the road who had tried to fix the washing machine. That boy was his next port of call.

As he walked back to the house he looked up at the mountains. He'd always wanted to visit New England. But not like this. Maybe one day, when this was all over, he and his family could come back and see the mountains in autumn.

He turned the corner to the house. His jaw dropped.

Sanchez's car.

He ran to the house. As he did, a muffled noise caught his attention. He looked around and found its source.

In the back of Sanchez's car, a teenage boy was banging at the window, yelling to be let out.

As soon as Sanchez's feet hit the bottom step, Annie and her mother, waiting in the hidden room, pushed the two stairs as hard as they could. Sanchez lost his footing as the ground was literally pushed out from under him. He reached for a railing, but there wasn't one. He landed on his behind and dropped his gun. His feet dangled through the gap left by the stairs. Before he realized what was happening, two sets of hands were pulling at his ankles, then at his calves.

"Let...me....go."

He fell onto the floor on his stomach and grabbed at the jagged concrete. He didn't know who was pulling him or where they were trying to pull him, but he was dammed if he'd let them win. He kicked at the hands and felt his boot hit the side of a face.

He pulled his body weight forward, and the mother and her daughter came out of their hiding place, still grabbing at his feet and legs. He kicked the mother in the chest, cracking her rib, and she stumbled backwards into a corner of the room. The daughter came at him, flailing and screaming.

Annie knew from the moment they began trying to pull Sanchez into Samantha's room that she and her mother could not win this battle. He was too strong and too angry; they were too weak and scared. But it was too late. Their ill-conceived plan had been executed, and there was nothing else to do but keep on fighting and hope that the gun, wherever it had dropped, was out of his reach.

She'd been hitting at him for a few seconds? Maybe more? All she knew was that time came to a standstill when she saw him pull back his fist and level it straight between her eyes. She felt herself fall to the ground and all light in the room went out.

"Who the hell are you?" said Annie's father, opening the door of Sanchez's car.

"I'm Theo," he said, jumping out and catching his breath. "I tried to stop him. But he shut me in. And now he's got them."

"They're both in there with him?"

"Yes."

"Sweet Jesus," he said. He started to run towards the house.

"Wait!" said Theo, opening the passenger-side door. "Sanchez's radio. We can call for help."

He handed it to Annie's father. "You're going to have to tell them who you are."

Annie's mother could not move out of the corner where she'd landed. It hurt too much. Her chest felt ripped apart. Stars flashed in her peripheral vision, like fireworks on the 4th of July. She saw Sanchez punch her daughter's face and helplessly watched as she fell to the floor. Sanchez picked up his gun. He came towards her and raised it.

"You never liked me," he said. "You think I didn't know that every time I went to your pristine little house I didn't know I wasn't wanted?"

"And still you came."

"That's right. It's called loyalty."

"It's called rude."

"You and your perfect little family, a shame it has to end this way." An awful smile crept across his face. "I'll miss the enchiladas."

"Kill me. I just want it to be over."

Sanchez hesitated. He knew it and she knew it. He inhaled and prepared to pull the trigger.

He didn't even see it coming. All he felt was the most excruciating pain of his life as Annie thrust Elijah Fabre's knife into the back of his shoulder. He howled and thrashed, trying to get at the source of his pain. Annie jumped at him and pushed. Her mother did not know where her own strength came from, but she defied the agony in her ribs and got to her feet. Within seconds Annie and her mother had pushed Sanchez into the hidden room, shoved the removable steps back in place and jammed the corner in the divot, making it impossible for him to open it from the inside. Sanchez's muffled screams and pounding shook the basement. Annie threw her weight onto the stairs, afraid to let go.

Her father and Theo appeared at the door to the basement. Her father descended first, quickly, and embraced her mother, both of them crying.

"It's okay, I'm here," he said. "I'm here."

Annie sat up and knelt in front of the stairs. She placed her hands flat on their surface, wincing at Sanchez's every sound. Theo came down on to the floor next to her, carefully, as if she might break.

"Annie?" he said. "Annie, are you okay?"

Annie dug her fingernails into the wood. "It's Samantha," she said. "My real name is Samantha."

Chapter 28

When Samantha awoke, she felt sure the recent weeks had been a dream. The voices of Oma and Chimi floated on the breeze above her. She was being rocked, just like Nessie used to do when she was a little girl. She opened her eyes, expecting to be in bed at Mont Verity. The sun stung her eyes and the air smelled of smoke.

"I hope they be where they said they be," she heard Oma say. Samantha squinted into the daylight.

"Oma?" her voice cracked. It hurt to speak.

"Miss Sammy?" said Oma. "She awake, Chimi!"

They helped Samantha sit up. She was on the back of a horse cart, rattling at a steady pace along a dirt road. Milo, the horse slave from her father's plantation, drove the cart. The sun was high in the sky. Behind them, smoke billowed over the horizon.

"Here," said Oma, handing her a canteen. "Drink this." Samantha took one sip and winced. Her throat was painfully dry and swallowing was instant agony.

"It gone be like that for a few days, Miss Sammy," said Oma, gently. Samantha put her hand to her throat. She could feel the dried blood on her skin and the bruising underneath.

"What's happening?" she whispered. "How did I get here?"

Chimi and Oma exchanged looks. "We almost stopping, Miss Sammy. We explain ever'thing then. You rest now."

Samantha lay back against the blankets and looked up at the clear blue sky. There were noises in the air that she couldn't quite make out, like the sound of a cheering crowd muffled by the distance. Soon, trees appeared overhead, their leaves dancing in the gentle spring wind.

She closed her eyes and let the sun paint red under her eyelids.

The wagon rattled over uneven ground. They entered a wood. A familiar smell filled the air. *Sawdust,* Samantha thought. *Follow the sawdust.* The wagon came to a stop.

Milo helped Oma and Chimi out of the wagon. Samantha sat up and took his hand.

"Well, I never thought I'd be seeing you again," said a cheerful voice.

It was Jem, standing on the bottom of the steps to his cabin, next to the barn that had been her shelter. It looked bigger in daylight, the woods surrounding it more verdant and alive.

Samantha came slowly off the wagon and let him embrace her, wishing she had the strength to put her arms around him. She looked at Oma, Chimi and Milo and tried to understand how they'd all come to be here, when she was the one who came here in secret only a few weeks ago. Maybe she had died after all and this was heaven.

"There's someone inside who wants to see you," said Jem. Samantha took a step towards the barn, but to her surprise, Jem and the rest walked toward Jem's cabin. Samantha felt unsteady on her feet as she followed. Milo held her gently by the arm and let her up the wooden steps. The front door opened and a figure held out strong, soft arms.

"Nessie!" Samantha fell into her arms.

"Oh, Miss Sammy! You here and you safe! Thank the Lord Jesus, he done answered every prayer I ever done said. Now, you come on in and sit down."

"Nessie's made herself at home," Jem said to Samantha, with a kind, but mischievous grin.

Milo shut the cabin door.

"Y'all have a seat," said Jem. "I'll get some coffee brewing."

Nessie's fingers hovered over the marks on Samantha's neck. Tears filled her eyes.

"I'm alright, Nessie," she said. "But please, can someone explain how and why you're all here. I don't know if I'm dreaming or if I'm dead. Or both."

Nessie, Oma, Chimi and Milo all looked at each other, unsure of who should speak.

Finally, Nessie said, "We free, Miss Sammy."

"You're free?"

"That's right. Your father done set us free."

"When?"

"Yesterday."

"But why?"

The four again exchanged glances. "Well," said Nessie, "we like to think it something he gonna do anyway, but I think Moses done convinced him when she tell him of her plan."

"Moses? She's here?"

Oma laughed. "I startin' to learn that Miss Moses be everywhere."

"You mentioned a plan. What plan?"

"Today's plan," said Milo. "Miss Moses work it all out. Once Master Weston know he couldn't do nothin' to stop them hanging you…"

"Wait, Papa tried to stop it?" Samantha's lower lip trembled at the mention of his name.

"Of course he did, Miss Sammy," said Nessie. "He did ever'thing he could to try and get you a reprieve, but they havin' none o' that. They say they wanted to make an example of you."

"But then Moses come along," said Milo. "She said maybe that the judge done us a favor making it a public hanging and invitin' whites and slaves along. So he free us, on one condition."

"What was that?" Samantha asked.

"That we muster up ever' Negro we could find, get to your hangin' and fight."

"What do you mean fight?"

"We was to wait until they pulled the lever on you, Miss Sammy," said Milo, "and then fight with whatever we could lay our hands on."

"Moses done call it an uprisin'," said Nessie. "And we sure did rise, didn' we?"

Nessie, Milo, Chimi and Oma laughed.

"We done create a riot so big those whites don't know what hit 'em," said Chimi. "Ever'thing destroyed. We done burned that whole courthouse down. When we was leaving, some were even pulling up bits of the railroad track."

Jem came in with a pot of coffee and tin cups. "Ah, come on," he said. "Y'all had some help."

"How am I not dead?" said Samantha. "The lever was pulled – I saw it and felt it."

"One of Moses' men, Miss Sammy," said Oma, "one of her white ones, he were the one tightenin' the hinge on the trapdoor so that it weren't gonna let you fall all the way down."

"And you wouldn't have known, Miss Samantha, but my brother was waiting to cut you down," said Jem. "He was the pastor in the front row, reading your last rites. It took a few seconds for the whites around him to get distracted by all the ruckus, but he got to you as fast as he could."

"We had no way of telling you, Miss Sammy," said Chimi, "but it was probably best that way. To be honest, we weren't sure we was gonna pull it off."

"In a way," said Jem, "the firing on Fort Sumter did us all a favor. The whites were so distracted, cheering the way they were. They didn't see it coming. I think some thought it was part of how people were celebratin' at first."

"It was an uprisin' that was a long time comin'," said Nessie. "But this started because of what you did for Odus and Amira. For settin' them free."

"Exodus," said Samantha. "He was there. I saw him."

"That's right, Miss Sammy," said Nessie. "He the one that took charge of rounding up the Negroes. Of telling them all what you done for him and his sister. Saying that there be lots of whites helping blacks get north and that if they was gone to make an example of you for freeing them, then we owed it to you to show we willing to fight."

Samantha stood up. "But where is he? Is he alright?"

"I fine, Samantha."

Samantha turned. Odus stood in the doorway. His left eye was swollen and shut, his right ear caked in blood. To Samantha, he was the most beautiful sight she'd ever seen.

As she walked slowly towards him the rest of the room disappeared. All she saw was Odus and all she heard was the beating of her heart. She stood before him and brought her hands to his face. As their foreheads touched and Odus' lean arms pulled her in, she knew she was home.

Chapter 29

Annie and Theo lay on Annie's bed and gazed at the stars on her ceiling. All the windows in her bedroom were open, letting in a sultry summer breeze.

"Your ceiling is still the coolest thing I've ever seen," said Theo. "What a great idea."

Annie laughed. "I think I might paint over it."

"Why?"

"I don't know. I feel like I don't need it anymore. I painted it because I thought...Oh, I don't know what I thought. When I first had the idea, I wanted to do it because I knew Jenna and Marcy would be jealous and wish they'd come up with it before me. That's a pretty shallow motivation."

"No, you've got to keep it. You know what they say. You can take the girl out of Virginia..."

"But you can't take Virginia out of the girl." Annie laughed. "I have a feeling if you knew me, how I was there, we wouldn't be talking right now."

"You can't have been too bad."

"Let's just say I can't ever imagine going back to how I was."

"Have you gotten in touch with more of your friends?"

"Yeah, I've talked to Jenna and Marcy a couple of times, and all my Facebook friends are still there. It's just...too much has changed. We don't have that much in common anymore. I think maybe we never really did."

Annie went quiet.

"What is it?" asked Theo.

"Mom was right all along. I became what they wanted me to be."

"Don't be too hard on yourself. We all do things that we look back on and wonder what the heck were we thinking. But that's how we learn."

"I suppose knowing what you don't want to be brings you closer to figuring out who you really are. Or something like that."

"I think you're closer to figuring it out than you know," said Theo.

She poked him playfully. "Closer than you, definitely."

"Ah, I'll get there. It's been one heck of a year, one way or another. I'll tell you what I still can't believe – that all this time your name is really Samantha. You must have been fit to burst trying to keep that one under your hood."

"A little," she smiled. "I mean, I would have wanted to find out more about her anyway, but the fact that she and I have the same name just made me feel like she and I were connected in some way."

Annie went quiet. Theo stroked her face.

"Just because we don't know what happened to her doesn't mean she had a sad ending. For all we know she lived happily ever after."

"Theo, you don't need to try and make it all happy and shiny anymore. Her life went one way and mine went another. I suppose I should be grateful our names were just about all we had in common in the end."

"How did you choose Annie? How long have you been Annie?"

"I became Annie right before we came here. I always tried choosing names that were made up in part from my real name or a mix of some of the letters. I was Amy for a while, then Senna. It sounds stupid now. But I like Annie. I think I might keep it. Although Dad can't seem to get used to it."

Her father's voice came up the stairs.

"Samantha! Theo! Dinner!"

Three months had passed since the day Sanchez came to Battenkill. Minutes after Annie put Elijah Fabre's knife through Sanchez's shoulder, Battenkill Police arrived, followed by the Vermont State Police, and then the FBI.

Sanchez was taken away in a stretcher, delirious from the loss of blood. Her mother was sent to the local hospital and treated for a sprained wrist and three fractured ribs. Annie, Theo, and her father were driven to Battenkill Police Station for questioning.

Theo was quickly released. Annie and her father were released late that night and told not to leave the state of Vermont while the investigation was pending. Annie's mother was interrogated at the hospital and sent home after three days. They all went back to the Jennings farmhouse. When they weren't being questioned as part of the evidence gathering, they tried living as much of a normal life as possible – shopping for food, getting books from the library and playing board games. They chucked the television and instead listened to classical music or NPR. Theo visited almost every day after school.

All of Annie's possessions were confiscated, including her backpack, which contained Samantha's letter and the Bible. Elijah Fabre's knife counted as evidence. Before she was acquitted of attempted murder, Annie was asked to identify the knife as her weapon of self-defense at her trial. The prosecutor put it in her hands. She read the familiar inscription and knew she would never see it again.

On the last day of May, an FBI agent appeared at the door. He explained that Sanchez faced two trials. One in Vermont, for breaking and entering, and grievous bodily harm. After that he would be sent to Virginia, where he faced charges for murder and people trafficking.

The family, he said, were now at liberty to go wherever they liked. They were free.

Annie, Theo and her mother and father sat on the front porch of the Jennings farmhouse, eating enchiladas and watching the traffic pass. It was a celebratory dinner, having received the FBI agent's news that morning. The sun angled over the mountains, giving the green that blanketed them a purple hue.

"So this is what they mean by purple mountain's majesty," said her mother.

"Beautiful, isn't it?" said her father.

"It felt like winter would never end," said Annie, "and now look at it. I've never seen anywhere so green."

"These are the best enchiladas ever," said Theo, taking an enthusiastic mouthful of chicken and tortilla. "How do you make them?"

Annie wanted to answer him, but her mouth was full. It was so good to be eating her father's food again. She had put on weight since he'd been back and could no longer count her ribs. Her hair had grown down to her shoulders and shone with health. Even after three months it still felt strange not to be keeping check on the food she ate, but it was a habit she was determined to break.

"Dad's secret mole sauce," she said, after she'd swallowed.

"Secret what sauce?"

"Chocolate," said her father. "Mexican chocolate and chili sauce. And actually, it's your mother's sauce. I stole it." He smiled at Annie's mother, and she smiled back.

"I have got to get this recipe," said Theo, taking another large bite.

"Thanks to you, all the ingredients for these are now at the store," said her father.

Theo laughed. "I'll bet we're the only store in New England that carries smoked paprika. You never know, maybe we'll start a trend."

They ate, enjoying the silence around them.

"So, Theodore," said her father, "what are your plans? Now that you've graduated from high school?"

Annie rolled her eyes, concealing her pleasure that her dad was relaxed enough to be a stereotype.

"Well," said Theo, shifting where he sat, "I kinda didn't get my act together with college applications. So, I guess the answer is, I don't know. I thought I might stay here. At least for another year. Do my applications right. Pick up Annie from high school."

Annie playfully threw her napkin at him. "That's right, you just keep rubbing it in."

Her mother set down her empty plate and picked up Annie's backpack. It had been returned that day with the contents more or less how she'd left them.

"So, this is everything?" her mother said, opening it up and gently rummaging.

"Everything we found. The Bible, the letter, the sign rubbings, the cotillion photo and what we've printed out."

"Everything except, you know," said Theo, referring to the knife.

"This is an incredible photo," said her mother, looking at Kate's picture of the cotillion. "Which one is Samantha again?"

Annie leaned over and pointed, taking care not to touch it. "There, the one in the middle."

"I wonder if she knew on that day how much her life was about to change."

Her mother put the photo back in the bag and picked up Bible. She carefully flicked through the pages. When she saw the inside cover, her mouth fell open.

"What is it?" said Annie.

"These," she said, lifting up the book to show them the list of numbers and letters. "You didn't mention these."

"We haven't figured them out yet," said Annie. "We think they're initials and dates of some kind, but we still haven't figured out for what."

"There's another set just like them in my barn," said Theo.

Her mother looked as though she might leap out of her chair. "I knew this kind of thing existed, but I never thought I'd see the real thing."

Annie, Theo and her father leaned in.

"What?" said Annie.

"Moses Marks. These are Moses Marks." Her mother was laughing. "I can't believe it!"

"You know what those are?" said Annie.

"Yes! You know the Underground Railroad?" She was too excited to see Annie and Theo nod.

"This was how a lot of station masters marked how many slaves and conductors went through their stop, by asking them to leave their initials and the date they passed through. No one really knows who started it, but it was supposed to help them keep track of which ones made it all the way and which ones didn't. I think, over time, it became a good morale booster – those traveling through could see the marks of those who had made the journey before them. Look," she pointed to the list from Theo's barn, "see how sometimes there's a second set of initials?"

```
AK - 12/4/56
JS - 12/4/56
M - 4/17/57
CT - 7/4/57, GB
ZT - 7/4/57, FD
AA - 1/8/58
DF - 3/12/58, M
HY - 9/23/58
GK - 7/4/59, DS
BR - 2/13/60
HN - 6/29/60, FD
GR -7/13/60
AF - 3/27/61
BV - 4/12/61
TG - 6/26/61, ESF
MO - 9/1/61
VX - 11/16/61, ESF
OY - 12/31/61
KJ - 2/13/62
GR - 6/25/62, ESF
VC - 1/6/63, ESF
KA - 1/6/63, ESF
HA - 1/6/63, ESF
PT - 4/11/63, ESF
```

"Those are the marks of the conductor. If they were traveling with the slaves they left their mark there."

Her mother studied the list in awe. "I saw a picture of some written in an attic in Pennsylvania, but I can't believe the real thing is right here."

"Mom, how do you know all this?" said Annie.

"Don't you know that your mother was a history major?" said her father.

"Well, yeah, but..."

"I did my senior thesis on the Underground Railroad," said her mother. "I thought it was fascinating. Can you imagine? To be a slave and just run away, not knowing where you were going or who to trust. For a lot of them the only thing they knew was to follow the North Star. Yet, somehow, so many made it safely to freedom. Some conductors made the journey again and again, even though they knew every time they did they might be caught. I just think it's incredible." Her voice trailed.

"What?" said Annie.

"Nothing," said her mother.

"Your mother won an award for her senior thesis," said her father. "They told her she should keep on going, get a masters and maybe even a PhD."

"Why didn't you?" said Annie.

"She met me."

"That's not fair," said her mother. "It's no one's fault. It was just how it was."

"No, it was my fault," said her father. "I didn't support you. I know you struggled when Samantha was little, being on your own so much. When we moved to Virginia I should have encouraged you, instead of holding you back."

"Starting your business was important."

"No, it cost us too much. I probably wouldn't have tolerated Sanchez so much once we got to Virginia if I wasn't trying to get his old police contacts to apply to work for me. I'm sorry."

"Honey, where is all this coming from?"

"A man who spends a year by himself on a mountain has a lot of time to think." He took her hand. "I never forgot, Julia. I just kind of lost hold of it."

"Things got in the way," said her mother.

"Like me," said Annie.

"Oh no," said her mother, "don't think that for a second. I think I thought at first that I could do it while you were little, but it just didn't work. And then I never really found my way back to it. I should have fought for it more. Instead I was just mad at everybody – at you for not remembering I wanted it and at Annie for not wanting it for herself."

"There is no shortage of colleges around here," said Theo. "There's at least six within a thirty-mile radius and I know at least one of them has a kind of 'university without walls' program. Hey – maybe you and Annie could go to college together." He glanced at Annie with a glint in his eye and Annie thought she might melt into the porch.

"I'm sure she has other ideas," said her mother.

"Actually," said Annie, "it's time I start looking at colleges. Weren't a few of the brochures you got me for colleges around here? We could visit them together. I can look at undergrad programs, and you can look at grad ones."

"I'd love that," she said, taking her daughter's hand. "I'd really love that." She turned to Annie's father. "That is, if you're happy for us to stay in Vermont for a few years at least."

"You're in charge," he grinned. "We can do whatever we like, now that I'm a free man," said her father.

Theo turned sharply. "What did you say?"

Her father looked at Theo, confused. "I said I'm a free man."

Theo's eyebrows furrowed. He stared at the ground. "Can I see the letters and numbers again?"

Annie handed him the Bible and the list. His eyes darted between the two.

"Free man," he said. "Free man."

"Theo?" said Annie.

Theo pushed himself upright. "I have to go," he said.

"Wait! Where are you going?"

He knelt down and reached for Annie's bag. "May I?" She nodded. He carefully placed all of their collection into the backpack.

Still kneeling, he took Annie's hand. "This is a long shot, a complete and total long shot. But can you meet me in the cemetery in an hour? The one behind my house?"

"Well, sure, but why?"

Theo stood up. "I think I know what really happened to Samantha Weston."

The sun was about to dip behind the mountains when Annie arrived at the cemetery. The grass was freshly mown and Annie inhaled its soothing scent.

Down the hill, Theo's truck sat in the drive behind the Store at Five Corners. Theo was nowhere to be seen. Annie waited among the old maple trees that kept watch over those whose remains fed the ground. Standing in the middle of the gravestones she wanted to take off her shoes and leap across the landscape, simply because she could. A few months ago she wouldn't have dreamed of just lingering in a place this open and exposed. That was when every sound made her jump, every rustle made her look. Now, she could just be. She could stay in this cemetery all night and not worry about who might miss her or who might see her. She spun around, delirious at the possibility of where she might go and what she might become.

She saw Theo running up the hill, carrying a manila folder. Annie felt her heart settle into the comfort of his sight.

"I was afraid you wouldn't be here," he said, panting.

Annie laughed. "If you told me to meet you on Mars I'd find a way to get there."

He smiled and took her hand, leading her farther into the cemetery.

"Where did you go?" Annie asked.

"To the Town Hall. Shirley was just locking up, but I begged her to let me in. And then I went home." He wavered. "To my mother's study. But first, I want you to see this."

He led her to a stone cross.

"Look," he said.

JENNINGS
Final resting place of
God's servant
Zachariah
Born August 20, 1799
Died December 3, 1862
His wife
Rebekah
Born July 5, 1805
Died November 12, 1861

"The Jennings that built my house?" said Annie.

"That's them."

"It's nice to know it's here, but I don't know how this explains what happened to Samantha Weston."

Theo brought her to a gravestone embedded in the ground. He knelt down and brushed away the leaves and moss.

"This one," he said. "Read it."

Annie knelt down beside him and read the engraving on the stone.

Here lies
Exodus Freeman
Writer and advocate of black rights
Who entered this life in 1843
And departed it on December 4, 1928

And his beloved wife
Samantha W. Freeman
Feminist and abolitionist
Who entered this life on June 21, 1845
And departed it on January 3, 1929

"I don't understand," Annie began.

Theo pulled the list of initials and dates from his pocket.

"See? The first date SW and EF appears is March 1861. But look, after that it's ESF. Exodus and Samantha Freeman. Moses Marks, like your mother said."

"So?"

"So, Samantha Weston did not hang that day. She lived. She became a conductor on the Underground Railroad."

Annie shook her head. "Theo, I want to believe it's her. I really do. But I don't know how we can be sure. How do we know that this Exodus Freeman is really the EF who left the Moses Mark? Or that ESF is really two people?"

"A few reasons." He took the first piece of paper out of the folder. On it was Theo's handwriting.

"E and S Freeman are in the town census," he said. "I looked them up. They first appear in the 1863 census and are there until the 1920s."

"Of course they are," said Annie. "Their grave is here. Why wouldn't they be in the census?"

He handed her the manila folder. "Here," he said.

Annie opened it. Inside were several pages, all freshly copied. She picked up the first.

Battenkill Courier
June 26, 1861
Marriages, Births and Deaths

-*Married: Exodus Freeman and Samantha Weston were married last Saturday by the Rev. Zachariah Jennings. We wish this extraordinary couple well in their new life together.*

"Samantha Weston," said Annie, running her fingers over the printed name.

"And this," said Theo, turning over to the next Xeroxed page. It was a copy of an old town photo. The caption read: *Battenkill Centenary, July 1876.* Annie squinted.

"What am I looking for?"

Theo reached into Annie's bag and carefully took out Samantha's cotillion photo. "Here," he said, pointing to a figure on the town photo. "Compare the two. It's the same woman." Annie's eyes darted between the two photos.

"Okay, they're similar but there's no way to tell that they're the same woman."

"Look at the man next to her, holding her hand."

Annie looked and shrugged. "He's black."

"Exactly. He was an escaped slave. That's how she ended up in your house. The Jennings farmhouse was a stop on the Underground Railroad. So was my barn. The Moses Marks are proof. Think about it, Annie – it all makes sense! Why she couldn't go home again…"

Annie interrupted. "She couldn't go home again because she killed Elijah Fabre."

"Yes, but think about why she would have done that! She said in her letter she was in love. All along we've thought it was with EF. And now we know who EF is. Exodus Freeman." He held up the photo and the newspaper announcement in one hand and the list of letters and numbers in the other. "We didn't think to look for her in photos or newspapers from here. But they were here. They helped slaves get north until Lincoln freed them in 1863. And then they stayed in Battenkill. Exodus Freeman was an escaped slave. He wrote about it."

He handed her a small brown book. On the cover, in embossed gold letters read:

"Where did you find this?"

"My mother's study. She has quite a few books written by slaves at that time. All kinds of books in there that I never used to look twice at, until I met you."

Annie took the papers from him. "But how did you know to come here?"

"Remember I told you how every year in school they made us come here and do grave rubbings? I know I told you I only ever did rubbings of my family, but I did used to look at other ones. I remember reading this one. At the time it didn't occur to me to think what it might mean, or who the people beneath the grave might be."

"It gets better." He showed her the final piece of paper. "It's the only one I found, but I'm sure there are more if we do some digging."

Battenkill Courier
September 19, 1868
Samantha Freeman to be published in The Revolution

Samantha Freeman of Battenkill, wife of renowned poet Exodus Freeman, is to be published in The Revolution, the women's rights weekly journal. Her essay Suffrage for Women and African-Americans: extending the vote to all will appear in the November issue.

"I'll bet we can find that essay," said Theo. "Wouldn't it be amazing to read more of her words? I wonder how many other things there are to find."

Annie was afraid to believe that in her hands she held the truth. But it was all there, in black, white, subtle shades of gray, and embedded into the ground on which she now stood.

"She did have a happy ending," she said, her eyes watering. "We both did."

Theo put his arm around Annie. Together, they stood above the grave of Exodus and Samantha Freeman.

"Isn't it amazing how your mother just knew about Moses Marks?" said Theo. "It's something she learned so long ago and yet she just held onto it."

"I can't believe you put all of this together. You remembered their grave." She touched Exodus Freeman's book. "You knew how to find this in your mother's study. She must have an incredible collection of books."

"Yes. She does."

"Do you miss her?"

"Everyday. I wish she was here. This was her book. She would have loved trying to find Samantha Weston. If she had been here we would have figured all of this out a lot sooner."

"But then you and I wouldn't be standing here right now. So I guess I have her to thank."

Theo nodded and they embraced, both hopeful, both hoping.

"Theo?"

"Yes, Annie."

"When we were looking for Samantha Weston and it was getting hard, you said you just wanted to know that some people can be found."

"Yes."

"Well, if we can track a journey like Samantha Weston's, maybe our next goal is to find your mother."

Theo leaned back. "What?"

"If we've proven anything, it's that no one disappears forever. They can always be found. I think if you and I were to put our minds to it we'd come up with something."

"I have to admit, I've been thinking the same thing. But Annie, you're finishing high school soon. And you've only just got your freedom. Isn't there something else you're supposed to do? Or anything else you actually want to do?"

Annie shook her head and smiled.

"You really want to do this?" he said. "For me?"

Annie nodded.

Theo's eyes began to water. She kissed the tears as they fell from his eyes, then hooked her arm through his.

"Come on," she said. "We've got some work to do."

The author would like to thank:

Yvonne Barlow – for her patience and insight.
Seth Fishman – for believing.
Dan Gunderman – for the ethics.
Erica Kennedy, Sam Korvin and Pat Trebe – angels in training.
Katya Batchelor, James Bishop, Gillian Buchanan, Clive Lonie, John
McBrien and Chris Walshaw – for reading, for listening, and for making
this a better book at every turn.
Alison Packer – for going above and beyond.
My husband, David – for making everything possible.

About the Author

Gayle O'Brien grew up in rural Massachusetts. After studying at Sarah Lawrence College and Oxford University, she was a youth organizer, health-care advocate, abuse manager, and part-time actress. She moved to London in 1999 and became a copywriter, which led to stints in Finland, Italy and the Netherlands. She has an MA in Creative Writing from the University of East Anglia and now lives in Kent with her dear British hubby and their two children. *Underground* is her first novel.

Lightning Source UK Ltd.
Milton Keynes UK
UKOW051235061112

201756UK00003B/3/P